Spaceship Over Vancouver

Alan Dean

Published by
Raincoast Images
Shirley
British Columbia
Canada
http:/raincoastimages.ca
ISBN: 978-0-9880382-0-2

For Pandora

Nature is Strange and Capricious

When Chepi's deep-space Sphere parked itself unexpectedly over Vancouver she didn't at first give it much thought. This wasn't surprising, as they hadn't actually hovered over an inhabited planet before, the significance just failed to register. Vancouver held no interest, this was simply one more destination in the endless stream of new places she'd visited from the very beginning of her time with the Sphere. In fact nowhere she'd visited had any particular meaning for her. She idly watched what took place, explored when she felt like it and dreamt the days away in quiet solitude. Nothing was new to her, or so she thought. Black holes, supernova, comets, colliding galaxies, red dwarfs and all kinds of exotic spatial anomalies populated her life endlessly with pointlessly beautiful images and visions, and so, in contrast, this latest destination seemed to be even more unremarkable than usual.

What did attract her attention at that moment was the sudden influx of gravity. It wasn't that she hadn't experienced it before, but usually she had some say over the matter, or at least a warning. This time, though, it appeared suddenly, and it'd been a long way from where she had been to the view screen inexplicably transformed into a solid, unyielding floor. The impact made her nose bleed. She knew the Sphere wouldn't care, so for several moments she stared uncomprehendingly at the city below and pretended not to notice. But, inevitably, that didn't last and Vancouver slowly vanished behind a red, painful cloud.

'Frak, what was that for?'

The Sphere didn't answer.

Ω

Although her arrival over British Columbia meant almost nothing to Chepi, it meant a great deal to the rush hour crowds streaming their ways around the city streets. Even for Vancouver, a large golden globe hanging over the city demanded some kind of response, though perhaps mindless screaming might have been considered excessive. Not that the wails of fear mattered too much, the crescendo of screeching metal welling up from lines of traffic stacking one against another in tattered, chaotic piles drowned out any personal moments of embarrassing loss of self-control. In the initial moments of the Sphere's arrival only cars had a say and pedestrians stood, gaped and were mown down in the frozen moments of the stunned mindlessness that filled those first seconds of realization that a Ferrari wasn't the coolest vehicle around, and Concorde had just been a plane.

$$\Omega$$

'I said why the frak did you do that?'
'You weren't paying attention.'
Chepi sighed.
'It's a lesson.'
'But was it really necessary?'
'Maybe.'
'Why?'
'So you don't forget.'
Chepi levered herself up onto all fours. She watched the blood drip slowly down to the pool of red already forming on the view screen. 'I never forget anything.'
The Sphere didn't answer. It had learnt that bickering with Chepi didn't get either of them anywhere.
'It hurts.'
'Then you will remember.'
'How? I can't think about anything.'
Resigned silence echoed back.
'It needs cleaning up.'
Lights flashed out and danced across the view screen. The blood vanished. Chepi waited hopefully, but nothing else happened.
'I said it really hurts.'
'It'll pass.'
She stood up slowly and gathered herself together, ready to present a face that even the Sphere would pity, but then something caught her eye.
'What's that?'
A 'thing' was hovering outside the screen. It was small, red

and white and hung in the air so closely Chepi felt as though she could reach out and touch it. It was the closest she had ever seen anything come to the Sphere.

'It's an aircraft. They call them helicopters. There are people inside.'

'What are they doing?'

'Living.'

Chepi crouched down to look more closely. 'What's it like out there?'

'Cold and wet.'

'Then why …?' But the question faded away. There was simply too much to think about.

Ω

The coastguard helicopter had taken only minutes to reach the scene. Initially the captain had instinctively started to head off in the opposite direction, but strained, distant voices far from the event and its consequences had thought otherwise. So, there he was, edging slowly closer and closer to something that would only seem friendly to someone on a long-distance radio link from Ottawa issuing the ludicrous order to investigate.

'What can you see?'

A large golden sphere.'

'Yes, but now you're closer. Try to be constructive. You're in a unique position. We're all counting on you.'

He didn't want them to count on him. He'd joined the coastguard because it had seemed kind of heroic, all that going out and saving people from tragic circumstances, he hadn't counted on there being actual, tangible danger.

'It's very golden.'

There was a long pause before an irritated, detached voice cut back in. He could hear clearly a growing glimmer of contempt. 'Anything else, any features at all, anything that could … that we might be wary of?'

He ignored the tone. They weren't there, otherwise they wouldn't ask stupid questions. 'Wary of, other than being confronted by a large, golden sphere that is hanging motionless in the air?'

'Yes, okay we appreciate it's unusual, but anything that looks

9

like a weapon. Anything that might show its intentions?'

'No, nothing … no … Oh, hang on ...'

Ω

Chepi stumbled backwards as the room began to rotate. 'What are you doing?'

'Making it more comfortable for you.'

Chepi bounced off the chair now sitting upright and fell onto her back with a scream. She got slowly back to her feet, checking herself for more signs of blood. 'And how's that exactly?'

'You should pay attention.'

'I didn't hear you.'

The Sphere kept quiet. For reasons it didn't quite want to admit to, it hadn't warned her.

'I said I didn't hear you.'

It didn't reply.

On any other occasion Chepi would have made more of the evasion. This time, however, standing and looking straight at the helicopter, which somehow made it easier for her to see clearly, her mind drifted. 'What if I …?'

'NO, DON'T!'

It was too late, Chepi waved her hand over the view screen and the crew of the helicopter got to glimpse the first extra-terrestrial ever to visit Canada.

Ω

The voice in Ottawa rose through several levels of pitch. 'WHAT? What's happening?'

'It's rotating.' He felt pleased with himself, even though he'd had to work hard to manage it he knew for certain that his voice had sounded calm.

His co-pilot thought otherwise. 'Take it easy Jack.' He urged.

'What, take what easy?'

'You're sounding a bit, you know, hysterical.'

Jack stared at this co-pilot with a vacant lack of comprehension until the distant unruffled, disconnected voice of Ottawa brought him back to the problem at hand. 'Did you say 'rotating'?

He pressed the transmit button. 'Yes, rotating.' He glanced back at the Sphere for confirmation, and instead of the same immaculate golden surface he saw a blurred image of Chepi staring back at him.

'Bloody hell!' He jerked the controls in panic and the helicopter baulked. The rotor blades almost clipped the Sphere. He pulled back and it stalled. As he struggled for control he glimpsed the hazy figure watching them intently. To the pilot she seemed as mystified as he was.

'What's happening?' The headphones screamed. Ottawa's cool demeanour fell away as quickly as the helicopter.

'There's someone in the Sphere.' The co-pilot replied.

'Someone? You said someone. What d'you mean 'someone'?'

'I think it's a girl. She looked ... surprised.'

The voice in Ottawa whispered to someone else. 'I think they're losing it.'

Ω

'They've gone.'

'They'll be back.'

'How d'you know?'

'Primates, they can't leave anything alone.'

'Oh.' She waved her hand and the screen shifted back to default opaqueness. 'Okay, what next?'

'We're staying.'

'But I've already seen it.'

'You've seen nothing yet.'

'Don't tell me this is another project?' She asked warily.

The Sphere smiled. 'Something like that.'

'Frak.'

Ω

Meanwhile in Ottawa, chaos and panic flitted around threateningly. Only fear of ridicule kept it at bay. Presentation was everything.

'What does he mean 'a girl'?'

A government minister on a brief but opportune official visit to the central control room frowned a superior frown. This was something of a gift, an instant chance to appear calm and superior at the same time. He'd only been there for a few minutes, supposedly enjoying a publicity opportunity, yet already he could step fearlessly into perhaps the greatest event in human history. He grinned at one more lucky break coming his way. 'I suppose he means a young female. Human as well, we should assume?'

There were rivals though, other people present who were looking for a spot in the limelight or a chance to score a few points. 'Yes Minister, but what d'you think it means?'

A question, and he hadn't even been briefed. Self-doubt crept in, had he played his opening card too soon he wondered? Should he have waited until they'd told him more? After all, being articulate didn't actually mean he knew anything. Not enough of the electorate had guessed that yet, about any of them. Eyes were watching and he needed to say something. 'I think it best not to jump to quick conclusions. Knowing that there's someone human on board is enough for now. At least that's something vaguely familiar among the chaos.'

'Not really Minister. Sorry, I mean being human, if she is, doesn't really tell us anything about her intentions. Different cultures different goals.'

The Minister, Marcoin, frowned even more deeply and locked his eyes on the speaker. It had always worked, everyone had doubts and direct eye contact tended to flush them out. 'Only in the particular, in general we're all alike. We want the same things and have the very same fears. Ask anyone in the opposition, they'll tell you if you're quick enough to catch them out. Not much difference when you get down to basics' Damn, he thought, what the hell am I doing? This is no time for bleeding heart confessions. He fell silent and hoped the moment would pass unnoticed.

John Lithgo, a junior air traffic controller, had an entirely different idea. 'But doesn't that mean competing for the same things, like someone else's air and food, or even their water and oil Minister?'

Marcoin almost panicked, water and oil were issues no respecting politician should ever be drawn into talking about, but he somehow coped. As every politician knows, the best way to disarm small but clever people was to ignore them, because if you did, for some unfathomable reason, so did everyone else. He turned away. 'Do we know what happen to the helicopter?'

A senior controller, Ford, answered automatically. Despite the fact that he has always thought Marcoin was moron and clearly as clueless as the rest of them, a chain of command however flawed offered comfort. 'Back on station just this moment Minister.'

'And?' He thought the tone was perfect. Pitched in that way that left no doubt as to who was in command.

'What can you see?' Ford asked the pilot.

The crackled reply was patched through the audio system. 'Nothing, back to just being the golden surface.'

'Ask them to confirm what they previously reported.' This was Marcoin flawlessly unrolling politics 101, where the first rule is that control gained is never willingly relinquished.

Ford obliged. 'Can you confirm previous report, over?'

'The sighting?'

'Yes.'

The pilot gathered his thoughts. 'The Sphere started to rotate and a small section became transparent. We both thought we saw a young female, over.'

Ford looked up at Marcoin for instructions. He basked briefly in the moment of deference before responding. Power was a source of pleasure as well as a method of control and every moment was something to treasure. 'Are they sure she's human?'

'Confirm human.'

'Looked human. Wait, over.'

Tension in the voice filed its way through the ether and filled the room. Marcoin began to plan his exit. After all, the situation could get out of control at any second and if he were still there then it would be his fault, the media would see to that. He needed to leave straightaway, make a quick exit before something went wrong. Cash in while he still clutched the imaginary prestige he'd slaved so hard to gain.

'Is there a problem, over?' Ford's voice wobbled, but he didn't notice. He was close to retirement and had nothing to prove to anyone.

'Sorry, the co-pilot said he thought she had … strange eyes, over.'

'Say again.'

'Strange eyes, kind of … hang on … very dark.'

'Very dark eyes?'

'For frak sake, what the hell does that mean?' Marcoin asked no one in particular. Vagueness in others is a politician's worse enemy. How could he ever respond to information like that and appear anything but unfocussed.

'Is that it, dark eyes?' Ford asked.

'Co-pilot here. Sorry, yes, that's just how they seemed. We think we might have got a photograph.'

Marcoin took the microphone. He knew he shouldn't, it showed weakness, and it was also illegal, but enough was enough. 'It's the Minister here, can you confirm she's human? If you've taken a photo maybe we can just sort out her eye colour later.'

'Affirmative. Looked human sir.'

Lithgo, the junior controller, had another moment of insight. 'Looking human doesn't mean human.'

By mistake Marcoin glared at him, thus acknowledging his existence. He wanted to look away but having started it he knew the only course of action left was to keep staring at him until he backed down or said something even more stupid.

He did neither, or the latter, depending on one's personal beliefs. 'Looking human might not mean actual human. Maybe she's just humanoid. I mean maybe from something like convergent evolution.'

This was dangerous territory for Marcoin, he didn't have a clue what convergent evolution was. In response he did the only thing he could, he carried on staring.

Transfixed by indecisiveness he began to sense a bead of sweat forming on his brow. It would run into his eye if he didn't do something, they always did, but he couldn't move as doing so would give it away, show he was stressed, and up until then no one had noticed. If he stayed motionless then at best they'd suppose he was thinking, and at worst being polite enough to let a relative nonentity have their say. In his world that was almost as bad as needing to pause to think, because although it would show that he was a thoughtful democrat, it could also indicate that he was prone to indecision at crucial moments.

Trapped in the glare like a startled rabbit, luckily, for Marcoin, Lithgo found more to say; it was always how these things played out for the successful politician. 'Like, you know, Star Trek, or Tolkien, maybe she's an elf, or something.' His voice faded away. He shouldn't have said elf, it was his favourite fantasy and now they'd know. It would have been obvious. They'd have heard it in his voice.

Of course, other than Marcoin looking for a way out of his imagined crisis, no one had heard anything, none of them had paid the slightest attention, but it was the chance he had been fervently praying for. 'Elves?' His eyebrows lifted and he glanced around the room. No one made eye contact. He turned and pushed his hair away from his eyes. The bead of sweat was collected and smeared away with a business-like rubbing of hands. 'And what can they see now?' He asked no one in particular.

Attention refocused on the radio and Lithgo was forgotten.

$$\Omega$$

When the Sphere next spoke to her, Chepi was showering away the blood and pain.

'They'll keep coming back.'

'Back where?'

'Here, to see what they can.'

'What's the point?'

'They need answers.'

'About what?' She asked. The Sphere didn't answer so she tried another tactic. 'Do they live long?'

'No.'

While she'd been showering she'd scanned the city trying to find out what, if anything, was worth the Sphere's attention. What she'd seen wasn't good. 'Then that's a blessing for them.'

'Why?'

'Their lives seem difficult.'

15

The Sphere remained silent.

'Am I anything like them?' She asked, unexpectedly, after several minutes had passed.

The Sphere was caught off-guard by the question but had no intention of showing it. 'Similar but strange, to them.'

Chepi was one step ahead. From the briefest glance below she knew already that she was like them, almost, and from long experience she had learnt that nothing that happened around the Sphere did so by chance. 'Is that important?' She asked with seeming innocence.

Despite its omnipotence the Sphere didn't immediately guess what she was getting at, so thought it best to be encouraging. It knew from experience that her attention span could be exceptionally short, so if it wasn't careful, without a second thought she could write off the whole human species in an instant. 'Yes.'

'I mean the difference?'

The Sphere was unsure where the questions were leading. 'Could be.'

'More specific, maybe?'

'It might give you some power over them.'

'I don't need power, do I?'

'That's for you to decide. I'm just a Sphere.'

The pretence was obvious, but it gave her the opening she wanted. 'I think, then, that maybe I'll not bother.'

'That comes as no surprise.' But the speed of it had. She'd outplayed it and long term that meant trouble.

She smiled. 'So, we can go now?'

The Sphere had no choice but to show is hand. 'No.'

'Thought not.'

Ω

The meeting had been hurriedly arranged, and the room full of Canada's most senior politicians and scientists reverberated with the chaotic sounds of random conjecture. Disorganised shuffling permeated the air as aids shambled by with piles of arbitrary documents in a forlorn struggle to create a paper structure to wrap around the frenzied minds bustling without direction from one place to another in the large but already over-full space around the table.

A hammer banged, crashing through the cacophony with a simple effectiveness no one could ignore. The room stilled.

When the gavelled echo fell away a strong, weighty voice rumbled forwards. 'If you have a seat please remain where you are. If not would you wait with the assistants outside until you are called.' No one demurred. 'Thank you.'

A murmur of disapproval rose like a plague of mosquitoes as those without a seat finally woke up to the reality of not being picked, of spending yet another day on the sideline. The moment they had long expected, their chance to bask in the aura of the powerful had been snatched away before they had had a chance to saviour it fully. They had not been granted even a moment to boast. After all the inconvenience of the long wait, no vindication of their importance, no public testimony of their worth. No nod from the powerful, just a bland, careless dismissal for being no one in particular.

The voice had some sense of this and wasn't yet ready to ditch them completely. As it knew, in a crisis you never could tell who would turn out to be essential. The trick was to keep as many of them happy as possible for as long as it mattered. 'We'll need input from you all I'm sure. Please be patient.'

The murmur subsided minutely, a gradual quietening until an almost silence returned, and then unnoticed they left, washed out of mind by the clanging and creaking of chairs being importantly manoeuvred into place by the lucky chosen few. Hushed voices ushered the others away and the door closed.

'Bloody cheek.' The speaker was Zen Macleod from the University of British Columbia. He said it quietly so no one would hear. Strong words, but whispered, as usual. Although totally disgusted in general with everything around him, both professional and personal, he feigned indifference, affected the pretence of cool detachment from the mundane problems of everyday life. 'Why am I even here?' He asked no one in particular.

'Just like the rest of us, looking for a chance to be important, scurrying around after half-educated politicians like we always do.'

Too often quick to judgement, Zen sized her up instantly. She was a hippy, obviously, he thought. His term for anyone who tried to flavour any mundane observation with something that seemed both radical and liberal but was usually neither. 'How original.' He

17

mumbled to himself. Fully expecting her not to hear he turned away.

'That's me, I'd rather be right than some misguided trend-setter.'

He turned back, but she'd moved away. Normally he would have dismissed her from his mind, but the fact that she was very beautiful made him hesitate, but only for a second, until he had the presence of mind to suck in a deep breath of objectivity and find something about her that he didn't like. Her hair was too short. He exhaled and glanced at his watch. The Department meeting started in 30 minutes and he couldn't be late, he was the chair, but despite what he might privately think, he had to stay. So far as he knew he was the only xeno-anthropologist there was, so he had to be able to make a contribution.

Actually, when the Sphere had first appeared, for a brief moment he'd thought it was because of him. That it, they or whatever had known about his work, had maybe even read his latest monograph 'Speculations on Non-human, Sentient Kinship Rituals'. His masterpiece, even the thought of it made him smile. He'd had endless arguments with his publisher about the direction he had taken. They'd thought they were getting a popular science book, a work of creative non-fiction, but alas not. The editor was sacked.

Across the room the head of archaeology, Rane Tantoning, a renowned and exceptionally pompous expert on human evolution, was watching him. 'And what's he doing here?' Tantoning asked.

His colleague shrugged, too wary to be drawn once again into a ritual character assassination of yet another colleague. A new post-doctoral appointment, he was still getting used to the sheer childishness of the average academic. Once revered, he now knew that a lifetime of learning meant nothing in terms of maturity.

Tantoning didn't notice his reaction, he was talking to himself as usual, nursing the offence he felt that a fringe idiot like Macleod should have been invited to the same meeting as someone as eminent as himself. He felt clearly that it somehow reflected badly on him. 'Bloody fools.'

'Maybe he'll have something to offer. You know, a blue sky thing.' The post-doc couldn't help himself. Still untainted by fear, failure, lost dreams and Machiavellian trickery, the words just tripped out.

Tantoning was unimpressed. 'The only bloody blue sky he's

seen is in his head.' He put his coffee cup down and turned to go. One thing was suddenly clear to him, he wasn't going to be called into the meeting despite his reputation. They were merely being polite. Whoever it was that had put him on the list was just giving him a quiet nod of approval, acknowledgement that he'd been noticed. It was corridor politics, and Tantoning, an expert on positive reframing, especially when he came to things affecting him, let himself believe that this invitation presaged bigger things to come, doors actually opening once the garbage had been cleared away. 'I'm off.' He said, please with the conceit he had conjured from nothing but believed in every bit as much as any fiction he had published on his way to minor fame and middleclass comfort.

'They might need you.' His colleague said. He tried to mean it but his eyes drifted away. It took considerable effort, purpose and some desperation for him to lie even partly effectively, and this didn't warrant any of them.

Tantoning wasn't listening anyway.

$$\Omega$$

The meeting came to order.

'Well, we all know why we're here so no need for an agenda this time, eh?' The Prime Minister laughed at his own joke, his large, red face beaming with pleasure and his eyes twinkling with the menace of power. 'John, start us off will you.'

John Marcoin cleared his throat. He knew that would happen, that he would be thrown in at the deep end. For a moment he wished he hadn't been at the airport when the damned Sphere had appeared. He looked down at his papers, but could still feel them all watching, waiting for him to tell them what to think. The moment paused while heavy, expectant eyes held him in the spotlight. That was enough, it was what he had been waiting for, as always he only needed to feel wanted, to know that they needed him. All the old reassurance came flooding back. Speaking first was a blessing. Do it right and the direction everything else took from that moment on would be his. He couldn't, didn't dare even for a moment to contemplate, reflect on, or in the slightest way allow the possibility of failure. The confidence of ignorance all politicians were somehow born with ensured that doubts were torn apart before they had time even to open their eyes and spy his destruction. 'We know very little. The helicopter crew have offered nothing more than is contained in the report in front of you.' He began.

A quick shuffle of paper followed as everyone hurried to be seen as taking the comment about there being a report seriously. They scanned the pages expertly, seeking the phrase they could hang their first comment on if they were asked. One of the oldest tricks, find a question, something to lean on and pretend it's worthy of attention. Anything would do, such as: 'Have we any ideas about the rotation Minister?' or: 'Are there any views on the fact it's gold coloured Minister?' There were always questions like those to show you have been paying attention. And if you've been skipped over until all the obvious points have gone then the response is simple: 'I think we've already covered the key points Minister, perhaps we could look at priorities, ways of moving forward.' Raised eyebrows at the end followed by an amiable glance around the room. It always worked. Executed properly it ensured that the speaker would then be free to choose arbitrarily something already mentioned, cautiously suggest it may be the most important, but concede the position immediately if anyone senior suggested anything different.

John paused to underscore how important it was to read his document. This was another strategy he used to coalesce the meeting around the things he knew already. He understood keenly, indeed had always known, that rarely would anyone say anything not directed at the content of a report placed in front of them. It was another of those things that he'd always grasped intuitively. Secretly he despised the trivialness of such transparent tricks, but they gave him power, and even more importantly they saved him from exposure. These tricks were the shield that protected him, stopped the others finding out the truth, that almost everything he did was made up, manufactured from drunken conversations, half-truths and damned lies peddled around in bars and political living rooms. He was a lie, but then he suspected they all were, that's why they conspired together in the silent exercise of self-importance and advantage. They were all hopelessly corrupt, but for some reason no one ever mentioned it. This simple fact of power cheered him and depressed him in equal measure.

'There are three key points to focus on initially.' He particularly liked the last word, it meant that if anyone did think of something else it would merely be a matter of priorities rather than the rightness or wrongness of anything he had said. With one word he'd managed to both open the door for anyone who knew more than he did, while at the same time protecting his own position. This was something everyone at the meeting both heard and understood. It was a standard opening gambit.

'So, firstly, why reveal themselves? He continued. 'Why make part of the Sphere transparent? Secondly, What does the rotation mean? Did they need to rotate to see the helicopter or could it serve some other function? And, thirdly, why gold? Was it there to protect them from our atmosphere, from the sun maybe?' Job done and baton passed on, he stopped and looked up.

Everyone looked down and ruffled their papers. It was too risky to speak. No one had the faintest idea of the scope of answer the situation required. Could they speculate wildly, or were they supposed to answer 'scientifically'? There were no clues and the safest bet was to say nothing.

The PM spoke out. 'Let's brainstorm; we're all caught out a bit by this so speak freely, all of you.'

'Brainstorm' a.k.a. the chance to commit professional suicide. They buried their heads further into their papers until time seemed to stop. Beads of tension bulged from sweated brows until out of desperation or misplaced ambition someone's nerve broke.

'I agree with the Minister.' A clever move and everyone nodded sagely in agreement. A murmur of content mumbled fraternally around the room followed by the expected pause, routine when the speaker had broken the ice but hadn't actually said anything substantial.

The room buffeted with a stilled moment of waiting. Would they be friend or foe after the next few seconds? Judgement hung in the air, approval partially granted but yet to be consummated. 'They obviously revealed themselves intentionally, and from what we know they appeared human. That must have been planned, to put us at our ease. Perhaps?'

The last word showed weakness and was quickly regretted. The speaker was a junior Minister, more an aide than anything else, and was thus at the stage when they still believed every word spoken was weighed carefully by the listener. The truth, as they would eventually find out is that no one ever really listens to anything that isn't about them in some direct or indirect way, or otherwise offers some reward or benefit.

'But can we really ascribe human intentions?' The PM responded. 'It could be a big mistake.'

Incomprehensible sounds of newly found doubt muttered their way around the table. The junior Minister sat naked under the bright light of contradiction. He had a million clever things to say, but the courage needed was greater than he dared. 'Perhaps not, but, well, it did seem, er, human.'

The PM moved slowly, but with the deadly purpose of any natural predator. 'And why is that exactly? Just speak your mind young Johnson.'

Johnson knew he'd blown it already. Never hesitate, that was the key to political success. He'd seen all of them do it time and time again on television and elsewhere. Speak quickly and with great confidence and no matter what the question was make sure you said what you wanted and not what the interviewer needed. Bluster if you must but never back down. That's what he'd been taught. If you needed facts then make them up, by the time anyone checks it's too late. Everyone knew that the public don't care enough anyway, and even if on occasion they did, one thing they hated even more than lying politicians was bickering journalists. So, faced with obvious failure, recklessness took Johnson over. A cunning move, the final card of the young. Somehow all politicians know instinctively that above all else youth, for a time, is always forgiven. Amongst the political elite, the unspoken acceptance of the reckless bravery of youth was timeless, after all how else could they be got to die in large numbers in the endless wars conjured from greying minds afraid of looming obscurity? 'It seems human sir.' Johnson said. 'After all, isn't that what we'd do, to get a better look at something., pull the blinds back, open the curtains? Just a gesture of sheer curiosity?'

Silent, tentative nods carefully weaved their way through the meeting. They admired the attempt, but until the PM spoke no one could be sure of its real worth.

The PM stared blankly into space. A false portrayal of thoughtfulness while the mood of the meeting eased its way through his thick, red desensitized skin. 'Mmm, yes, I see your point.'

An unheard sigh echoed. The meeting was opened for the

first time. The initial salvos played out and the tone set. The skeletal parameters were established and words began to burble out liberally. Much time was wasted and the experts outside became increasingly toxified by hopes of imminent inclusion and endless cups of cheap caffeine.

Ω

'What are they talking about?'

'Who?' The Sphere asked.

'All those people watching us.' The crowds had grown over the last few days. The centre of Vancouver had become almost impassable at any time of day or night. Tens of thousands had flocked in from all over Canada and beyond. The Government was considering a ban on both domestic and international incoming flights to British Columbia. They trembled, though, at the concept. Traders would be outraged at being held back from such a valuable source of extra wealth, but that had to be balanced against the enraged traders who would no longer be able to get to their stores and offices.

Once the tents started to be erected driving became impossible. The police had done as much as they were able to, but once religious interpretations of the Sphere's presence began to abound the Provincial Government staggered into inactivity on the grounds of a citizen's right to freedom from religious persecution. They were also playing safe for other reasons. After all, they reasoned in private, sometimes doing nothing was better than opening the door to endless unseen problems, which in the case of an alien visitation would no doubt be limitless.

'They're trying to work out what we are. Some think we're aliens ...'

'We are, aren't we?'

'… who've come to bring about the end of Mankind, and ...'

'You mean Humankind. They have two sexes don't they?'

The Sphere sighed. 'The word 'Mankind' is their social term, in the language here anyway. The males are dominant.'

Chepi frowned. That didn't seem likely, she thought. Why imbalance a perfectly good arrangement by making one of them more powerful than the other. 'Are you sure?'

'Yes.'

'Why?'

'It's a primate thing.'

'They really are still primates?'

'Yes.'

Chepi had known their evolutionary history but hadn't thought such a distant thing would still be significant socially. Swinging from trees was a long way in their past. 'Why, haven't they evolved from that yet?'

'They can't, it's a brain stem problem.'

'Shame.' And then something else occurred to her. 'And this is the reason they're obsessed with sex, power and status?'

The Sphere quickly grasped the thread of Chepi's thought. It was a distraction from what it had intended, but this was too good a chance to miss to get her to think seriously about what humans were, the reality underneath all the bright lights, tall buildings and totem poles. 'The males, yes, the females are more obsessed with babies, finding the right mate and making a home.'

Chepi feigned interest. 'So they're after different things, and in competition with each other most of the time?'

'Conflict.' The Sphere corrected. 'Most men want to rule everyone else and have sex with as many beautiful women as they can.'

She shrugged. 'Why do women even need men? Sounds like a lot of trouble to me.'

'To get pregnant, fulfil their sexual desires ...' The Sphere could see Chepi shift uncomfortably. It tried to forestall further unnecessary distractions. 'Yes, but maybe not all of them, I'm generalising a bit, but in most cases ...' It waited but she didn't say anything. 'The majority of women want to be looked after and provided for.'

Chepi laughed out loud. 'I don't think so, from what I've seen they can provide well enough for themselves. Seems to me they only need the sex and the sperm.'

'Perhaps, but they like each other, most men and women anyway. They like being together, and, anyway, you'll find there is often a lot less to them than you might expect.'

'Why in particular do they like each other?' She knew the Sphere wouldn't know.

It paused for a millionth of a second. Not long, but long enough for Chepi to notice. She smirked at being right. 'You don't have any idea, do you?'

'No.' It replied defensively. 'Only a human would know. It's just their nature.'

'And I guess old habits die hard.'

'Sex is almost everything to them. It permeates everything they do, build and all they ever want. Whatever you do, don't forget how important this is to them, or ever underestimate its power.'

She shrugged again. 'Okay, but why does any of this matter to me? To be honest, I don't find them all that interesting.'

'Maybe you'll change your mind.'

'Don't think so.'

'You will, and, anyway, there's someone down there I want you to meet.'

A long silence filled the Sphere before Chepi little by little got to her feet. 'Meet someone?' Her voice trembled. She'd never met anyone, not even once throughout her whole existence. 'Meet ...' Even the concept confused her. Meet? Meet what?' In her head she ran through the meaning of the word to check for some kind of misunderstanding. There wasn't any, it did mean some kind of encounter; 'their lips met', an expression she had once read that still made her shudder. 'In the flesh?' Another phrase, one that disgusted her even more. 'You mean meet someone physically?'

The Sphere understood her fears. 'You won't have to touch them.'

She felt nauseous. 'They smell.'

The comment came as a surprise. 'You've taken samples?'

'Yes, the air around them, all those hormones everywhere, it's enough to make me sick.'

'Why?'

'Why, because of all the clouds of disgusting fumes surrounding them that make them completely irrational. There are young humans walking around half naked in the cold just because they've caught a whiff of some obnoxious odour from the armpit of someone they might not even know? They are not rational you know. Their brains are okay, but sadly for them their bodily odours get everywhere and drive them crazy'

25

But the Sphere wasn't going to be distracted. 'I mean why the samples?'

Chepi switched to evasion. She didn't even understand herself why she'd bothered. 'I wondered how they could breathe with all that stuff around them. Thought it must be ... somehow attractive in some way, but unfortunately, no, it's not in the least bit pleasant. To be honest, they disgust me.'

The Sphere thought about explaining olfactory fatigue, explaining how the ability to smell them would wear off over a short time, but it guessed Chepi already knew that it would, so the disgust wasn't about the smell itself but the fact of them smelling of anything in the first place. The Sphere blamed itself for over-protecting her, for thinking her sensitivity was weakness when anything but that was the truth. It had taught her to be too cautious, and now there needed to be change. 'Not this person, she doesn't smell at all.'

Chepi scoffed. 'Impossible. Their hormones are in everything around them, their food, where they live and work. They even cover themselves in animal hormones. I looked into all of this carefully, so don't try lying to me, as usual.'

The Sphere ignored the insult. 'But this one isn't like them, she's ...' The Sphere held its breath, she wouldn't like what was coming next, finding out that something important had been kept from her for so long. There was no easy way to tell her except to do it her as fast as possible and then run. Leave her to find some exaggerated conspiracy behind the deception she would be able to confront it with later. That way at least there would be a starting point for a discussion, otherwise she would just sulk for millennia. The Sphere breathed out with trepidation. 'She's my avatar. The only one I've ever had.' It added quickly. 'She's been here for a while.' It switched its attention away and ran to hide, but not fast enough to miss Chepi's eyes grow wide with astonishment. Anger followed, but by then the Sphere was watching the stars and humming to itself.

Ω

Zen Macleod hadn't left. Staying had been more about apathy than anything else, he told himself, but in truth his was an act of unconscious desperation. He was already 38 and still hadn't been offered a permanent academic post. In his twenty-something imagination he'd foreseen a brilliant academic career unfolding, but life hadn't worked out that way. His friends blamed his wild choice of specialisation, after all where could xeno-anthropology lead him in a world where close ties with fellow researchers was the only way to survive let alone prosper? He was the only person in the world with his interests and, more importantly, that meant that he was only one who cared whether he survived professionally or sank without a trace. Except, of course, for the inhabitants of innumerable web sites for conspiracy theorists who listed his every move as though they were somehow as important as the sad bedroom habits of some idiotic film or pop star. The truth was his career was grinding to a halt, but as his options faded, along came the Sphere and his call to the meeting. He weathered a long nervous wait until at last came a tap on his shoulder and doors literally opened before him.

The doors creaked slowly inwards, revealing a smoke filled room of faces that were all too readily familiar, faces that judged, that would give him at most a minute or so to prove himself. The age-worn glances of no second chances followed his progress into the room.

'Pull up a chair. Dr Macleod, isn't it?' The PM sounded almost friendly, but he knew not to let that fool him.

'Yes, ...' He was about to say sir, but didn't dare in case it made him look inferior. It was a stupid thought, but one that had already caused a noticeable pause. He recovered quickly. 'Prime Minister.' Then he blushed. For some inexplicable reason the words sounded stupid, as though he had made a mistake, a huge gaff, that it wasn't the Prime Minister at all, but the figure away at the other end of the table merely smiled in response and so he eased himself into an available chair and began to shuffle the papers conveniently placed in front of him by some silent angel of a bureaucratic saviour.

'Dr Macleod, Dr Nitunakiwidinok has said you might be able to help us with a bit of an impasse we've come to.'

At the name of his until then unknown sponsor Zen looked

up and across the table. The name conjured the image of an old, wise, aboriginal man. He followed the gaze of the room around to their destination with a sense of comfort and familiarity. His eyes sought an ally, but instead they found the young woman with the too short hair he'd insulted outside. He gawped at her; she didn't even look native Canadian. The eyes, maybe, there was something about them that ... He felt himself drifting.

'Dr Macleod?'

He turned quickly back to the PM. 'Yes.' He gestured back to Nitunakiwidinok as coolly as he could. I'm afraid we've not met before, Prime Minister.'

The PM frowned and leaned forward in what to Zen seemed an avuncular fashion. 'But judging by your reaction you soon will.' He laughed at his own wittiness. He had long known that creating a bit of discomfort kept people in their place, stopped them becoming too sure of themselves.

Zen did his best to look blank. Not saying anything was always the best option in these kinds of situations.

The PM's smile faded as the quiet laughter subsided. 'As I said, Dr Nitunakiwidinok believes you might be able to help us sort out a few minor problems we've come up against.' And then, just in case that suggested too much importance. 'We won't keep you long, just one or two small things we'd like to resolve before we move on. So, Dr Nitunakiwidinok, over to you.'

The words meant he was momentarily handing over control but he had no choice, he didn't have the faintest clue what they had been talking about for the last 30 minutes. Calling in Zen had been merely a trick to switch the discussion in a way that, he hoped, would enable him to regain a grasp on the increasingly obscure discussion that had evolved. And, anyway, with Macleod arriving most of the discussion would have to be replayed, giving him valuable breathing space.

Nitunakiwidinok turned and smiled. It said a million things and made Zen bitterly regret ignoring her before. It was a wise smile, a knowing look, some pity wrapped in amusement. Only the eyes were a problem. They knew him, he didn't know how but they looked deep inside as though they were gathering secrets from places even he had forgotten existed. Fleetingly they paused and an instant later they shifted to something else, to interest at his answer to the question her lips began to frame around her perfect white teeth. The moment stretched out and around him in a strange embrace, and then it was gone, dissolved into ordinary words.

'Can we know truly know anything about an alien culture? Not observe, not note behaviour, but understand from just reasoning about it?' The last bit was for the audience, she knew he would have followed her drift from the third word onwards but ordinary people needed a little more.

His heart raced. He knew the answer; this was exactly what he knew. 'I'm glad you said know 'something' ...' She didn't smile. 'Because we could never know everything.' He looked away from her and turned to the PM. It was a good move, it showed respect, but, more importantly for him, it also meant he wouldn't have to weave out his answers under her ridiculously distracting gaze.

The PM nodded encouragement. So far so good, he thought, plain language.

'If their lives share any of the same interests and activities we have, then there would be some chance we could understand the purpose behind what they do. Well, at least in part.' The latter was an expression he always used, it was an academic 'get out of jail free card'.

The Minister, however, was well versed in verbal tricks. 'But how big a part?' The Minister asked.

This was easy. Zen smiled to himself. Rule two in putting forward unusual ideas was to keep everything general and tentative. 'Depends on how close their lives are to ours. A whale, maybe not much, but with tool using, spacecraft building explorers, because that is at least a part of what they are, we should be able to generalize in a useful way. First, though, we should be clear about what we want to know, what questions we want to ask because these will determine what we find out. Do we have any idea of what is thought to be important at this stage?' He let the question hang in the air for while, but no one responded. This wasn't unexpected, and it gave him a bit more room to manoeuvre. 'They've come here from a long way off so that shows that they have the same kind of curiosity we have, wanting to leave their home country to explore, learn about other cultures and species and new find resources.

'Our history hasn't been too good on that.' The speaker was a large hawkish looking man in a uniform. Zen smiled and tried to respond, but he was cut off. 'If you're saying they share our interest in going out and finding things they want then that doesn't sound too good for us given the way we've gone about that process in recent times.'

'No, that's true.' Zen responded. 'But I'm not saying that they are here to take anything, not at this stage anyway, I'm just giving an example, and an abstract one at that, of the kind of process we could use to help us think about what their purpose and motivations might be.'

'And, from what we do know, these could be?' The PM asked, not a little apprehensive at the change in tone. The last thing he wanted was some mass display of paranoia. That was the trouble with academics, always speculating as though it was all a game. Either that or one minute they were promising limitless free energy and the next predicting the end of the world. Always the same, they needed a firm hand to stay on side. 'Let's try to keep focused on what we already know, can we.'

Zen groaned inwardly. It was always like this with politicians. All they ever wanted was comfortable platitudes, justifications for what they had already decided, and for everyone else to look the other way so they could carry on supporting corporate interests while the rest of the planet went to the dogs. Whatever was said they always had a knack of turning things around to make scientists look as though they were just empty-headed dreamers or enemies of the state. 'What I meant Prime Minster is that they are here in something they've built. They must have come a long way and have highly developed technology. In a way it's a bit like the wooden ships from Europe arriving on the American coast. Explorers searching for the new.'

The room panicked. Beaded eyes swivelled frenziedly across the room and lined up angrily in his direction. He felt each glassy reflection of alarm burn into him with malevolent intent as whispers of fear brimmed quietly in every hissed gasp of surprise. Zen paused in confusion, what had he said? His nervous glance swept by Nitunakiwidinok and then it dawned on him, the plagues, genocide, the sweeping away of indigenous cultures in the name of progress. A surge of adrenalin whirled out of control as he struggled to find words to save his moment of glory. 'But, of course, that doesn't mean they're like us in every respect, I'm just … speculating.' He stammered hurriedly.

The PM looked at him long and hard. When the words came the warning was obvious. 'Maybe we should put wild speculation to one side for a moment.' His eyes narrowed either in anger or for dramatic effect, it was impossible to tell. 'So exactly how much can we know for sure?' He folded his hands together slowly in what he hoped was a gesture of perfect ease. 'After all, it's not helpful to suppose too much, now is it Dr Macleod.'

Zen needed no further warning, this chance was too important to blow so quickly. For once he managed to rein himself in. 'No Prime Minister, I was merely … demonstrating the kind of thought processes we could employ.'

'Well then, perhaps we'd better wait until we know more. We don't want the public panicking now do we?' He guffawed loudly, to make clear how preposterous the thought was. They joined in quietly, tentatively at first as though they were somehow testing their own feelings, but then the sound of their own laughter gave them strength and the room quickly resounded with manic cackles of relief at a crisis avoided.

$$\Omega$$

Chepi screamed wordlessly at the walls. And then once again, but the Sphere couldn't hear.

She wandered over to where she could look down at the strange throngs of people milling about below.

'An avatar? What the frak does it want with one of those? The whole thing was way outside her experience.

$$\Omega$$

Zen sipped his beer. He was sitting uncomfortably in the Urban Pit, a bar not far from the University of British Columbia. He had Nitunakiwidinok for company, but it seemed more than obvious that she was anything but willing. They'd both been bungled into the same private plane and flown straight back to Vancouver to 'collaborate'. Zen took that as a slight on his reputation. He had never had to collaborate with anyone before so he didn't see the need now. The irony of being offended because she felt the same way escaped him.

'I haven't got long.' She offered at last, having until then only proffered non-verbal responses to everything he had proposed or suggested. Her shrug was particularly well practiced he thought.

Perversely, her lack of manners and obvious complete disinterest in anything he had to say began to cheer him up. As much as he felt insulted on the surface, he began to realize that at last he had encountered someone with even less skill than he had at playing the political game. It wasn't that he recognised this consciously, instead her behaviour left him with a feeling of superiority he wasn't particularly used to experiencing. Instinctively, he felt that at last he'd found someone he could look down on in the great hunt for academic status.

At least that's what his unconscious mind silently whispered to him, but it was a notion quickly extinguished. An instant later, before he even had the chance to tell her he didn't have long either, Rane Tantoning happened to pass by. As he glanced at Zen he automatically conjured the glazed expression senior people everywhere use to flick over the unwanted with a clear but immediately false signal that they haven't been seen. The glance gave out two signals, one, that he had been seen, and two, that he didn't count. All would have been fine, the game played and ended, but then he caught sight of Nitunakiwidinok and stopped just that bit too quickly. Not that he noticed. Already his face had fixed itself into a leery smile of gushed excitement. His face trembled with the flushed pleasure of the smitten middle-aged. 'Nitu, my dear, I thought they'd kept you back in Ottawa.' He danced a little dance, waved his hands about in unknowing excitement and offered to buy her a drink. Which was, as it always is in such situations, a plea to be included, to sit with her, to join in and get just that little bit closer.

'Rane, hi, I've got one thanks. Sorry, but.' She gestured to Zen. 'I'm tied up just now'

At the inclusion Zen felt a warm glow of pleasure, which almost, but not quite, countered his frustration at seeing how chummy she was with senior management. Conversely, the rejection left Tantoning feeling stupid. His confidence vanished, leaving him feeling like a small, sad puppy. It had always been like that, rejection hit him hard, but then that had been what had fuelled his ambition for as long as he could remember. Being wanted had been everything for the sad loner of his teenage years, and that meant learning how to please those he needed, which as luck would have it was also the most essential trait ambitious people could possible have, more important by far than either ability or professionalism. 'Well, another time then.' He acted out the facsimile of an unintended pause. 'And you must come over to supper, Jean's always asking after you.'

'She smiled and dazzled both of them. 'Sure, I'd love to visit. I'll phone Jean. Say hi to her for me.'

Tantoning stepped lightly from one foot to the other while he worked out whether or not he could leave without appearing to have been brushed off. Feelings of unease bristled upwards, but then she smiled again and touched his arm briefly. He was released, and no one but the two of them even knew anything had happened.

'Didn't know you knew him.' Zen said, as Tantoning's back disappeared across the bar.

'Yes, he can be really helpful.'

'Not your department though, is it?' Zen realised he didn't even know where she worked. UBC was a big place.'

'Archaeology.'

That was all she offered, one word and then she clammed up again. Zen was finding it hard work. 'Oh, right. That's near me. Haven't seen you around.'

'Just came down for this, seemed like it might be fun.'

Down?' It was like pulling teeth.

'I do fieldwork, up in the Yukon.'

'Oh.' He wasn't in the least bit interested and it would be dangerous to ask any more. It was always the same with archaeologists, ask a question and before you knew it they have bits of old bones and arrowheads all over the place. They were all the same, mind crushingly obsessed with wild speculation about scraps of indistinguishable junk they had found that were so small and indistinct, to everyone else they looked like the kind of garbage the dog brings in, or the cat after a successful night of randomly killing unknown numbers of endangered bats, toads and endless other victims of their insatiable, murderous obsession with death. So far as he was concerned the whole discipline was pure invention, conjured up by too many over active, adolescent minds wrapped in academic pretensions. To Zen they'd simply never out grown a childhood fascination with treasure hunts. 'I see.' It was all he could manage.

He paused long enough for the obvious to come to mind, if what she did was all so pointless, why her, what was she doing at the meeting, and Tantoning too? 'So what were you doing at the meeting?' Neither tact nor patience were his strong points.

'Invited.' She sipped her beer and then sprawled back into her chair. She crossed one leg across her knee and waited.

'Yes, but why? I mean archaeology is obviously important.' He surprised himself by not smiling even a small amount. 'But what's it got to do with alien spheres?'

'Could ask the same. What's xeno-anthropolgy got to do with it?'

He felt affronted. Surely that was obvious to everyone. 'I thought what I'd said in the meeting showed that, what it could offer I mean.'

In truth she'd thought that what he'd said was vacuously obvious, but to her surprise they'd actually taken him seriously. And that, she felt, just showed once again that in academic life packaging was everything. 'I don't want to be rude, or anything, but wasn't all that bloody obvious?'

Those were the words he feared the most because they had been used before, over and over and he still did not know if it was true or not. In the past he had rummaged through colleagues papers to see if there was anything fundamentally different in their basic approach from his, but he couldn't see one. He was hopeless at self-criticism, always had been. He suspected they all were and they only survived through some grand conspiracy of mutual self-protection. Other than his own work, which was carried out without any support whatsoever he always reminded himself, he believed that everything else, the whole of social science research was nothing more than a huge exercise in collective vanity publishing; worthless mush with no scientific value at all.

'Well, it was wasn't it?' She asked.

'Bit hard don't you think? After all they were just politicians.'

She didn't laugh. 'Don't underestimate them.'

Ω

The Sphere sneaked its attention back to Chepi and watched silently as she scanned through some pages of text on her computer screen. 'I know you're watching.'

'You couldn't possibly.'

'You don't know everything about me.'

That was true. Chepi's mind had four times as many neural connections as there were particles in the universe, which made it four times smarter than a human mind. Even the Sphere couldn't compute its activity at that level. That had been one of its intentions, a small one over all, but on balance it liked the fact that it would never know all there was to know about her. 'Maybe.' Was all it offered in reply.

'You don't and you know you don't, so why play games.'

'I came to see if you'd calmed down.'

'No, but I'm busy now. They're trying to talk to us.'

The Sphere hadn't known that, it had purposely left any direct contact to her. 'I'm surprised they took so long.'

'I think they've probably been waiting for us. After all, they'll have supposed that we travelled all this way with some purpose, not to just hang around above them doing nothing.'

'True, I can imagine they would think that. Even I would if it was the other way around. 'What do they say?' It asked.

'Welcome.'

'Anything else?'

'We offer you no harm.'

'That's good of them.'

Chepi tutted. 'Well, don't forget they did see me, those people in the helicopter, and I must have looked as shocked as them. Hardly anything to threaten them anyway.'

'You might be surprised.'

Chepi sensed the Sphere was withholding yet more she should know. 'Meaning? What else should I know?' She sounded impatient. The Sphere decided not to prevaricate.

'To them you look like a mythical character. Something they think came from their imagination, or a spirit or something that lived thousands of years before them.'

'Something evil?'

'No, something powerful and superior, and ...' It knew she'd like this part. 'Something more beautiful than their imagination could describe.'

'And that's some kind of coincidence I suppose, that they just happened to imagine something like me? I don't think so. Is that what your avatar's been up to?' Of course she took for granted that she'd be more beautiful than they could imagine, it wasn't worth even acknowledging.

'Yes.'

There was something in its tone. 'And more than planting stories?'

'It has findings, bones and things, that might make it seem to them that people like you actually lived there.'

'When?'

'When what?'

'When did your avatar find them? And was that its purpose?'

'About a month ago, and yes, it was one purpose.'

'Nice timing. So it's a she?'

'We thought so. And yes, it's a she.'

Chepi wanted to ask why it was female, but if she did she knew the Sphere would use the opportunity as a means of feeding her misinformation. She decided to work it out herself later. 'Skip the 'we', she's just an avatar, just a ...'

'She's not, well was, but she's completely sentient now, her own person. Anyway, I didn't mean her.'

'Does it have a name, and does she know about me?'

'Nitu. And she doesn't know anything about us.'

Chepi mentally flipped through all the Earth languages she'd had time to look at so far. 'Oh, so original, and Native American just to make it even more grounded in their pre-technological cultures. There's a whole mythology you've been playing around with isn't there?'

'Aboriginal Canadian, and I said there was.

'You have been working hard.'

'There's a purpose. You'll work it out.'

Chepi didn't respond. The beginning at least was now obvious. The avatar had found remains of beings previously believed to be myths and then at almost at the same time the Sphere appeared, and by 'chance' she'd shown herself. She could guess what they had been thinking. The avatar would be bound to have told them by now. Then, something else fell into place ... 'So that was the purpose of that childishness, making me fall and break my nose so I'd do something rash.'

'You needed spurring on, you weren't showing any interest.'

'It's immoral to manipulate me like that.'

'Yes, I'm sorry.'

'Sorry doesn't change anything.'

'I know.'

'And who did you mean by 'we'? If its not the avatar then who?'

It wanted to lie but couldn't think of anything plausible. 'Illiaeth.'

Illiaeth, the name came as a surprise. Chepi needed time to think, and she was in no hurry.

The silence grew between them and lasted until the Sphere was forced to speak. It needed to maintain the momentum until Chepi took control. 'What are you going to say to them?'

She didn't answer.

'To their message?'

'Things are going to have to change around here.' She said.

'I know. But now, what are you going to tell them?'

Still annoyed that things had been decided behind her back Chepi's thoughts formed themselves slowly into four words. They appeared on the screen in front of her and then she beamed them down to those waiting below. 'THERE MUST BE CHANGE.'

'Bit cryptic, and they might see that as a threat.' The Sphere remarked cautiously.

'It's ambiguous, it's how they work.' Of course she didn't just mean the human's below, if the Sphere could play games so could she. 'They'll be wary, but not too threatened because they can't know for sure what it means.'

The Sphere's image transited in colour from pure white to sea green blue.

'I knew you'd like it.' And then she swivelled her attention directly at the Sphere. 'So what's all this about Illiaeth?'

Ω

'You found what?'

Nitu didn't offer a reply, she just watched him evenly and waited. It always took time for the news to sink in.

'One hundred and twenty-five thousand year old remains of a human up there in the Yukon?'

She nodded. 'Possibly older, we can't quite fix the date. And they're not quite human.'

'Wow, early humans here that long ago?' Despite his contempt for archaeology the idea gripped his imagination. There was nothing like the merest hint of a large grant cheque to quash the most entrenched doctrinal contempt.

Nitu hesitated, she wasn't yet ready to share the findings with anyone. 'Perhaps.' She offered.

She fell quiet again. It was almost too difficult to talk about. So far she'd kept all news of the find to herself, and she'd intended to carry on like that for as long as she could. She feared the involvement of others would mean an influx of pre-conceived ideas and she wanted to stay as unburdened as possible, at least until she had had time to complete an initial analysis. She knew, though, that time was running out, once they saw the possible connection with the Sphere it could all be over for her, someone else from the government would take charge and she would be side-lined or cut out completely.

She knew she needed to work faster while there was still time, but for that she needed help, someone to bounce ideas off and work through with her what to do next, but how far she should collaborate wasn't clear. In her world no one could be trusted, probably not even Macleod with his suddenly glowing cheeks of excitement. Her choices were limited. She glanced over at Zen and wondered if she was wrong about him. Like her, he was an academic loner, and his career choices so far suggested that he didn't care in the least about career advancement. Maybe he could be trusted she thought. With no little time left to act, she took the risk. 'Maybe pre-human, but it doesn't fit any of the current models.'

Zen laughed. That was obvious, one hundred and twenty-five thousand years was way earlier than any other record of human life up there, but at the same time the remains should have been far too late to be anything but modern human, Neanderthals only existed in Europe, and yet she'd said not quite human. He knew this was big news, if she had found another branch of hominid around in North America at that time in human history the news would shock the world. Still, there was more than a slight chance that she might be wrong. He decided to play safe for the time being. 'I guess not, and, the remains aside, we have data to show most of the area covered in ice back then, don't we?'

'Most of, but not all, and we don't understand everything about what was going on.'

'No, I guess not.' He could see her mood shift. She was starting to clam up. 'But modern humans were still in Africa at that time, and didn't they almost become extinct?'

'That's what we've thought until now. Basically, the samples don't fit anything we've got at the moment This is all so crazy I'm playing it low key, so I haven't had chance to check everything.'

Zen couldn't believe his luck. She hadn't told anyone! 'You're keeping this to yourself?'

She shrugged. 'Maybe.' But nothing could be gained from lying. 'I don't want to make a fool of myself in case I'm wrong.'

Zen wondered what kind of fool was she thinking of, the 'simple mistake' kind, or the raving lunatic variety? 'Wrong about what exactly?'

She looked at him long and hard. His reply and expression betrayed the obvious 'say anything really weird and I'm out of here'. 'How much weird can you take?' She asked.

It was his turn to hesitate. Without the obvious potential for fame, wealth and lifetime tenure her research would surely bring if proved to be valid, he would have already made excuses and left. The fact that a giant golden sphere had appeared from nowhere also could not be ignored; it was, after all, a game changer. Taking everything into consideration, the choice was obvious. 'We've got a giant golden globe hanging above us so how much more weird can it get?'

'Did they show you the photograph?' She knew they hadn't, this was absolutely 'eyes only' to a few. She'd been shown, but only because of Tantoning.

'Photo, no. What photo.'

'Something on the Sphere showed itself to the helicopter crew.'

'I know, I heard that.' All restraint vanished, he sat upright in excitement. 'But they've got a picture? Bloody hell, what's it like.' Bizarre images of improbable shaped aliens flashed through his mind too fast to capture. 'Have you got a copy?'

She started to open her bag and Zen had to fight the urge to help. 'I copied this, even Tantoning doesn't know, so ...'

'Yeah, sure, you have my word.'

'This is serious Zen.'

'Sure, I know.' She had used his name for the first time. He smiled.

Nitu saw the smile in a different way. 'Really, it's state secret stuff. If they find out you can just forget about whatever it is you're planning, they'll ...'

'I understand.' He offered more soberly.

She fixed his gaze with serious intent. 'They're afraid of public panic.'

Zen felt his stomach clench. He wondered what could they have seen to make her so afraid of showing him a photograph.

Nitu handed him a photocopy. He paused and she nodded encouragement. He glanced down, and then laughed. 'Is this a joke? It's way out of focus.' He screwed his eyes up to see if it helped. 'Hard to make much out, but if anything, the figure looks like something out of Lord of the Rings.'

Her face drooped slightly in disappointment. She wondered what he had expected, some amorphous grey blob or a giant insect perhaps? The blurred outline seemed more probably to her, and would have done so even if she hadn't made the find in the Yukon. Nearly every culture had myths about creatures like this one, some strange, fabulous, ethereal human type figure that lived above and beyond the human world. Tolkien had drawn on that, creating figures drawn as much from the collective mind as his own imagination. 'It's a figure of myth. You're an anthropologist, you should know that.'

'Sure, but are you certain this is real and not a hoax, something pulled out of a box because of the familiarity, something not in the least threatening but appeasing for the fearful throng?'

'By the politicians?'

He nodded.

'Not likely is it? 'That wouldn't last long if the visitor decides to show itself.'

'Then how about the aliens, could it be them manipulating us?'

She smiled. 'Except for what I've found in the Yukon.'

He stared at her and the penny began to drop. He'd missed that she was actually slowly drawing some connection between the sphere and her work in the north. 'You're not going to say that you've found one of these?' He asked incredulously.

She smiled hesitantly. 'No, can't be that sure, but this does look a bit like my remains, as though they are similar beings. I can't ignore what I see.' She was going to say more, but she needed to know she could trust him first.

Zen wondered if she was pulling his leg for some reason, perhaps testing him. 'They could know about what you've found and fitted this fake picture to that. Not quite human remains and a humanoid alien.'

She frowned at him. 'Because that would make people less scared you mean, having one up there and one buried one hundred and twenty-five thousand years ago in the Yukon?'

He pulled a face. 'I see what you mean.'

She could see the time to hold back had already been passed. 'And we have to consider the DNA too.'

His eyes grew round in surprise. 'You got DNA?'

'Yes, and very well preserved.'

'And?'

'Well, let's just say we're probably more closely related to the chimpanzee than we are to whatever this is.'

'Frak. And you've not told anyone?' He found that hard to believe.

'No one, except you.'

'Why?'

'I don't really know.'

'You can't keep news like this from them. I understand why you'd want to but this isn't only an archaeological dig anymore is it? They'll expect you to share everything with them, and they will definitely expect us to collaborate, come up with ideas about the Sphere, but how can we do that now knowing what you've found unless we, you come clean with them?'

She shrugged again. She had known sharing what she had found would lead to this point. 'They didn't show you the photo did they, so you don't owe them anything.'

'Fine, I see your point, but I don't get to make the rules, and anyway, giving input will be hard when we will have to censor absolutely everything we tell them. '

She looked at him strangely. 'You afraid of them?'

He shrugged. Unconsciously he had already started to mimic her. Nitu noticed the gesture with irritation, she wasn't looking for yet another admirer. 'Maybe I shouldn't have told you.' She said.

'It's a matter of global security. At least that's the way they will see it.' He replied. 'They're not going to back-pedal if they think someone's a risk, are they.'

She wondered why men were always so melodramatic. Personally she didn't give a toss for boy's games. 'I'm interested in the ideas not who shuffles themselves into some stupid position of international importance. Have you noticed they've not let anyone in from outside Canada yet? They're keeping it for themselves. Frankly I don't think they can believe their luck, that the Sphere turned up here.'

'I thought you just told me not to underestimate politicians.'

'I don't think you should, but that doesn't mean letting them put you under their thumb. I meant they're cunning, that's all, and good at word games, making themselves look smart at other people's expense, that doesn't give them the right to know everything.'

'You're even more cynical than I am.' Zen said. Privately he began to wonder whether she was slightly less mature than he had first thought.

Comparisons with other people made her even more irritated than being liked for how she looked. 'Don't assume you know me.'

Zen checked himself before responding. She wasn't the kind of person to give him a second chance. 'Sorry.'

Awkwardness descended and she began to fiddle with her bottle of beer and glance around the room.

'What are you going to do?' He asked.

She hadn't known until he asked. The question triggered the resolve she'd been looking for. 'Go back to Yukon.'

'And what about us, I mean the collaboration? They'll be expecting something.'

'Not really, they're like journalists, they cast a wide net and run with whatever comes up first. Give it a couple of days and they'll have forgotten all about us.'

Unexpectedly, the words hurt, but he knew they carried some truth. The invitation had been to run with an idea and see where it led, so if they slowed even the smallest amount they would be left behind. The only real leverage he had was what she had just told him, but that card could only be played once, and no one likes a sneak. She was the key, without her he had nothing. And, anyway, if he had to take sides he knew he would take hers. There was no contest. 'I guess you're right. So, you go back to Yukon and then what? Stay there until it's all over? Find something even more amazing than the remains and then tell them? Write a book? What's the plan?'

'I don't have one, I'm not going back because I want to do something specific, I just need time. I want to watch what happens, see if I can find some link. Maybe someone or some thing intended that I find the remains. Before I open this up to everyone I should work out some of these issues first. If I tell anyone now, more time could be wasted while they catch up.'

Zen heard only the bit about her find being driven by destiny, or alien influence. 'So you're like, what, a chosen one? Chosen by the Sphere or some mythical alien species to uncover their past?' The idea that she might think she was made him nervous.

'Maybe.' And then she smiled. 'And anyway, it'll be a lot more fun to find it out myself than just hand it all over to them.'

That was something he couldn't argue with. He suddenly felt envious. 'Can't blame you. Want another drink before you head off.' His voice sounded full of false joviality.

She leaned over and fixed his gaze for several long seconds. Then she nodded to herself. 'Want to come?'

His surprise was honest and direct. 'What, me?'

'Can't leave you here with my secret.'

Ω

'The message says what?' The PM took his glasses off and glared aggressively at his aide. Even in the 21st century messengers were still being killed, if only metaphorically.

'There must be change.'

'And what the frak does that mean?' Alone with a junior all pretence at joviality, kindness, consideration, sensitivity and charisma were abandoned. This was the man laid bare in all its private horror.

'We're not sure Prime Minister.'

'Well get frakking sure. What does that idiot Marcoin think.'

The aide inwardly cringed. It had been a 70 to 30 call that the PM wouldn't want anyone from the Cabinet to know before he'd been informed. Sadly, yet again, he'd got it wrong. It amazed him how often the odds fell against him since he'd taken the post. It was as though the laws of nature somehow didn't count around the PM. Either that or, in traditional style, his true purpose was to take the abuse the PM couldn't off-load anywhere else, to play the role of whipping boy, one of the oldest professions, and another, more hidden form of prostitution.

'He's not seen it yet Prime Minister.'

His eyes glared and his red face deepened to purple. 'And why the frak not, is that bastard skiving off somewhere again? I swear I'll skin the bugger alive one day. Get him on the phone, now.'

The aide found courage from somewhere he hadn't known existed. 'I'm afraid it's my fault, I thought you'd ...'

'Don't think, just get the bastard on the phone.'

'He doesn't know about the message. So I ...'

The PM glanced a look of pure malevolence. A terrifying glimpse into what madness, ego and naked ambition it takes to lead a modern democracy. 'Get him on the phone.'

'Yes PM.' The aide left the PM's office and threw the papers into the waste bin by his desk. He walked out into the bright, busy street in downtown Ottawa. In comparison to the office he had left, the air tasted like cold Sauvignon Blanc sipped from a glass sparkling with frost. He walked away and never looked back.

Ten minutes later John Marcoin caught the full force of the

PM's pathological ego and learnt once again that being at political ground zero is not the best place to be in a crisis.

'John, how many frakking times do you need to be asked to give me a simple comment?'

Marcoin recognised the tone instantly, he hadn't a clue what it was about but instinct suggested deference and prevarication. 'Sorry PM, I was caught up with sorting it out. Got several things to run by you, so which d'you want to go through first?'

'The bloody message of course, the rest of that crap hardly matters right now does it.'

'No PM.' He almost panicked. 'The message, yes ...' He shuffled quickly through the papers on his desk to see if anything gave even the slightest hint. He couldn't find anything. He could feel his sphincter squeeze tightly. 'I'm afraid ...'

Frakking hell, hasn't that idiot of mine given it to you yet?'

Marcion almost hyperventilated with relief. 'Afraid not Prime Minister, maybe he's ...'

'Maybe nothing, get yourself over here.'

The phone slammed down and Marcoin streaked from his desk towards the door. Every second counted, take an instant too long and the PM would get someone else, his moment of opportunity would be gone. Survival meant being there. The veins in his temple pulse wildly and a new, even more profound headache effortlessly supplanted the one that had been slowly killing him since the Sphere had first arrived. His fears clouded it out, and even the pain in his chest went unnoticed.

Two minutes later. 'Well, what should we make of this message?' The PM asked belligerently. He hated delays, so when Marcoin arrived he'd been half way through phoning for someone else, but a being great believer in fairness, when he'd arrived at the last minute the PM decided to give him another chance. His own generosity made him smile and that countered the anger he felt at having to change his mind about finding someone else. It was good to be kind, he knew this made him a great leader, and a popular one too, everyone said so.

Marcoin squinted through the blackness of the pain engulfing him and slowly made out the words on the PM's screen. It didn't help that the screen was almost completely turned away from him, but he didn't dare acknowledge that, it could only worsen an already risky situation. The PM didn't like people who fussed. 'There must be change.' He read out cautiously.

The PM sighed impatiently.

Marcoin tried to hurry. Having read the words he knew that this was his chance to shine. He had a degree in philosophy from a minor rural college, and so he felt especially well equipped for linguistic ambiguities. Admittedly that was before his career in school catering, but in his own mind at least, it nevertheless remained one of his key strengths. 'Suggests caution, perhaps.'

The PM looked at him with renewed enthusiasm, that was exactly the kind of thing he wanted her hear. 'Caution, thought so myself, but what gives you that idea?'

'The use of 'must', they could have said 'will' but presumably chose not to intentionally.

'Mmm, I see. Good work John. So they are …?' He left the question unfinished. It was always better for someone else to take the risk of actually being clear about something.

'Perhaps making a suggestion, or preparing us, getting us ready to consider something they'll raise next time?'

The PM smiled and nodded, this encouragement spurred Marcoin on. 'And they could be referring to change for themselves, they must change in some way.'

'Don't get carried away John.' He barked. The PM didn't like anyone to show too much confidence, he believed it made them careless. In his world of small carrots and large sticks the rewards were few.

'No, of course not, but it could mean us, that we should change. Or even the planet must change. There's all this talk about global warming, maybe they mean something like that.'

Global warming was the last thing he should have raised. An agreement with the US mean that no reference at all was ever made by the Cabinet to anything even remotely 'environmentalist'. It simply wasn't allowed, at least not until they'd scraped out all the remaining tar, felled all the trees they could keep from becoming pointless nature parks that no one ever went to except by way of the witlessly narrow tracks that spindled their way through otherwise impenetrable moss covered, dank, dark wooded wildness (the PM loathed forests with particular venom), and, finally, mined everything that turned a quick profit for some trust fund or other.

'We don't think they're some kind of intergalactic Green Party do we John?' He scoffed, with more than a bit too much spittle-hung hatred.

'No PM, just trying to list the options.'

'Well don't, not in that direction. Word gets out that one of my people thinks they're here to save the planet then we're all bloody done for. Keep ideas like that to your frakking self from now on.'

Marcoin wanted to explain that it wasn't his idea, that he was just trying to be thorough, but reasoning with the PM was like trying to massage a hippo, no matter the effort the impact was zero and every single moment was a life put at risk. All he could do was agree.'Yes, Prime Minister.'

'Good. Well, anything else?'

The pressure on John's chest grew unbearable. Even the chance of a lifetime couldn't distract him any further. He wheezed and then the world blanked out. The PM watched him fall and hit the ground with the vacant indifference of children watching a cartoon mouse stumble dazed from some elaborate, unlikely ambush. He stared emptily while his usually unoccupied moral sense eased itself with difficulty to the surface. Slowly a fat, lethargic hand reached for the phone. 'Send someone in, that bloody Marcoin's fainted.'

Ω

'So when do I get to know where we're going?'

Zen and Nitu were walking through Whitehorse airport. Since he had agreed to join her for the trip back to her dig in the Yukon, it had been a continuous hectic whirl of secret plans and barely adequate packing. Since she'd invited him he'd tried everything he could to get the location out of her. Even his old grandmother needing to know where he was hadn't worked. At each attempt she had just smiled or scowled, or sometimes both and simply paid no attention to his almost constant feeble pleas and entreaties.

'D'you know that's about the thousandth time you've asked?'

'I know, but I do have some kind of right, don't I?'

'No, none at all. If you don't like it then go back, but, for the very last time there is no chance whatsoever I'll tell you anything until we get closer.'

'Why?'

'Like I've said a hundred times before, you might change your mind and I'm not having you going back with that kind of info.'

'But I could go back anyway, once you've shown me.'

That was a new line of argument. Before, he must have thought it would be too risky. Threats like that could mean being abandoned on the spot. 'Upping the pressure are we?'

'I just think I have ...'

'The right to know, but you don't. And keep asking and you might just possibly get left behind.'

'There's no reason to overreact.' He pouted.

She stopped and looked at him with an expression he didn't quite recognise. 'Don't be childish.'

He almost reddened with embarrassment. 'Yeah, right, okay.'

She turned away and once she was sure he wouldn't see she allowed herself the briefest smile at his gullibility. Luckily a pile of newspapers were stacked against the entrance to the gate, so she swept one up to distract herself, but the headline caught her eye and the mood quickly shifted. She stopped dead in her tracks. 'Holy frak!'

Zen turned indifferently. 'What, your dividends gone down again have they?' Then he caught sight of a whitening face. 'What?'

She showed him the paper. The headlines glowed ominously from the page: 'Minister Dies of Fear? Alien message causes panic in Government.' They huddled together in a shared sense of dread. They read down the page, speed reading for any clues about what had actually happened rather than what journalist thought would sell papers. 'Unconfirmed Government source says PM received message from alien Sphere ... horrific content ... is alleged that ... possible warning ... public fears ... is benign stage over ... military on alert.'

'They don't know anything.' Nitu summarised what they were both thinking. The throng of passengers growing around the newsstand had other interpretations. A piercing scream shattered the mumbled reserve of hushed voices that in the Canadian way had been quietly ignoring any suggestion that they should be alarmed. A moment later a woman fainted and as though a trip switch had been thrown, panic began to ripple urgently through the crowd.

'Let's go.' Zen eased his way through the crowd towards their departure gate.

Nitu followed and rummaged her cell phone from her bag. 'I'll phone Tantoning.'

'Good idea.'

The phone hardly rang before someone picked up at the other end. 'Rane? It's Nitu, what's … I'm at Whitehorse air … going back to … didn't think I'd be any … you sure because … yes but … look you don't … Rane there's maybe something up here … I'm not keeping anything …. you will, I'm just … but the message … fax, I haven't … they'll … tell them, what? They won't … you're kidding … But Zen Macleod's here … oh, right … because I need … not now Rane … he's an anthropologist … Rane, he's standing right here … sure … yes … sure … I will … about two weeks … no … no Rane, not yet … don't want to make a fool of myself … I know it's a crisis … I've got a sat phone … this number. Yeah, fine … bye Rane, and thanks.' She hung up and looked around the terminal with a sweeping, urgent glance. 'We need to find a RCMP office.'

'Why?'

'Rane's going to get the message faxed to me. To us, he knows you're here.'

'Guess he's not to pleased to hear ...'

'Not now, this isn't about you.'

'No, sure.' He bit his lip and tried to pretend she hadn't put him in his place for the second time in only a few minutes.

'Sorry, shouldn't have said that. We're both cleared to know what's going on.' She shook her head in disbelief. 'Can you believe all this?'

Actually, Zen could, he'd always known something really interesting was going to happen to him. 'No, not really.' He agreed. 'Is there some kind of password or something?'

She stared an inscrutable stare. 'God you boys, you're all the same. Come on.'

'I mean to show the police ...'

'Yes, there's a password. Once only use so we'd better hurry in case some spy's intercepted it.' She giggled privately under her breath.

'Yes, I see.' Zen agreed eagerly.

'I'm kidding. They have our photos and fingerprints. I think Rane likes this Boy's Own stuff as much as you seem to, don't know why you two don't get on better. Like peas in a pod.'

Zen kept quiet.

They found the RCMP office easily, and faces of hushed authority seamlessly gave way to solicitous helpfulness once their identities were confirmed. They were ushered into a private room to read the documents that had been faxed through. The local Superintendent had been dragged from lunch to receive them himself in a locked room. He handed them over with a mixture of awe and irritation. Nitu looked liked a twenty-year-old college student and Zen some kind of drop-out artist. It wasn't what he'd expected when he'd been hurriedly told that VIP's needed his urgent attention. It just confirmed what he'd suspected, that the Government in Ottawa had truly lost the plot.

Nitu ripped open the envelope and Zen, judging the need to regain some kudos, sat back calmly and waited.

She rested the paper in her lap and looked at him with a puzzled expression. 'It just says, "There must be change".'

'What, the Sphere's message?'

'Yes, look.' She handed it over.

'Well, either Marcoin was very highly strung or his death has nothing at all to do with this. Well, not directly anyway.'

Nitu nodded in agreement. 'I bet that bastard of a PM killed him. Harassed him to death.'

Zen gave her a strange look. 'Why on earth would you say that?'

'You weren't in the meeting long enough to see how he treats everyone. He's disgusting. You wouldn't believe it, so don't be taken in by his public shows.'

'But still, he can't have hassled him to death, can he? Not literally anyway.'

'Yeah, well, I just don't like him. Anyway, what d'you make of the message?'

'Bit innocuous don't you think?'

'A threat?'

'Mildly phrased if it is.'

'I suppose so.'

'What do the other papers say?' Zen asked. There had been more than the message in the envelope, and so far Nitu hadn't taken any notice of them.

She scanned through them. 'Not much, what you'd expect really. Don't talk to anyone, don't discuss anything, don't talk in your sleep or phone your mother, you know, that kind of thing. And, oh, the PM's reflections on what it all might mean. Or his minion's at any rate, but it has his signature.'

'And?'

'See for yourself.' She handed the documents over.

Zen flicked through the papers. 'Not much is it. About the same as we came up with, basically the message might be a threat but why so tame.'

'Tantoning wants us to go back.'

'Both of us?'

'Yes, you too.'

'I mean, are you thinking ...?'

'No, I'm not going back, he knows that. You heard the call. I've got the sat phone so I'll call him later when, if, we've got anything to say, or even if we haven't, just to shut him up. But you can go back if you want.'

It didn't even enter his mind to go back. Two weeks in the wilderness with her was something that didn't warrant even a moment's reflection. Even playing spy's games couldn't compete. 'No, we're in this together. You asked me to help out and I will. Anyway, I loath meetings.'

She looked at her watch. 'We've probably missed the flight by now. We'll have to find a hotel. I'll go and ask someone.'

But the flight had been held for them. As they walked down the aisle of the aircraft under the quizzical gaze of the other passengers eager to know who the VIPs were they were being held up for, Zen felt about ten feet tall. One glance and the passengers took Nitu to be some kind of celebrity, and Zen her gofer. Nitu didn't care one way or the other what anyone thought while Zen, enjoying the attention, basked in his misconceived moment of glory.

Ω

'Something is happening.'

'Yes, a disturbance of some sort.'

'There's some kind of panic. A lot of them seem to be trying to move away.' Chepi looked more closely at the throng of people below. 'There isn't room. Some of them will be hurt.' She turned away. 'What d'you think is going on?'

'I'm not sure.'

Ω

'How did it get out?' The PM wasn't in any mood for prevarication. A clean, straightforward admission by someone was the only permissible reaction.

'We think it was one of the cleaners.' Offered Peter Smilie, Minister for International Cooperation.

'And how exactly could that be Peter?'

'There were three of them cleaning the outer office when the paramedics arrived. We're trying to find out which one, but you know what journalist are like when it comes to protecting their sources.'

The PM stared at him long and hard. Smilie returned the eye contact without flinching. 'Okay, we'll let it go for now, no point in creating more attention by going after bloody cleaners, but someone's going to pay, and I don't give a flying frak who it is, but for now one of you had better be doing something frakking positive.' He glared around the table, daring anyone to disagree. Smilie made a note. In the next couple of weeks the career of some unknown pawn, who could even be have been on holiday when the leak happened, would come to an end in a blaze of hostility and criminal charges.

'Anyone want to say anything?' The PM asked. No one did, Cabinet wasn't a place for discussion, it served solely to do what it was told. Increasingly, the only purpose this supposed cradle of democracy had was to give the semblance of government to a system that pandered exclusively to the needs of an increasingly vane and deluded manic who had somehow won an election victory despite the fact that most Canadians couldn't stand him. In truth, democracy was dead, but few dared utter a world, and those who did tended to be arrested while protesting peacefully anywhere outside their own living rooms. The sole function of Cabinet in modern Canada was to dole out tax breaks, government grants and control over vast swathes of the last remnants of the Canadian wilderness to any corporation vaguely associated with the ruthless exploitation of forests, oil or any other commodity that made foreign businessmen rich and powerful beyond anyone's craziest dreams. Canada was for sale, and democratic accountability was not going to be allowed to spoil any deal that could turn a quick dollar or two.

Responding to the expected silence that followed his invitation to anyone to add to the discussion, the PM turned back to the message. 'We need to think about the reply, and quickly, so all your ideas are needed now and anyone holding back will be found something else to do up north.' Exile, it was one of his biggest threats.

Still held in the headlights of the PM's attention, Smilie spoke first. 'Maybe we should follow their lead Prime Minister, keep it general. Not vague exactly, but open to more than one interpretation.'

The PM laughed with what might have been open amusement but no one was sure, it didn't happen that often. 'Well, nothing new there then Peter. I'm still trying to make sense of that last proposal you sent me, that frakking Big Elk Raincoast conservation business, more caveats than fat on a pig.' His eyes narrowed. 'So, this time, do we have anything specific in mind?'

It was actually the Great Bear Rainforest project, but he knew the PM was only pretending not to know. Denial that something existed, even in the most trivial way, was all a part of the vast Ottawa conspiracy against anything that could even remotely have a bad effect on oil, mineral or logging developments. 'Not as yet PM, I'm just trying to get the ball rolling.' He smiled disarmingly and gave up gracefully as he always did.

'Anyone else?' The PM asked, but no one spoke.

Someone decided to act quickly and pass the buck. 'What about those two academics from UBC, Nitu something or other and that scruffy Macleod guy, anything from them?'

Muffled replies buzzed meaninglessly around the meeting. To fill the vacuum the PM's new aide spoke up. He'd only been in post for three hours and his voice almost cracked with the strain. 'I believe they're in the Yukon Prime Minister.'

He turned to the Defence Minister. 'Whose bloody idea was that Ken? Anything I should know?'

Ken Crawmish, startled by the sudden attention, jerked his head involuntarily in the PM's direction. As Canadian defence was mostly a USA affair he wasn't used to being spoken to at all at meetings. Cautious about this break in accepted protocol he waited to see if it was a mistake. But the PM had the power and experience to wait longer. 'Sorry PM, should you know what?' Crawmish asked at last.

'About Nitu bloody what's her name. What's she doing in the Yukon? Anything to do with you?'

Crawmish began to relax. He had no idea what the PM was talking about and he was certain that his department knew nothing about anyone being in the Yukon. 'Absolutely not PM. Nothing to do with my Department at all.'

The PM turned his glare back to Smilie. 'Must be your lot then Peter.'

'Not that I know of PM.'

'Well get them back here.'

'Yes PM, right away.' He turned to his aide sitting behind him. There was only the briefest gesture and the aide sped away and out of the room.

'Right, so that brings it back to us. So I want suggestions. If we have to we'll go around the room one by one.'

Still no one spoke. They hadn't been trained for anything so unusual and that made it far too risky.

'This might be the last time we get the chance to take the lead gentlemen, and women, of course.' He smiled discouragingly. Women had no place in government so far as he was concerned. Give them an inch and they'd take a yard his father had always said. Far too argumentative, too much time discussing reasons instead of getting on with things. 'The international community wants in on all of this and we can't put them off forever.' His beady eye swept across them, but there was no answer.

'Shall I tell you what our allies, and others have suggested? Might trigger something, perhaps?' He said sarcastically. He unfolded a piece of paper that had been kept carefully stowed in his jacket pocket. Everyone could see immediately that it was a list. A list meant demands and that usually meant trouble, but the PM looked relaxed. They sensed with the survival instincts of rodents that somehow the game had shifted.

Feelings of panic at some possible betrayal rippled around the room. The PM's calm manner when faced with an international list of demands or suggestions could only mean one thing, in front of their very eyes he was about to begin a play for the ultimate prize in a politicians life. He was about to bid for international statehood, to be a world leader, one of the few of the few, an elder figure in the grand game of who gets to sit on the biggest chair of them all, to sit side-by-side with the richest and most powerful. He was turning the alien visitation into his own great moment, something to mirror the most immense rhetorical moments in recent history. The hint of something Churchillian wafted through the room and mingled unpleasantly with the stale air of fear and ambition.

He heard the murmur and knew they'd guessed. So, then, it was up to them. He could see his big chance just ahead and all it needed was for one of them to give him the words he'd failed to find himself. He wanted inspiration and they had better find it or be left behind.

The room watched him closely for clues. Slowly for some and more quickly for those desperate to please, the realisation spread through the room that unless they found what he was looking for he'd cut them out and play to a bigger audience. Their political senses whirled madly in a frenzy of alarm. This was perhaps the best chance any of them had to grasp hold of the coat tails of a potentially great man.

He placed the list in front of him and smoothed it out dramatically. The implication was clear, they had to come up with something better.

He began to read from the list.

'The US: "Change is something we will always be happy to negotiate."' He looked up. His expression was unfathomable. They all looked down.

'The UN: "The people of the planet Earth would welcome opening a dialogue with our illustrious visitors."' Again he looked up, and again he met a wall of silence. He'd known it would play out this way. They'd wait until some kind of pattern emerged that showed them the scope of what they could think about. Then they'd tinker slightly with the wording of one of them. Lastly they'd find that it wasn't enough, that he wanted much more. He chuckled inside at the fun he could have if he played his cards for long enough.

'The People's Republic of Eritrea.' He liked this one especially, it gave him a warm feeling to give prominence to such a small and, so far as his political ambitions were concerned, insignificant country. "Welcome brothers and sisters."

'It doesn't cover change.' Someone called out.

'No, clever that isn't it.'

'France.' This bought whispers of both approval and disapproval from the French speakers at the meeting. It gained approval because France had been included in the top few, but disapproval at the fact that once again they hadn't been first. "Nous adorons le changement et la nouveauté! dans mes bras, mon ami et bienvenue sur la planète Terre!" The PM read.

There were some deep sighs of approval but mostly hushed silence as almost everyone waited for a translation. 'Bit postmodern isn't it?' Someone said.

The PM banged the list down onto the table. 'D'you want to stay in this meeting Smith, or is there something else you could be doing?'

'No sir, I just meant ...'

'I know what you meant, and you can frakking well keep it to yourself' His grandmother had been French Canadian and he was very proud of the fact. He stared at Smith with unconstrained vehemence and then turned back to the list, but not before making a mental note to sack him the moment the meeting ended.

'The UK: "An interesting idea, please tell us more."' They all laughed, the Anglophones because it was what they would expect from the Brits, and the Quebecois because on behalf of their French cousins they still hadn't forgotten Agincourt, the 100 years war and Britain's inability to accept that they were European and not a satellite of the USA '

The PM continued down the list until his persistence flushed out the last of their resistance. It began with fidgeting, and then progressed to sighing, glazed eyes and constant inspection of the trolley of tea and coffee that had long since been emptied.

Well everyone, I've got a few dozen more, but a dare say you've all got the gist of what most of the rest of the world thinks, so now it's up to us. In a few days at most we'll have to convene some kind of international committee, stands to reason, won't have any power of course, not if we get this right and lead the discussions with the Sphere, but there will be a committee and that will make life a bit more difficult, to say the least. So last time of asking, any suggestions?'

Smilie knew it would be him who would have to speak first. He was nearly always the one to start the ball rolling and this time would be no different, not now Marcoin was gone. What a relief that had been for him, that Marcoin had been at the airport. For once he'd been able to sit at the back and snipe at others. It'd almost been a holiday, but now the bastard was dead and so he was thrown back into the front line again, the stooge to everyone else's great moments. 'I like the Brits idea, keep it vague.'

The PM smiled broadly. It was ghastly sight., it always made Smilie think about wart hogs with lipstick. 'Yeah, good at that the Brits, a thousand years of practice.' His grandmother had hated them. 'But I take your point. Want to put some meat on that idea Peter?'

He hated that expression. Vacuous 'new speak', lazy, shiftless ideas slurred thoughtlessly by people with no inclination to think. It was nothing but graffiti filling minds that didn't care about words anymore. He hated all of them. 'They mention change but we don't know what kind of change they mean. We need them to say more, so, best to stall, draw them out, find out what they're really thinking.'

'Look I bloody well know that Peter. I know what frakking 'vague' means, I didn't ask you for a frakking demonstration. D'you have something to offer or not?'

Bastard, Smilie thought. He began to hope that somewhere along the line the aliens, whoever they were, would find a reason to kill him. The thought motivated him to find something more, something the PM would want to use, something that would put him in the firing line. 'How about: There are many changes?'

The room went quiet. In a rare gesture, the PM rubbed his chin thoughtfully. They all waited.

'Frakking hell Peter, you're a genius. No frakking idea what it means; it's even more vague than the Brits. Type that up will you.' He said, turning to his aide. 'Fantastic, I like it, well done.'

Smilie grinned in return, but to himself. It was his first act of intentional treachery and he liked its taste. He knew for sure that no one else in the international community would take to the suggestion for a second, it was too abrasive, sarcasm with too hard an edge, exactly the way the PM operated. He would be exposed, isolated, perhaps even got rid of sooner than anyone might have hoped.

The PM waved a large hand and more tea, coffee and cakes appeared as if from nowhere. They began to dash eagerly to their feet but his hand paused mid air and they all stopped, frozen to the spot. 'Now we've got the small issue of the message sorted out, we need to attend to another small matter. We've got this crap photo of the alien, and we need to have a little discussion about it.'

They all began to sit down again. He waited until they were almost comfortable once more before he gave the pretence of noticing that they'd returned to their places. 'No, that's fine everyone, get some coffee, or whatever, we'll start again in a few minutes'. He sipped the coffee the aide had already laid beside him. The rest moved with relief and gratitude towards the trolley. He beamed at them. He had them just where he wanted them.

Ω

They were over two hours out of Old Crow, north of Porcupine River, when the sat phone warbled. Nitu fished it out of her bag. This caused Zen considerable alarm. At that very moment they were flying extremely low along a riverbed walled in on both sides by towering rock faces. He hadn't known she flew her own aircraft, if he had he'd never have agreed to the trip. Of all the fear-filled minutes that had passed through his life up to this point, this was by far the worst of all.

'Look, let me take it.' He squawked.

'No, it's fine.'

'No it's not.'

'Shhh.'

Zen began to realise what rigid with fear actually meant; each muscle locked as tight as steel in its own hellish embrace. The experience was tiring beyond description, but his unconscious mind somehow found the effort worth the discomfort. In a small way it created a balance to the headache creeping slowly across his skull.

All he wanted was to land and sit with a cold beer in front of a television somewhere. After this he knew for certain that he could never love her completely, it just wasn't worth the level of terror she brought with her.

'They want to know what we think of the reply they've come up with.' She informed him breezily.

'I don't give a shit.'

'Sorry, Zen's a bit preoccupied. Can I call you when I get down? Sorry. Yes, in flight. Yeah, fine. Bye.' She put the phone back in the bag.

To Zen it took an eternity before she sat upright again. 'Did you have to do that?'

'The phone rang ...'

'I know, but why the bag ... No, never mind.'

'You look a bit pale. Air sickness?'

He threw her a venomous glance. 'No, just fear. D'you know how high we are.'

Nitu looked casually down at her instruments. Says 52 feet but there's always a bit of an error around here, the instruments play up a bit in these canyons.'

He closed his eyes tightly. 'D'you think maybe you could look out of the window. Not sure indicators show rocks and .... Shit.' She pulled up, turned the aircraft on its side and banked into an enjoining canyon.

'Shit, shit, shit.'

She pulled back on the stick and Zen felt his brain squeezed like a blancmange in a vice. 'We can fly a bit higher here, there's not much turbulence and we'll be out of the canyons soon.' She unhelpfully explained.

Zen didn't reply.

'You sure you're okay?' She asked.

'Not really.'

'Don't like flying?'

He didn't answer for several long seconds as he struggled to bottle up his true feelings. 'I thought I did, until now.' He managed, eventually.

'Light planes can be a bit scary if you're not used to them.'

He wanted to scream but instead bit the inside of his cheek until the pain kicked in to provide a welcome distraction.

'Want to know what they wanted? Might take your mind off things.'

'It'll keep. If it's okay with you I'd rather wait until we got to the airfield.'

'Oh.'

Despite the terror one small, still functioning part of him didn't want her to think he was some kind of total wimp. 'It's just that I think better with tarmac under my feet.'

'Oh. Well, anyway, we'll be down soon.'

They flew on for nearly half an hour. Against all the odds Zen managed to drift restlessly into a half doze. Only in a half dreaming state did he feel even remotely safe, but just as real sleep beckoned, pokes and jabs into his ribs pulled him back to reality.

'We're just coming into land.' She said cheerily.

Afraid of seeing what height, speed or attitude she'd got them into he glanced down reluctantly. There was nothing but rocks and water everywhere. He looked around anxiously trying to spot the welcoming sight of an airfield. There was none, for as far as he could see there was nothing but broken ground cut through by a narrow, endlessly winding river. ' I can't ...'

She knew what was coming. 'Look, sorry, this is bush flying. It's fine, just fasten your safety harness, close your eyes and we'll be down before you know it.'

'Down where?'

'It's a floatplane, surely you knew ... look, never mind. She lands really well on water. I do this all the time.'

'Not the river, tell me you're not going to try to land on that tiny, minute river?' But he knew that's what she meant, that at this precise instant his life had become irrevocably arrowed in on a miniscule ribbon of water winding its way through a remote valley far too far from help and safety, and worse of all there was nothing he could do about it

'Done it loads of times.' She chirped. 'See, its 's' shaped, so I can always ...'

'You're frakking crazy.' He closed his eyes. 'Please just make it quick.'

She wasn't sure whether he was talking to her or saying a prayer, but it didn't matter, flying was easy, she'd always been able to do it, even from the very first time when her mother had been around. In her minds eye she could still her long golden hair and the endless smiles of encouragement and gentle coaxing. Her face was never clear but Nitu didn't mind. The memory as it was always made her warm inside. She slid down onto the water in a perfect landing. 'We're here, you can open your eyes now.'

'Don't lie, I ....' He opened his eyes and looked at her in amazement.

'Tents up, then salmon and cold white wine for dinner, how does that sound for an apology?' A smile shone out of eyes glittering with excitement.

'You love all this, don't you.'

'It's my ... it's me, what I am. Just look at this ...' Her lean, bronzed hand gestured to the world outside the windscreen. There was no need for him to reply.

Less than an hour later the tents were erected and Nitu was grilling the salmon she'd brought with them. Zen had poured them both a glass of the promised chilled wine and was sitting back watching the sun begin to sink behind some mountain in the far distance. He began to see what she liked about being out there. Knowing how remote they were made a difference. Its stark, wild indifference had an enchantment he couldn't have expected.

'I can see the attraction.' He said.

Nitu looked around them in a slow, appreciative way. 'This is a special place.'

'Yes, it is.'

'No, I mean more than being wild, untouched.'

The tone of her voice caught his attention. 'Because you found the remains here?' He prompted.

'No, not for that, not just the remains, whoever they belong to.'

Zen could see what she meant. 'This is a spectacular place.'

She emptied her glass and poured some more. 'Yes, but that's not all I meant. They ... look, best if I show you.' She stood up hastily, as though she wanted to complete something before she changed her mind. 'Follow me.'

They walked for several minutes before cutting through a small gap in the side of the adjoining canyon. There was a dense stand of trees of a type he couldn't recall ever having seen before. They were spread out widely in every direction. He was about to comment on them when Nitu disappeared into the wood and started to work her way down a steep bank. He tried to get her to tell him what was so urgent but she said that he'd have to wait and see. It took around half an hour before they broke out of the trees and into a wide, open meadow. When he saw what stood in the centre about half a mile away his jaw dropped open in shock.

'Christ is that some kind of joke? A film prop or something?'

Nitu shook her head. 'No, it's real. I've had it dated. Where it's standing, it's relationship to everything around it, every kind of dating I could think of and it's real and it's 200 million years old.'

His shocked face turned slowly towards her. 'That's a joke, right?'

'No, but it gets worse.' She laughed nervously. 'Or better, depending on your point of view.' Not quite believing it herself, she paused for a brief moment.

'What could be worse or better than this?' He looked back at the towering standing stones that filled the centre of the meadow.

'The remains I told you about.'

'Yes, but, they don't ...' His already paled face turned ashen. 'You mean ...'

'Some of them date the same. There's the one that is one hundred and twenty-five thousand, and others that are millions of years old. Couldn't tell you back there, you'd have ... well, you know what you'd have thought.'

'That you were insane.' He tried to work out what it could all mean. 'But they couldn't have survived that long.' He turned away, not waiting for an answer, he started walking towards the stones. He hesitated. 'D'you mind? This is your find but I ...'

'Go ahead, but be prepared, they make you feel strange.'

'Strange, that's a myth isn't it?' He said, thinking about myths surrounding standing stones.

'And so was the idea of million-year-old civilisations, until now. And bones that don't erode.'

'Good point.' He fidgeted excitedly. 'I'm going to take a look.' And then he paused again. 'What 'strange feelings' exactly?'

She looked hard at him. She thought of telling him about the voices she thought she heard. They were like whispers she couldn't quite make out, but then thought better of it. 'You'll see. Might be different for you.'

She let him go ahead and then followed him through the grass and wild flowers she'd never seen before she found the relics, and hadn't yet had time to catalogue, until they got to the edge of the circle. She knew that at any other time he'd have noticed how strange even the plants were, anyone would have, even to a casual inexpert glance they'd look alien, but the huge stone circle with its long aisle of enormous pillars, some of them hundreds of feet high, leading off to the west was simply too overwhelming. It made Stonehenge look like a ring of toy blocks.

He touched one lightly. 'This is impossible. Even if you're wrong about the age this simply just can't be here.

'We have to rethink everything.' She said.

'Even human evolution.' He added.

'I don't think it was humans.'

'No.' He laughed. 'The dates don't fit. I was thinking that maybe we had a helping hand.'

'It's possible.'

He moved around the column, touching the surface in awe as he examined small etchings covering its surface. 'The Sphere, you think its them?'

'Yes. I find this, and then a few months later they show up. After a few hundred million years that can't be a coincidence.'

'That's why you're not so into all the government stuff?'

'I wouldn't be anyway. But, yeah, this is big and it's probably linked and no frakking politicians should get their secretive little fingers on it. It belongs to all of us.'

'Maybe the Sphere has another idea.'

'Then why go to Vancouver?'

He laughed. 'How should I know, they're aliens.'

She smiled back at him. It looked like her gut feelings about him might have been right after all.

While they were talking he'd traced a line of symbols around the column. He thought he could discern a pattern. 'You worked out what any of these mean? I think I've got a pattern here.'

She heard the whispers again. She shook her head in frustration. 'No, not yet, not had time, been doing all the dating first.'

'Yeah, course. Maybe we can try to work something out while we're here?' He cautioned himself to go slowly. It was her find and he knew he wouldn't last long if he tried to take over.

'I'd hoped you'd be interested in that.' She shook her head again. 'Look, d'you feel anything? Being this close to them?'

He paused and looked up thoughtfully. After a few moments he nodded. 'Like … sort of like the wind, but not really.'

'Like whispers.'

'Maybe.' He glanced around. 'There's no wind, is there?'

'No.'

Then briefly a word seemed to form itself out of the chaotic sighs of the unreal wind. He heard it clearly. Startled, he jerked back from the stone.

'What?' She asked.

'Nothing, I just thought I heard something.'

She waited but he turned away and began to look closely at the stone again. It was obviously pretence, something to cover his reaction and deflect her attention. It didn't work. 'What? What d'you hear?'

'Must have imagined it.'

She had to know. 'I hear things too.'

'Yeah, you said … I mean, you said 'whispers', so ...'

'And words sometimes.'

He turned back to her. 'What words?'

'I can never make them out.' She lied. 'What about you.'

He smiled disarmingly. 'You'll laugh.'

'Won't, promise.'

'Well, okay. You sure you promise?'

'Sure.'

'Well, probably just imagining it but, well it sounded like 'unhuman'.'

'Unhuman? What kind of word is that?' But she knew only too well what kind of word it was. At the beginning they'd whispered that to her over and over, but she wasn't going to tell him that, nor anyone else, at least not yet.

'Don't know. Don't blame me, you asked.'

'Yeah, sorry.' She feigned indifference and made as if she was taking in the whole vista around them. 'So, what d'you make of it?'

'Still can't believe it's not some kind of elaborate fake.'

'That was my reaction at first, but I've done the science and it's been here a very long time.'

'And the remains?' He asked. 'How do they fit into all the rest of this?'

'Let's go back. I need another drink and I'll tell you everything I know and what I think it means, but it's not much.'

He wanted to stay, but it made sense to go back. It would soon be dark and he had a morbid fear of being killed by a bear. He'd had nightmares as a child and they still haunted him. 'Sure.' They started walking away. 'You got any guns?'

The question startled her. What else had the stones said? 'Why? Strange question, if you don't mind me saying so.'

He was going to lie but couldn't think of anything quickly enough. 'Oh nothing. Well, it's not really anything, except ... Look, don't laugh, but I've got this thing about bears.'

She gave him a strange look. 'Really? Well, don't worry, I've never seen any around here.'

'What, never, no signs at all?' To Zen this was too good to be true.

'No, none, and no mosquitoes or black flies either.'

Zen thought about it for a moment. Being bitten endlessly had been his second fear, just before his third, cougars, and it was true, no wind and yet no bites. 'That's weird, isn't it?'

'Yes.'

Ω

'What are those stones?' Chepi asked.

'Your ancestors left them behind.'

'My ancestors?' This was the first time Chepi had ever heard of them. 'I didn't know I had any.'

'You were to discover them at the right time.'

Chepi didn't probe any further. There were things the Sphere would never tell her and she knew from its tone that this was one of them, and more to the point, she knew it didn't know the reason either. She wondered if it had been instructed not to find out, or at least asked politely not to, or just acted on instinct when it saw a chance to annoy her. Either way it didn't matter, it was just one more thing she had to find out for herself. She changed the subject. 'I'd like to meet them.'

'Then go down there.'

'I'm afraid.'

'They can't hurt you.'

'Are you sure?'

'Nothing can happen unless you want it to happen.'

Ω

'Okay, how did those stones and relics last through various ice-ages and erosion by the wind and rain?'

'In the last ice age, even in the coldest periods, not all the area was covered in ice, perhaps earlier incidents were the same.' Nitu replied. 'And did you take in the layout of the valley? The whole thing is completely enclosed. I've walked the whole of area. It took me about a week but other than the small entrance we got through it's essentially sealed from outside.'

'You think it maybe has its own eco-system?'

'Did you notice the plants?'

Zen shook his head. 'No, not really.'

'Take a look round tomorrow. There's stuff there I've never seen anywhere else.'

'This place is a gold mine.'

Nitu looked at him cautiously. His choice of words made her nervous. 'I thought I could trust that you'd keep it ...'

'I will, but ... well ... you could have hundreds of people out here trying to solve this.'

'Promise?' She asked.

'Yes, definitely.'

'You could easily make your name from any small part of what there is here.'

'What, drop the xeno-anthropology just when an alien's turned up, you must be kidding.'

They both laughed.

Zen managed to catch his breath. 'Isn't there something you've supposed to have told me about the Sphere? The phone call in the plane?'

'Oh that. They want to know what we think about their answer to the alien message and the photo.'

'Who are 'they' exactly?'

'Some aide from the PM's office. They're in one of their meetings and under pressure to let the US and the Europeans in on the act. Obviously ...'

'So we're into game playing and they want to get as much done first as possible.'

'Something like that. No doubt they want to keep control, take the lead, show true statesmanship. At least that's what they said on the phone. 'It'd be in Canada's interests ...'

'Apart from the obvious reification, I can see their point.' Zen offered. He knew he'd be no happier than anyone else if teams of people from the south and Europeans started taking over. Maybe she hadn't realised that yet. 'You wouldn't want anyone else taking this over would you? Throwing money at it until you got squeezed out?'

She gave him a piercing look. 'No one knows about it.'

'I know, but we still have to face the fact that if we find some connection to the sphere you'll have to tell someone eventually.'

'When I'm good and ready.' Her look endured long enough to make her point.

'Yeah, sure, I'm not going to say anything.'

'Frakking right, so let's get back to the message and the photo and stuff the politics.' Her eyes glinted at him, reflecting the red of the setting sun. 'Remember, there's only one way out of here.'

He laughed, but she didn't. 'Sure, so what about their stuff?'

'They want to send back "There are many changes."'

He waited, but there was nothing to add. 'Just that?'

'Yes, apparently. Something about trying to out-cool the Brits.'

'Is there a point to that?'

'Who knows, politics is full of childishness. Anyway, what we need to do is plug our brains in and get back to them.'

'Yes, true.' He paused. 'First reaction, it's too vague. Maybe that kind of comment would go down well if we were dealing with other human beings, but there's no way of knowing what aliens will make of something so cryptic. They could misread the intent completely and take it as permission to do something we'd have no control over.'

'Maybe their message was some kind if test, to see if we understood why they are here.'

'What would you have said?' He asked.

'The problem is in choosing.' She turned and smiled. 'Then they have to answer and reveal something of their motives.'

'Yes, but doesn't that commit us to change? It's agreeing that there does have to be change.'

'And would either of us disagree?'

'No, but should they know we're so open and flexible?'

'Perhaps flexibility is useful in the face of the unknown? You know, keep doors open?'

'Okay, I agree. We want to keep the communication malleable, and we can't try to second guess ourselves too much.'

Her head straightened almost imperceptibly, she hadn't expected that he would go along with her so quickly. 'Okay. Should I say it's from both of us?'

'That's hardly fair, it's your idea.'

She shrugged. 'If we're going to collaborate then who cares?'

'That's generous.'

'You'd do the same.'

It wasn't a question. Zen hoped he could keep up.

'So, next.' She said. 'What about the photo?'

'I think it might be a hoax.'

She looked surprised. 'Oh, okay. And that's what you think we should tell them?'

'I think so, at this stage. It's all a bit obvious don't you think? They conspire to show themselves when we have to assume they didn't have to, and they happen to look like something out of Tolkien. From what we can see anyway, but the photo is so blurred it's not really possible to be sure. What it does do is nicely muddy the whole contact, just like their obscure message. Or they could be trying to give us a reassuring image to work with. Lull us into believing they're benevolent.'

She pondered for a moment. She could see that he had good reasons for believing what he did, but only because she hadn't yet been fully honest with him about the remains. She knew she would have to tell him. 'Except that, and sorry I didn't tell you before, but I did some facial reconstruction on the remains I found, they looked similar to this one.'

Zen felt shivers run down his spine and across his arms. 'You're kidding, right?'

She shook her head slowly and deliberately. 'No, afraid not.'

He looked bewildered. 'This is frakking awesome. It's almost too unbelievable.'

'I know, that's why I wanted someone else in on it.'

'Yeah, I can see that.' But he could see problems too. 'So, what're you going to do? Tell them?'

'No way.' Of that much she was certain.

'Don't they, you know, like have the right to know? They are the Government after all.'

'Is that a joke?' From his expression it obviously wasn't. 'This is and always was 1st nation land and no European land-grabbers have any rights whatsoever so far as I'm concerned.'

There were many things he felt he could say in reply, but decided to keep it simple and to the point. 'Bit hard to insist on that if they find out. They'll probably imprison you for treason.'

'You keep saying stuff like that, but they can't find out, can they.'

'Who knows; don't they have satellites that can see stuff like that? And what about Tantoning, won't he work something out. Got to be pretty weird you coming up here in the middle of everything.'

'Good, I like that, you're as paranoid as I am, but there's nothing to worry about, satellites can't see it, I've checked. And ...'

'Checked, how?'

'Got this friend of mine to scan the area, told him I was looking for somewhere to land. He didn't see a thing.'

'You have friends with satellites?'

'Sort of.'

'Bit risky though, wasn't it?'

'I had to know. So, anyway that's not a problem, and Tantoning's an idiot that somehow thinks he's in with a chance.'

'That doesn't actually mean he's an idiot.'

'Whatever. Anyway, I'm not telling them anything.'

'Then what's the point of all this? Biggest find in history and we do what, nothing?'

'It'll give us chance to see what the sphere thing is up to.'

'Just like that?'

'Yeah, just like that.'

Ω

The PM was sitting in his overlarge office behind a desk that could seat a mammoth. The size of the desk was something that both pleased him enormously and caused him endless doubts and inconvenience. The upside was that a desk of that size imparted great status. Even foreign leaders of countries far more important than Canada gushed with amazement when they saw it for the first time. He made a point of always being behind it when they arrived so he could maximise its impact as he carefully eased his enormous bulk from around it to greet them. Lesser visitors were treated differently, they sat on the other side, lost in the far distance like abandoned children in a museum. These were the things he liked about it, its power to either impress or subdue, as the mood took him, or convention dictated.

When he thought about the advantages it brought, he touched the desk lovingly and wondered by what miracle of physics it could one day be fitted into his modest Ontario home. Other times, when doubts beset him, instead of a treasure it became a grotesque liability. Suddenly the focus of his devotion became his enemy, a source of ridicule and contempt. The expanse he had admired became a bottomless trap. It was simply too large. So large in fact that no matter how hard he worked, how many papers he read, reports he signed, letters he opened it always looked empty. Some visitors had even commented on how nice it must be to have an empty desk, and then laughed as though somehow he managed to run a country without actually doing anything.

No matter what he did, there was no escape from this peculiar trap of his own making. He'd been brought up to blue collar work. Learned all the tricks he knew in the kitchens of ocean liners and oil tankers. It had been a life of grind with only one rule, always look busy, but now he couldn't, the desk never allowed it, not even in the middle of a crisis. In such moments he experienced a deep, unwavering, hopeless sense of failure. He wanted to be remembered with affection, instead there loomed only ridicule. People would snigger at his laziness and question everything he had ever done in their name.

Such is the madness brought on by too much power, and this is the man who orchestrated 21st century humankind's first ever encounter with an alien presence. In truth, though, it has to be said that throughout history, leadership has tended to be handed to the maladjusted. After all, they are the only people for whom it has value, and we are too distracted and self-interested to make it otherwise.

Ω

When there was a knock on the PM's door only minutes after the meeting about the message had ended, his thoughts were far from morbid. He was pleased with himself and as some kind of reward he had happily and unconsciously shuffled all his papers into neat, orderly piles. He was sitting back elated. His eyes scanning the desk with deep satisfaction at the way it spread out before him like a new conquered land, or the vast stretch of water that secretly all Canadians wished lay between them and the USA.

'Come in.' He gruffly beckoned through the warm smugness of his imagined success.

'Are you busy PM?' The new aide asked.

At the word 'busy' his confidence vanished. He turned purple with a myriad of unnameable emotions and with shaking hands he impulsively shuffled the newly formed piles of papers into a chaotic, unusable jumble. 'Of course I'm frakking busy. Who the frakking hell d'you think runs this country.'

The aide stood transfixed. For a moment he thought the PM was going to burst into tears. 'Sorry sir, I just meant ...'

'Well don't just mean frakking anything.' And then he caught the look in the aide's eye. He'd seen that look before. For someone with a fairly advanced but undiagnosed and exceptionally rare offshoot of Asperger's syndrome, the PM found such moments were precious. He'd been taught to look for them by his mother, and when he took the time to notice they helped him modify his behaviour slightly so he would appear merely callous and cruel instead of insane and viscous. It wasn't really his fault, after all many men had various forms of Asperger's, and amongst leaders everywhere it tended to be both effectively universal, always extreme and often linked to a form of psychosis that led them to suspect their very thoughts could without hindrance change material reality.

'Sorry sir.' The aide said. Not a little afraid of what might come next, he then stood and waited patiently for the PM to recover himself.

Minutes passed, and as he slowly and carefully rearranged the pile of papers on his desk into a pattern that covered almost all its surface, the PM's face gradually returned to normal. Though he didn't dare show any emotion whatsoever, this greatly amused the aide because so far as he knew it hadn't previously been suspected that the PM also had some type of an obsessive, compulsive disorder. At least he hadn't been briefed on that particular quirk. Not that it was funny per se that someone would be ill in that way, the aide reminded himself, but it did explain why the PM was so fixated on his desk. Of course, as the reader now knows, it wasn't anything to do with that at all, but being wrong has never stopped anyone from starting a rumour too good to resist.

The paper shuffling grew quiet and the PM looked up, his gaze keenly tuned to any sign of disapproval, censure or disgust. During those moments he was vulnerable to anyone, but the aide kept his expression passive and his eyes averted. 'So, what d'you want?' He asked at last.

'We've heard from Drs Macleod and Nitunakiwidinok.'

'And what the frak do they want?' Secretly he was pleased they'd got back to him. He was clever enough to know that a successful politician occasionally needed an expert view, but he was also cunning enough to realise that it was best never to let anyone know that in case it was seen as a personal weakness. The fact that, on the contrary, not to admit that expert opinions were invaluable was a great weakness never occurred to him. 'Not another madcap idea I hope?'

The fact that neither Macleod nor Nitunakiwidinok had ever, so far, made any madcap suggestions didn't escape the aide, but the last thing he'd do would be to tell the PM. As a professional administrator he had long since become totally immune to political rhetoric. He saw his sole function as being responsible for diverting and diluting whatever madness they put his way. He had no interest whatsoever in either their morals or honesty. As with all administrators, he saw them as nothing more than a necessary evil, an essential barrier between those who actually ran the world, business leaders and government administrators, and the great, volatile unwashed public. So, he did what he always did, and smiled broadly. 'Hope not Prime Minister, but you never know with academics.'

'Skip the frakking philosophy and tell me what they want.'

'They have a suggestion about the message.'

'Oh, really?' He was trying to add sarcasm to his repertoire, but to anyone listening it carried exactly the same tone of disgust as almost everything else he said. The aide smiled again.

'Well, sir, you know what they're like so maybe we shouldn't hope for too much.'

The PM was going to remind him yet again that his opinions were of absolutely no interest, but a sudden wave of tiredness at invariably having to correct everyone overwhelmed him. Instead he shifted himself into a comfortable and familiar baleful glare. 'And?'

At this juncture the aide decided that discretion was better than the full truth. Their response was a little too forthright for the PM's current mood. 'They feared that the committee's reply might be too subtle for an alien mind. Their culture could be too different for them to be able to understand the delaying strategy implied.'

The PM almost understood what was meant, which cheered him enormously. 'Meaning we should be more direct I suppose?'

'In a way, PM.'

The PM found the aids response almost certainly a bit too clever. There was just the slight possibility that he might, after all, be left behind if he let the conversation go on too long. 'No need to be vague just spit it out.'

'The problem is in choosing.'

'I bloody well know that, we've just wasted hours with those idiots on the committee and ...' The aids expression filtered through the PM's instinctive outrage at having always to make so many life and death decisions. 'You mean that's their suggestion?'

'Yes PM.'

He knew without having to think about it too carefully that their answer was brilliant. In one simple sentence they'd thrown the ball back into the alien's court. For a second admiration almost spilled out and overwhelmed the pathological disregard he usually reserved for anyone but himself. And then he remembered that approval gave people too many ideas. 'Humph, well ... what d'you think? Pity we didn't have this a few hours ago.'

'Throws the ball in the alien's court, sir, and, if you don't mind me saying this, if it doesn't produce a positive response it won't impact direct on you in the same way the committee's response would.'

The PM's eyes bathed him in a malevolent glow of warm approval. 'We'd have to make it clear that under the present conditions ...' He paused, waiting for the aide to take the responsibility for what had to follow.

'Yes PM, that you had no choice but to draw on the leading experts in the field.'

'Exactly. Get Tantoning to put his name to this will you.'

'At once PM.' He whirled away hastily on one foot and strode off with squared shoulders and a smile of pride at having deftly survived one more encounter with the maniacal political beast that for some unfathomable reason the universe had decided was his fate to meet and serve.

The PM smiled and began to tidy his desk, and at the same instant Chepi read Nitu's response.

Ω

'The problem is in the choosing? What do they mean?'

The Sphere guessed. 'They want you to say more?'

'I know that, I mean what does it mean for them? Do they find every option equal, or does it imply that they don't know what to do?'

The Sphere didn't know. It was far too human an issue. Chepi was a closer species by far, so it was her job to work it out. 'What d'you think?'

'I believe it's rhetorical.'

The Sphere stayed silent.

'Why didn't they see my message as a direction?'

'Is that what you wanted?'

'I wanted to see if they would.'

'And now they haven't, so you did get the kind of answer you wanted, didn't you?'

At this point Chepi decided not to commit herself to any specific kind of interpretation, especially as it might turn out that they had out manoeuvred her. 'I think they should have taken the message a bit more seriously.'

Ω

Nitu shone a light directly into Zen's face. Although it had never happened to him before it instantly became his least favourite way of being woken up. 'Don't do that.'

The very lameness of such a submissive response cut straight through her enthusiasm. Whenever it sprang up inappropriately, boyishness always stopped her in her dead in her tracks. It was something to do with constant surprise at the inexhaustible ability of men to prioritise rest over almost anything else. 'This is important.' She hissed softly.

'Can't it ....'

'No, it can't wait.'

He struggled to sit upright. Nitu marvelled at the miracle of convergent evolution. How it came about that in reality men hadn't evolved from tatty, flea-ridden bears instead of graceful primates she'd never really understood.

'Just lie there, I haven't really got the time or stomach for all that scratching and farting.'

'What d'you ...?'

'I just wanted to tell you that they've sent our message as the answer. It's caused a big international stink, particularly with the Yanks and Brits, apparently.'

'Why?' He lay back with a sigh. The effort to move had been too much. He sighed again, grunted, scratched and worked himself into the most comfortable position possible under the circumstances 'Oh, I see, he didn't consult, did he.' Zen said.

She grinned. Even in the dark he could sense it spread across her face.

'What?' He asked. 'What's that for?'

'Yeah, they're all pissed off, but there's more.'

'Not nuclear, they're not thinking of ...?' This had been his real fear from the first moment he realised Canada was probably going to try to go it alone.

'No, it's the aliens. We seem to have really shaken them up. The Sphere's vanished and in it's place there's this apparently frakkingly awesome spaceship. Tantoning says it looks like something out of a Tim Burton film, or that guy who did the stuff for the Alien films. Really out there, very scary apparently.'

Zen sat bolt upright. Years of evolution passed by in an instant. 'And that's amusing to you? Look that sounds very much like ...'

'Yeah, I know, we've got them moving.'

'But they're threatening us now, aren't they? How's that good for ...'

She shone the light on her own face so he could see her amusement. 'Thought you were an anthropologist.'

'What's that got to do with anything. Look, what time is it?'

'Three am, still sleepy are we?' She giggled and Zen lay back again.

'That's better.' She patted his leg, and for the whole of the rest of his life Zen never worked out why. 'If they wanted to kill us don't you think they could do it with a Golden Sphere?' She added.

'Not necessarily.' He weakly offered.

'Okay, where did this new ship come from?'

He shrugged. 'Been in orbit?'

'Possible. So, suppose it was, can't it shoot at us, drop bombs or fire missiles from there?'

'Mmm, okay, see what you mean.'

'Seems to me we've got a clear answer. They want us to get our act together and do something.'

'About what exactly?'

It was her turn to shrug. 'That's the bad news. They, the politicians, might have boxed them in, boxed us all in. With all these alpha males around they'll never simply ask for anything, it'd seem too much like giving in. They'll want some show of strength. They'll think it'll give them a chance to negotiate.'

'Maybe they don't want to negotiate.'

'That's my view as well.'

'Is that what you told Tantoning?'

'No, I told him to send us some photos so we could think about whether the shape could tell us anything.'

Zen looked at her long and hard just to make sure. 'But that's bollocks isn't it?'

'Yeah, course.'

'Then why ask?'

'I'm interested in their aesthetics. Want to see if there's anything in the design that matches things I've found in the dig.'

Zen shook his head slowly. 'You're being pretty cool about all this.'

'I think they've been here before and that could be a way of proving a link, and that could be the best way we've got just now for working out what their motivation is.'

'And what d'you think Tantoning will make of it?'

'The PM's giving him hell, he hasn't got time to think.'

Ω

'Why did you do that?'

'They're a bit too complacent.'

'I know, but why that?' The Sphere insisted.

Chepi didn't reply.

The Sphere shrugged. 'What d'you think they'll do now?'

'Something.'

'You mean "anything"?'

'Maybe.'

'You've not thought this through, have you?'

'I want to see what they'll do next.'

'So you haven't.'

'You've told me lots of times that doing something is better than doing nothing.'

'I've never said any such thing.'

'Inaction gets you nowhere? Remember now?'

'Thoughts are actions. I meant literally doing nothing.'

'Is it possible not to think?'

'It's possible to keep thinking the same thing.'

Chepi was about to argue, but for the first time she got the point. 'Oh.'

'So, what now?'

'I can't undo it.'

'Why not?'

Chepi didn't know. 'Won't they think it a bit strange. Maybe indecisive?'

'Who knows, maybe they'll think you have some exotic, alien plan.'

'And that being better than no plan at all? Which is what we've got now thanks to you.'

'You never had a plan.' The Sphere sighed.

'It was, of sorts.'

The Sphere hated bickering and seeing the possibility looming it changed the subject. 'I thought you wanted to meet my avatar?'

'Is that a hint?'

'No, just a reminder that you did have some other kind of plan, once.'

'So you think I should?'

'No, it's up to you.'

'Then I shouldn't?' The thought was more worrying than she'd expected. If that also turned out to be a bad idea then she definitely had no idea what to do. Might as well leave, she thought. But that wasn't half as interesting as she'd have thought it was days before. Despite everything she quite liked watching all their dashing around making noise, and deep down she knew she was going to have to do something about them.

'It's for you to decide.' And then Sphere left, too quickly as it happened, but there was no chance of changing that. It should have left casually, as though it wasn't really trying to set her up to do something it wanted. As it was, it knew Chepi would have noticed its haste and she'd jump to the wrong conclusion as always. It was too late though, and all the Sphere could do was hope that despite the weird trains of thought she would inevitably go through as a result, in the end she'd do something useful. Maybe even something not in the least bit impulsive.

$$\Omega$$

As Chepi stood watching Nitu and Zen talking in the flickering light of their campfire, the dark ship she'd swapped with the usual appearance of the Sphere, vanished from sight.

Ω

The PM's phone jangled harshly in the dark bedroom shadows of another restless night. His thoughts still caught up in the terrors of endlessly dreamed images of his own political destruction, he reached out in dread for the vehicle that he knew would one day soon deliver the suffocating, airless news that would end everything that in quieter moments of delusion and misguided desires he'd hoped and expected. One day the phone would ring and a voice he'd never heard before would tell him hat it was all over, that his career was finished. Night time phone calls terrified him.

'What? What d'you mean it's gone? What does ...? I see. No, keep them on alert but off the streets. I'll be in ... Soon, soon, I'm in frakking bed.' He banged the phone down. 'Indecisive bastards.' He muttered quietly.

Ω

Nitu's satellite phone warbled emptily in the blank, still, almost dawn that spread away into the dark beyond the warm light of the rekindled fire. Chepi was standing watching them only a few yards away. The sound made her jump and murmur in fear. She dreaded the strange sounds of unknown creatures, especially things that flew invisibly around her. Small organic beings of hidden purpose terrorised her thoughts whenever she left the Sphere. Once, long ago, the Sphere had forgotten about her momentarily. She was only a very small child then, but that didn't matter. The memory of buzzing, dazzling, dangling legs brushing her face with unknown purpose still menaced her whenever she went outside after dark and left herself open to whatever could sneak in unseen and invade and molest her.

The Sphere said the answer was easy, she could just erase the memory, but for Chepi that was worse. She was her memories, so change those and she'd be nothing but some random script written by the person she had been but wasn't any longer. Let that happen and she would become authored by a stranger, be no more than a fiction of her lost self. So she shuddered at shadowy insects concealed by the night, while at the same time revelling in the freedom and awareness that made it possible.

Zen heard Chepi's gasp and caught by his own childhood fears he whirled quickly in the direction of the sound.

Meanwhile, Chepi was busy with the phone call. 'What d'you mean it's just vanished?' She hissed with quiet urgency.

On the other end of the call Tantoning started in surprise at the tone. Last time he'd spoken to her she hadn't appeared in the least interested in the fact that the Sphere had been replaced in an instant with a menacing dark object of clearly evil intent. If that had seemed strange then her latest reaction was even stranger. Despite being besotted by almost everything about her Tantoning began to sense strongly that she wasn't, after all, being completely straight with him. "Why does this suddenly matter so much? Last time we talked you didn't appear to care at all.'

The question caught Nitu off guard. She held her hand over the mouthpiece. 'He wants to know why it's so important to me.'

Of course Zen had no idea what she was talking about. 'Why, what's important?'

'Never mind.' She snapped impatiently. 'All these changes.' She hissed back to Tantoning. 'You keep asking my opinion and then the next minute it changes again. This is hard you know.'

Tantoning felt like pointing out that it wasn't easy for him either, having to deal almost minute by minute with a deranged politician who clearly had some kind of bipolar disease, but he liked her far too much, and instead suggested that she must be tired, and told her he'd call again in the morning.

When the phone clicked into silence Nitu stared at it with a hostility even she hadn't known was possible. 'D'you know what that bastard Tantoning has just said to me?' She asked vehemently.

Zen had no idea but could see from her face that he was definitely about to find out. 'Get back to Vancouver?' He guessed.

She glared.

'They've pulled your grant?' The thought of that made even him nervous.

'I must be tired so he'll talk to me in again in the morning. The patronising bastard.'

Zen had no idea why that would be a problem. He was tired and would prefer to talk about absolutely everything in the morning. Luckily he knew better than to say so. Instead he grunted and threw a log on the fire.

'Can you believe that?' She asked.

'No, I can't.' He answered calmly, because of course he couldn't.

'Bastard.'

'Yep, never liked him. But, well ...' This was the tricky part. One mistake in trying to find out what Tantoning really wanted and he knew she might never tell him. 'Why'd he say that?'

'Just because I ... how should I know, you're a man, you tell me.'

Which of course Zen had no intention of doing, even if he ever did work out what she was going on about. 'I mean, so what did he phone for?'

'Oh, that.' She'd lost track. 'That other ship, the dark one, it's vanished again.' She added as indifferently as she could.

'Oh, and the Sphere's come back?'

'No, I don't think so.' She glowed with slight embarrassment as she realised she'd never asked.

Her omission was too obvious even for Zen to miss. 'You did ask?'

'No, didn't need to. He'd have mentioned it.'

Given how short the call had been Zen thought that was unlikely. 'You sure?'

'No, but it doesn't matter to us does it. The big thing is that they've taken the other one away and we haven't got any good photos of it. It was almost night when it turned up and now it's gone.'

'They'll have something though, won't they?'

'But not the detail we'd need, surely?'

'Maybe, who knows; anyway, do we need real detail?'

'I'd guess so, for the etchings, on the sides. The details, like on the pillars in the stone circle.'

'I don't understand. We don't know if it had any etchings, do we? Wasn't that just speculation, or d'you know something else you've not told me yet?'

She was about to answer impatiently when she realised she didn't actually know why she'd thought it had, it'd somehow seemed obvious. 'I don't know to be honest, it just seemed kind of, well, like it would've been. You know, like the pillars.'

'I don't see why.'

'No, nor do I really. I just … I don't know, kind of thought about the design and thought maybe there'd be some type of hieroglyphs on it somewhere.'

Zen couldn't see the connection. 'I guess so.' He lied. 'Why not, many cultures adorn their weapons, so why not them? It was a good idea, pity we'll never know now.'

Chepi decided it was time to say something. 'It wasn't a weapon.'

Zen whirled around in a kind of jumping, startled leap backwards. Nitu froze momentarily.

Chepi laughed. 'I'm not dangerous.'

Nitu turned her head slowly towards Chepi but it was Zen who spoke first. 'You shouldn't sneak up on people like that.'

'I didn't sneak.'

Gathering his composure Zen sat back down again and let his eyes run cautiously over their visitor.

Nitu did likewise. She saw a young female about her own age or a bit younger dressed in a long cowl that made her look like some stray member of a nearby temple. The hood hid most of her face. Only her eyes were clearly visible. They rested easily on Nitu, and even in the grey light of dawn, their intelligence sneaked through.

Zen failed to see those nuances, but others were all too obvious. To him she looked distinctly like a yet another hippy.

Chepi kept her eyes focussed on Nitu and broadened her smile. 'I told you I'm not dangerous.'

'Appearances can be deceptive.' She replied.

'Not usually, if you know how to look.'

'A cowl doesn't show much.'

'It could show everything.'

'The need to hide for one.'

Chepi laughed lightly. 'Or modesty?'

Zen's increasingly mystified expression switched back and forth between them. 'Maybe we could start with a simple hello first?'

Nitu glance at him and then turned back to Chepi. 'Is there a point to this or d'you make a habit of sneaking up on strangers in the middle of nowhere to play word games?'

Chepi's smile weakened. 'If anyone's going to be rude it should be me.'

Zen decided to nip whatever was happening in the bud before in got too out of hand. 'Hey, c'mon, give each other a chance. Look, why don't you sit down.' He started to stand and offer Chepi his seat near the fire, but she waved him down.

'I'm okay.' She shifted her weight easily from one foot to the other. She looked relaxed but watchful. Zen couldn't help noticing how she kept one eye constantly on Nitu.'

'Do I know you?' Nitu asked.

'No.'

'Then why d'you keep looking at me like that?'

Zen interceded again. 'You do keep looking at her. We're not really used to being stared at where we come from.'

'I can speak for myself.' Nitu said.

Chepi ignored her. 'I don't care too much for conventions.'

Hoping it might switch the mood Zen hastily poured some coffee. He handed a cup to her. 'So, anyway, what brings you out here?'

'No thanks.' She waved it away. ' I came to see what you two were doing.'

'And offer opinions about private conversations.' Nitu added.

Chepi shrugged. 'I don't think that dark ship was anything private. Everyone could see it.'

'How d'you know that?' Nitu asked.

Chepi shrugged again. 'On my phone, like you.'

'How d'you know I've got a phone?'

Chepi looked at her for several seconds. 'Are you paranoid or something?'

'Don't change the subject.'

It was down to Zen to play peacemaker once more. 'C'mon, don't start arguing again. And, well, you do sound a bit, well defensive.' This remark turned out to be perfectly misjudged.

Nitu glared at him. 'Frak, didn't take you long did it.'

Chepi frowned. 'Don't be like that to him, he really likes you.'

Nitu's head swirled angrily back towards her. 'Mind your own business.' She sipped her coffee impatiently. 'So how long have you been spying on us?'

'I'm not spying.'

'So what are you doing here? It's not as though you just

happened to be walking by.'

'I saw your campfire. Thought I'd come and see what you were doing.'

'Saw it, from where? ' Suspicion surged back to the fore. Working in the area for over 12 moths she'd flown over every bit of land for at least a 50 miles radius, and even if she hadn't, from asking around she'd learned that no one had lived within many miles of the artefact for as long as anyone could remember. It was a wild, exceptionally remote area, almost never visited by anyone.

'I'm camped a few miles away. I saw the light of your fire so I came over to see what you were doing.'

'I've been coming here a lot and I've never seen you.' Nitu retorted.

'I know.'

'What, that I come here often or that I've never seen you before?'

'Both.'

'And?'

Chepi shrugged.

'So you pick now to come over?'

'This time there were two of you. You've only ever been here on your own before. And then there's that dark ship like etching on the circle, so I thought maybe that's why you'd come back, except you were here before it appeared so, maybe not, but then I thought you might think there's a link to the Sphere. So, anyway, there were two of you and I thought you might be up to something interesting.'

'And why would that concern you?' Zen asked.

'Never mind that.' Nitu interjected. 'What etchings on the pillars?'

Zen had been trying to be less obvious. Not knowing who she was, he thought that it might have been better to have moved a little more slowly. Nitu's need to rush, and her whole attitude since the stranger had arrived was as unhelpful as it appeared to be out of character. 'Maybe that's got nothing to do with us.' He said meaningfully.

Ignoring Nitu, Chepi turned to Zen. 'Because I was here before either of you, and I suppose that makes me a bit territorial.'

'No way, no one's been here before I found it.' She paused.

The idea that someone else had found the circle before her wasn't easy to grasp. 'If you'd been here before me others would have known and I'd have seen signs, your camp from the air or footprints or signs of work, or something at least. Everyone leaves a mark and I don't miss things like that.'

'Sorry but I have and you do.' Chepi had never lied before, there'd never been any need to, except to pretend she was hiding something from the Sphere, which was pointless but nevertheless didn't stop her trying from time to time. The lie made her feel strange, like she'd lost a part of herself somehow. Immediately she wanted to make amends, to tell the truth. Feeling uncomfortable with herself was too strange to cope with. 'Well, maybe not quite in the way it sounds, and I come and go easily so no one can tell, it's not your fault.'

But in trying to undo what she'd started she only managed to make it worse. 'I don't need patronising.' Nitu responded almost sulkily.

'I don't want to argue with you.' Chepi offered, in some dim hope it might make a difference.

'Thank God for that.' Zen threw in, trying yet again to change the subject. 'What is it with you two? You've never met before and yet you can't stop bickering. Sure your not related or something?'

'No way.'

Chepi looked at her with a surprised expression. Zen couldn't tell if it was genuine or just another ploy to annoy. 'Don't start again.' He urged.

'I was just going to say that we might be.' Chepi calmly responded.

The Sphere heard and turned its attention away.

Nitu coughed with disgust and rubbed her eyes. 'Sorry, maybe I'm being a bit crazy. Or I've maybe not been sleeping enough, but how the frak could we be related?'

'Well, not really. I just meant, who knows?'

'Well I do, and we're not.'

'Okay, I'm not saying we are. Look, maybe I can sit down after all?' Chepi asked.

Without speaking Nitu created some space and Chepi slid in beside her on the mattress that was spread over the log she was sitting on.

'Thanks.' Chepi said.

Nitu looked at Zen. 'What?' But he didn't need to answer, the question was rhetorical and, to his relief she turned back to Chepi. 'Sorry. I'm Nitu.' She held out her hand.

Chepi took her hand. 'Nitunakiwidinok. I know, Daughter-of-the-Wind.' Her smile was broad and open.

Nitu's face showed more surprise than it had for years. 'You know Chippewa?'

'A little, but I wouldn't have known the meaning of your name except for you, your work. I've read about all your stuff on stone circles.'

Zen had no idea what had triggered the change between them, but he embraced the shift with open relief. 'There you go, give her a chance and you've got a fan instead of an enemy.'

They both glanced at him in an exaggerated way. The message was obvious. He offered to make breakfast but neither replied, so he made it anyway. He always saw cooking on an open fire as one of his specialities, but then so did every other man on the planet.

$$\Omega$$

The three days that passed after Chepi's unexpected arrival turned out to be a time of exceptional hard work, both physically and mentally. Chepi's respect for them both grew quickly. She'd been used always to being able to link to data in the Sphere whenever she wanted to, think a thousand different things simultaneously at twice the speed of light and access anything she needed from hundreds of millions of other cultures. Even without the Sphere's help she was seventeen times smarter than any human who would ever live. Inevitably she soon discovered that the human way of working ideas out one at a time was quite different. Having to cope with constant forgetting and frequent mental tiredness made their work slow, hard and painful. Nonetheless she continued at their pace, and eventually learned to admire what they were able to achieve with so few resources.

When they'd gone to the stones together on the first morning Chepi had shown them the faint outline that looked like the dark ship that had quickly come and gone. That led to efforts to try to translate the hieroglyphs surrounding the image. For that even Chepi had to work from basics. She wanted to know the answer as much as they did. Although the Sphere had always been able to build black ships Chepi wanted discover its history. She couldn't ask the Sphere as since she'd arrived on the surface it wouldn't talk to her directly, and searching data bases wouldn't help until they'd coordinated as many extracts of the text as they could find. Until then any random trolling for meanings would be like trying to find a lost pin in the whole of the multiverse. They worked long hours, and after three days Nitu made a breakthrough.

'Chepi, look at this.'

She peered over Nitu's shoulder. 'What've you got?'

'I think it's a reference to a golden globe.'

'Let me see.' At the same time she asked the Sphere if it knew about any reference to it being on the circle but it refused to answer. Chepi checked Nitu's work and agreed that it did appear to make reference to a golden sphere. Whether or not it was the exact same one as their visitor, it was impossible to tell.

Further work didn't give them anything more. The reference was vague and they had to admit it was possibly ambiguous too. They even had to concede that there was a small chance that the reference could refer to the sun, especially when they unravelled a bit more and found reference to a child being "sent" to it as a gift. That disappointed Nitu particularly, as it seemed like a clear reference to some kind of human sacrifice. Chepi's reaction was personal and somewhat different, it made her skin shiver with unformed fears and speculation about her childhood.

Nitu looked up. 'Hey, you okay? You look really tired and cold. Maybe you should wear more? Just having that cowl isn't really enough out here, is it?'

It was a subject they'd talk about before. Neither Nitu nor Zen could understand why she wore the cowl all the time and kept the hood up whatever the weather. In the end she said it was to do with her religious beliefs, but they doubted that, believing that if it had been true she would have said so earlier. Zen wondered if she had some kind of physical scars she was uncomfortable revealing.

'No, I'm fine. It's warm. I'm okay.'

Nitu was unconvinced. 'Look I know it's not really any of my business, but if you do get ill out here there's no one but us to look after you.'

'I'm fine. Please. You know why I dress like this.'

Nitu wanted to argue further but knew it wouldn't get her anywhere. 'Okay. I'm just worrying about you. Anyway look, it's lunchtime. Let's take a break and have something to eat?'

Zen joined them and for a time they ate in silence, each lost in the problems relating to their own bit of the project and also reflecting on the news they received several times a day about events in Vancouver. Zen and Nitu offered advice to whoever called whenever they could, but since the Sphere had disappeared there came to be less and less they, or anyone else, could say. They began to suspect that Tantoning only phoned for support in having to deal with an increasingly deranged PM.

They'd tried to involve Chepi in their post phone call discussions, but as she never showed any interest they'd stopped bothering. They differed in reaction to her response. Nitu thought it a little strange but Zen argued that she'd probably lived away from cities so long that what happened there hardly mattered to her anymore. His real motive in offering any opinion at all was to steer Nitu away from starting an argument again. Not that she'd given any indication of wanting to since the beginning, but he could sense some odd kind of tension between them lying so close to the surface he feared it would erupt at any moment.

The silence continued. After eating they all lay back in the long grass and closed their eyes, each reluctant for a while to break the stillness. In the end it was Chepi who broke the spell.

'Why are people destroying this beautiful planet?'

'It's not just now.' Zen answered. 'History shows that human beings have always destroyed the environment, it's just that now we do it more efficiently and in greater numbers than before.'

'Does the difference matter?' Chepi asked.

'And is it even true?' Nitu added. 'What about Native Americans? They never destroyed anything.'

'Only because they were few in number; get a bit of population pressure and then you see what people are capable of. A few thousand people in a wilderness isn't the way to see what we're really capable of because, in the end, it's all about survival. And just like dear old Darwin taught us, when life gets tough every single one of us will fight for the whatever we can get.'

'Fair point.' Nitu conceded.

'Then it's as simple as that?' Chepi asked.

'It's not exactly simple. There's ...' Zen replied.

But Chepi wasn't open open to excuses. 'Sounds like it. There are just too many of you.'

'Of us, you mean. You're included.' Nitu corrected.

'I've never destroyed anything.'

Zen sighed. He'd had this argument with students many times. The more they had the less they understood. 'Only because you've never had to.'

Unnoticed, Chepi stared intently into the sky, trying to see some trace of the Sphere hanging ten miles above them. She wanted to ask it a million questions about human beings, but right then, during those moments the three of them were together, she didn't want willingly to give up anything they were sharing, the solitude especially. She wanted it to intervene unasked, but she knew it wouldn't no matter how hard she strained her eyes. They closed and she thought in the darkness instead. 'D'you think I'd destroy a planet to stay alive?'

'It's not as obvious as that, it takes time, it's a slow process, almost invisible so we never notice or think it's us that's the cause.'

She didn't know which one of them had said that. Sometimes their voices sounded so strange she couldn't put a face to them. 'Nothing is slow.'

'What does that mean?'

That was Nitu. Her questions could be so much more direct than his ever were.

'It's all about what you're thinking about.' Chepi replied.

'Deep.' And that was Zen, trying to appease once more. What was it they believed about the differences between men and women? Then again, Nitu wasn't really one of them. She kept forgetting that.

'Don't trivialise.'

That was Nitu again. Chepi had grown really fond of her. 'If the ocean is a circle then something deep is also its surface.' She answered.

'Even deeper.'

There was a pause, heavy and undecided. And then Chepi laughed. 'I just meant that it's obvious that time isn't objective.'

'So it's neither slow nor fast?' Nitu asked, deciding at last to go with the flow.

'I mean that the destruction is eternal, no matter how long it takes. So, the time that passed to achieve it is irrelevant and, for those who come after, well, they wouldn't even care, the event would be what defines all reality.'

Nitu grimaced unseen. 'But that doesn't matter does it? Zen's saying that people carry on the way they do because they don't see the changes. Not in any day-to-day sense. So, well, the metaphysics don't count. Not in this sense, the sense you're implying. If you know what I mean.'

Chepi thought long and hard. If Nitu really meant what she said then humans weren't at all aware of the cosmic consequences of what they did. She couldn't believe that was true. 'You mean people don't think about these things.'

'No. Except a very few.' It came in chorus from both of them.

'You sure?'

'Yes.' They chorused back.

'So everything is only about local physical things?'

'Material things.' Nitu corrected. 'Like possessions, cars and houses, and even bigger houses and clothes and ...'

'Planes.' Zen added.

'I need that, for my work.'

Zen laughed. 'That's what everyone says; 'but I NEED it.''

'This isn't funny.' Chepi said.

Nitu didn't understand where Chepi's sudden sombre mood had come from. 'I can understand why you, well, anyone, would be worried about this stuff, but why now. I mean, it's a beautiful day and we're making great progress, so why the pessimism? We might even find an answer to some of these problems. The ancients could teach us how to be different.'

'If people could learn to be different, wouldn't they have done so by now?'

'Perhaps.' Zen agreed. 'But there is something to be said about enjoying the moment.'

'What?' Chepi asked. 'What's to be said about that?'

Zen sat up, his face serious. 'If we don't, then what is there left?'

'D'you really mean that?' Chepi asked. 'You work hard and try to achieve something. You don't seem to act as if it's all fun.'

'I enjoy my work.' He answered.

At that moment Chepi saw how it was for them, billions of individual searches for a utopia of the senses. Striking alliances solely to gain something. The Sphere was right after all, they loved physical things too much. What she didn't know was what the purpose of it all was, and now she understood that lost as they were in their evolutionary well of limited possibilities, they couldn't tell her. This would be true for all of them, Nitu, though, was another matter. 'Nitu, I want to show you something.'

Nitu responded cautiously. She'd half expected from the beginning that Chepi knew things about the circle she wasn't sharing with them. She'd had an unspoken fear from the first moment Chepi had arrived that at some point she'd reveal something that would undermine or make redundant all she'd put together so far. 'What?' She murmured.

'Can't tell you, but I can show you.'

'What, now?' She hoped whatever it was it wouldn't be so bad that she couldn't move around it in some way. The research was everything, all she'd ever wanted.

Chepi glanced up at the sky again and wondered what the Sphere would think. Not that that would change anything, this was her call, her world now so, in the end, all that mattered was what she would sometime soon decide. 'Might as well.'

'What about me?' Zen asked.

'No, not you.' Chepi replied. 'Sorry.' She liked him and one small part of her didn't want to exclude him.

She stood up and after the most fleeting hesitation held her hand out to Nitu. 'C'mon.'

With some uncertainty and not a little confusion Nitu held out her hand in return and Chepi pulled her to her feet. 'What now?' She asked.

'This way.' Chepi stepped in the direction of the river. Nitu hesitated but firm pressure from Chepi's hand urged her to follow.

Zen watched them walk away and shook his head in surprise and bewilderment.

They walked in silence. Nitu twice tried casually to let go of Chepi's hand but the attempts were ignored. This sudden, persistent attention made her feel awkward but she was at a loss at how to respond.

'Why are you holding my hand?'

Chepi looked at her in surprise. 'Sorry, I hadn't noticed.' She let go immediately. 'Didn't mean to make you feel uncomfortable.'

Nitu's hand quickly cooled. An impulse almost made her reach out to have it held again. 'I just wondered why, that's all.' She said.

'I'd forgotten. Sorry.'

'It didn't matter. I was just curious.' She pushed her hand into a pocket and wished she hadn't said anything.

They walked on until they got close to the river. An early morning mist still lingered and spilled out from the water, consuming the banks in light, grey and silver patterns. To Nitu the shapes looked like strange creatures dancing behind silver veils. The effect made it hard to see where they were walking.

'Where're you taking us?'

Chepi reached a hand behind her. Nitu's slipped out of her pocket and took hold of it. It felt cool and strong. They walked on for several steps and the mist thinned. Nitu could make out a kind of bivouac close to the river.

'Is this yours?' Where you camp?'

'Yes, sort of.'

'But you said …?'

'I know, I just didn't want you to know where I was.' She turned, let go of Nitu's hand and smiled broadly. 'I'm a bit secretive. Sorry.'

Nitu's hands pushed themselves into her pockets. 'That's fine. You can trust us, but, well, a woman out here on her own, I can see that, that, you know, you'd want to keep yourself safe.'

Chepi continued beaming the smile at her. 'Thanks.'

The smile was somehow disconcerting. It seemed to say that there was a secret about to be shared. Nitu held her breath. 'And?'

Chepi frowned. 'And what?'

'The reason we're here?'

Spaceship over Vancouver

'I've got to show you something. It's a bit, well, strange, but I think you should see it. Well, someone I know wants you to see it and I've been asked to show you. Well, take you there actually, if you agree.'

'Somewhere here?'

'No, well, yes.'

'Yes or no?'

'No.'

'Then how d'you expect to get there, walk?' It's a wild place out here. Maybe you've noticed? And why bring me here to tell me all this?'

'Yeah, I know that, and why here? I didn't want Zen to know.'

'Why? Aren't we all in this together?'

'You two, I don't know, but me, no, not really, I just wanted to see the stones, see what you've found.'

Nitu tensed. 'Your not some kind of frakking spy?'

'No, at least I don't think so.'

'What d'you mean you don't think so?'

'I don't know, but it's really not important. I've got something to show you, take you to and then I'll leave.'

'Take me and then leave?'

'No, not that, I'll bring you back.'

Nitu's mind was running ahead. 'Is it something to do with the site?'

'In a way, yes.'

'Then you knew about this place before?' The connection seemed obvious and once again Nitu felt a tense fear at the possibility someone had found the site before her.

'It will be easier if I can show you, if you'll let me.'

'I don't know.'

'You have to say yes.'

'I don't have to say anything.'

'I mean you have to say yes before I can show you.'

Nitu shook her head. 'I have to agree before you can show me.'

'I know, that's what I mean.'

'Are you some kind of religious freak? Is this a cult thing, because if it is then forget it.'

93

'No. To be honest I don't really believe in very much.'

It all seemed a bit farfetched to Nitu. After all, she reasoned, where could they possible go to in the middle of the Yukon wilderness without any transport, but on the other hand she did want to know what Chepi was hiding. 'Okay, I agree.'

The wind chilled suddenly. A sense of expectation filled the air and bristled through the trees, rustling the leaves as though in warning. The light dimmed as clouds suddenly scurried across the sun. The chill deepened into feelings of dread that tendrilled their way into Nitu's heart. She backed away in fear but Chepi only smiled more broadly. The mist returned but this time it had substance. Nitu could feel it trail through her fingers like silken threads too small to grasp. She could feel them against her face as they thickened, causing her to lose sight of Chepi. Stars came out briefly, glimpsed despite the mist, flitting between gaps in the clouds. They were large, larger than they should have been, too large for Nitu to grasp. They shone brightly for one instant in millions of shades of colours she'd never seen before, and then they were gone, leaving behind a blackness that screamed at her, promising to drive her insane with its cloying grasp on everything. It reached into her mind and clutched another part of her that lay even deeper, something that until then had been hidden. And then the blackness too was gone, replaced by greyness and sudden warmth that claimed her. Slowly she began to see again.

Chepi still faced her. Bright red barked trees spread around them, and shining green ferns sparkled and shifted with alien movement filling the spaces left between the mad scramble of plant life that had suddenly erupted from the dank void of moments before. She tried to breathe but the air felt cold and insubstantial and her vision faded as blackness returned. This time there were no visions and as she slumped to the ground unconsciousness rescued her.

Chepi's eyes reflected momentary surprise before they settled back once again to excited anticipation. She sat down and took Nitu's hand again and waited.

Ω

'That scientist, the blond one with the name, where's she got to?'

'Nitunakiwidinok?'

'Don't be bloody clever.'

'She's disappeared.'

'Dis-a-bloody-peared! What d'you mean disappeared. We're in the middle of a frakking world crisis here. No one disappears unless I tell them they can, is that bloody clear?'

'Yes, PM. Except that … we can't find her.'

'Get onto that idiot Tantoning, he'll know where she is.'

'He's the one who told us ...'

'He told you did he? Well I don't give a frak. There's a frakking meeting of the G20, NATO, the UN, the African Congress and God knows who the bloody hell else in two days. I want briefings by everyone. Find her. Find everyone. Get them here. Now get the bloody hell out.'

As the aide walked away down the corridor the manic shouts continued to echo from the walls of his mind, and, he increasingly feared, his very soul.

Ω

The meeting of world leaders went very badly for the PM. Having deferred to his claim that he had the right to Chair the meeting he mistakenly believed that gave him some kind of status over the rest of the 87 world leaders in attendance. On that score he quickly saw his error. It was clear from the start that the US, Germany, France, Russia, China and the UK had already decided singly or between themselves the outcome they'd accept. On some issues they shared full agreement, while on others lines were being drawn for future battles. His ideas weren't criticised or rejected, as such, no, it was much worse than that, whenever he spoke there was a silence followed by bright smiles of encouragement from one or other of the group of six. Others tried to intervene, whether out of conviction or pity he wasn't sure, and it did help, for a time, eventually, though, the Chinese offered a view that contradicted the NATO position and from then on it was clear that whatever else happened the outcome of the meeting would be decided by the result of that particular power struggle.

Of course, he knew that deals had already been played out in trades, exports, imports, tax concessions, gifts, endowments, holiday homes and impossible promises of support for fantastical claims over land or treaties or committee membership. Everything that had made the West so rich and powerful, and which promised the same to China and certain other favoured developing economies was thrown into the pot. The fact that Canada was a major trading partner, exporter of oil and other costly non-renewable commodities didn't count for anything. The PM had taken his eye off the ball. He'd been planning world leadership while they had been cajoling, begging, bargaining, wheeling and dealing and throwing around the odd threat. They'd called in old favours and signed new ones in blood. He hadn't stood a chance and no one had told him.

'They stitched me up.'

'It's all about old debts and networks PM.'

'But it isn't is it, not this time?'

For the first time the aide almost felt sorry for him. Of course it wasn't all about alliances, pay back and promises, but if that was taken away there wasn't much left. The PM seemed small and vulnerable for once, and the aide almost apologised for not telling him, but there had been orders from some software company with ties to MI6 and the CIA. They wanted an inside track on any alien equipment that came to light and the PM wasn't running things the way they'd wanted so it had been decided that the best thing was to get rid of him. Misinform, that had been the instruction, and then watch him burn. Despite loathing him for more reasons than he could count, the aide couldn't bring himself to tell him openly, so he prevaricated. 'Not entirely PM.'

'But mostly?'

'Afraid so. At least that's how they see it, just another opportunity to trade favours.'

The PM thought he understood. 'Can they honestly believe the aliens will give us technology. That they've come here trade?'

'Not sure exactly PM, but perhaps. Isn't that what explorers do, like Marco Polo, find new trade?'

'Like the spice wars, and slavery you mean. Trade in people, take whatever else you want and beat the shit out of anyone getting in the way. We could do that, that's the whole point of keeping it here.'

'You have a point PM.' He was swearing again, back to normal. The aide started easing his way towards the door.

'But they know that as well as I do, so what the frak are they playing at?'

'Reshuffling the pack, trading off old debts and making new ones. Everyone seems to think they've done well out of it, well all the big players anyway, so it'll probably set the stage for years to come.'

'Unless we get the shit blown out of us.'

'That could have happened anyway. I doubt anything that has happened here will change anything they've already decided'

'But we might have done something else.'

'What, exactly?' The aide placed his hand warily on the door handled. The PM was still facing away and didn't notice.

'Some kind of defence plan led by Canada.'

'They've done that, PM. It's in your notes.'

'Everything on alert, is that it?'

'Not much more they can do without knowing more about the thing, it's capabilities.'

'There was a chance here for something else.'

Of course what he meant was that there was a chance for him and the oil, mining and forestry companies he owed for his career. Or at least there should have been. He was pining for something lost that he had never had, and the aide knew better than anyone that there was nothing more dangerous than a needy and scorned politician. 'Maybe we should play along with them for now. We've not missed out completely PM. We've still got trees and oil. They'll want them whatever they do.'

'The bastards haven't deforested Indonesia and Brazil and a hundred other places yet, we'll have to wait our turn.'

'But there's still the tarsands PM.'

'Not if those alien bastards have some miracle fuel the rest of the world can get their hands on.'

'What is it you want me to do PM?'

Being a politician, when he needed to the PM could shift positions as fast as greased lightening in an ice rink. He had an idea, it might not bring him international statehood, but it could make him very rich. 'Get them together, all of them, my team, Tantoning too, and especially that Macleod and Nitu woman. Tomorrow, first thing.' He barked.

The aide saw the PM's spirits rise, and feared for the worse. He decided to stall. 'She's still missing. No one's seen here.'

'Well find her.'

The aide danced nervously from one foot to the other.

The PM noticed, he hated any sign of weakness, it distracted him. 'And stop bloody well doing that will you.'

'He's stuck in the Yukon sir, Macleod. She left him out there apparently.'

'Left him?'

'Yes sir.'

'In the Yukon?'

'Yes.'

'And why the frak would she do that. Why not leave him at home or in a bar somewhere, like normal people? Bloody academics.'

'I don't think it was like that. They were working out there.'

Alarms rang out in the PM's already paranoid mind. 'On what?'

'Ehm, no one really knows.'

He swivelled his chair and stared the cold, wet stare of an insect with its prey. 'They bugger off in the middle of all this for something no one knows anything about?'

'Yes sir, I ...'

The PM could smell fear, and most of it was his own. 'Academics don't sneak off when they get a chance like this, and if they do they don't just bloody well disappear. I'll bet the yanks are behind this, or the Brits, or all of them.' He wiped his hands together nervously. If they've got their fingers dirty on Canadian soil then I'll have the buggers.' He added uncertainly. 'Get a plane out there, get Macleod back here and find out what they've been up to.'

'We don't know where he is.' The door handle turned under a sweating hand.

The PM just stared.

'The Yukon's a big place PM.'

Big, fat hands gripped the sides of the desk.

'He won't tell us where he is. Something to do with

confidentiality.' The aide continued.

'Charge the bastard with treason and get him back here.'

He wanted to ask how, but his nerves couldn't take any more. 'Yes PM.' The door handle slipped and squelched as he wrestled it open. 'I'll keep you briefed sir.' The door closed silently behind him. The PM didn't notice.

Ω

The day after the PM hatched his plan for Canada to stand against the rest of the world's preoccupation with global trade and corner any potential economic benefits for the sole use of Canada the Sphere reappeared. Not over Vancouver as the first time, but over the Yukon. It was spotted by a satellite in the early hours of the morning and once again the empty echo of a night-time phone brought the news.

The PM ordered an immediate state of emergency to be called across the Province. Events to follow would show that in doing so he made his biggest mistake of all time. If he'd waited only a few hours longer, world history would have followed an entirely different path. Alas the rash steps he took following the political setback he experienced during the Sphere Meeting of Governments subsequently proved to be an impossible barrier to any retreat to more considered options. His aide had cautioned him to act slowly, consider every option, but he never heard. The news was more than he'd dared hope for, but worse than he could have imagined. The Sphere reappearing over Canadian soil turned out to be his great undoing. His great dread had been that it would rematerialize somewhere else, the UK or, God forbid, the USA, but it arrived back on his native soil and from that point on the world would change in ways no one could ever have predicted.

Ω

Troops moved into the Yukon only a few hours after their orders came through. They placed an impenetrable barrier around the Sphere's ground zero before daybreak and hermetically sealed the Yukon by noon the following day. There were the expected protests and demonstrations, and it was from that point on that the arrests began. There were only a few dozen at first, but by the next morning thousands had been locked up on the grounds of national security. The PM suspended Parliament and formed a war council. The dark days, as they would become to be known, had begun, and amidst the worst times, most of the PM's attention was focused squarely on Zen Macleod.

'What's he got to say for himself?' The PM asked.

The aide shrugged. It was a new habit, one that made him feel somehow detached, as though everything he said or did was magically enclosed in parentheses. The conceit helped him pretend to himself that nothing he did was in any way his fault. He suspected that the PM was already growing tired of seeing it, but that only made him shrug mentally even more deeply. In truth the PM assumed he was cracking up, he'd seen it many times before and every other time he hadn't cared in the least. On this occasion things were very different. He needed the aide; there was simply no time to find a replacement. So he clenched his teeth, metaphorically looked the other way and allowed the insubordination to continue unremarked. Of course the aide knew all this and he didn't care either.

'Macleod says it's nothing to do with him, or words to that effect. It was Nitunakiwidinok's project, he was just along for the first time to help.' The aide reported.

'And she's bloody well disappeared.'

'Yes PM.'

'Any idea where? No chance he's murdered her? You know what these academics are like, kill their own grandmother for a research grant and probably eat their own children for a favourable book review.'

'Possible of course, but he's not behaving as though he did.'

'Could be insane.'

'Had him assessed. Other than the usual self-obsession and narcissism academics generally demonstrate, there's no evidence of any serious abnormalities.'

'So, where is she?'

'Other than what you know already, there's nothing else to report. She went off with some young woman wearing a cowl two days ago and she's not been seen since.'

'And she left that plane of hers?'

'Yes. Still parked where she left it.'

'Any chance she's been working for someone else all along?'

'No real idea PM, but even if she was you'd think the sudden appearance of the Sphere only a dozen or so miles from her dig would get her back pretty quickly.'

A sticky stillness filled the air. 'You're not being insubordinate again are you?'

'No sir, sorry, I'm merely trying to help, make suggestions as they come to mind.'

'Frankly I don't really care what you meant, just find her. There's some link between the Sphere and those stones and I want to know about it now, or even sooner. This is the chance we need. If we work that out, find the reason the Sphere's gone there, the rest might fall into place.'

'And our allies? As you know, they're not at all happy with what's going on in ...'

'I bloody well know that. You keep telling me every few bloody minutes. Let them wait. This is Canada and we do things my way.'

'They're beginning to make very hostile noises sir.'

'Frak them, I want to know what Macleod knows. Beat it out of him if you have to.'

'I don't think he knows anything sir.'

'We'll know that when you've finished with him won't we? Now clear off and do as you're told.'

Ω

Zen was used to dealing with idiots, after all he'd worked in a university most of his life, and although real and implied threats from the hallowed halls of learning did not involve actual violence they could be very damaging to person's mental health.

Faced with this new kind of abuse, Zen did his best to ignore most of what they threatened. After five years of trying to tutor engineering students on the basics of culture he had developed some considerable immunity to irrational pleas, abuse, and character assassination. If fact, as yet another drop of spittle blasted his face and the hot breath of one more faceless idiot who thought shouting was the key way to put forward an argument scorched his eye brows, he reflected on the fact that they could learn a great deal about interrogation from the daily lives of university teachers.

'I don't know where she is. I keep telling you.' Despite the fact that it was somewhat stressful to be shouted out for hours at a time, he knew that he could take what they had thrown at him so far for hours to come. 'I've told you time and again. They'd simply walked off, hand in hand and so far they haven't returned.' He said the same words over and over again, and even they began to admire the way he could repeat the same statement for hours without any sign of fatigue. Clearly they had no idea of the depth of repetitive ability teachers garnered over endless years of listening to their own voice. He was well within his comfort zone, but what he wouldn't find so easy was the thing that happened next, or more accurately, the thing that happened after the thing that happened next.

The shouting stopped, the door opened and a slightly built, immaculately dressed young man in a dark blue suit entered. He spoke to the older man who always stood at the back of the room and then, and this was the part that scared Zen, looked over at him with an expression that in one glance conveyed pity, remorse and a kind of existential resignation. The expression chilled him, someone he'd never met was telling him simultaneously that he was sorry but what was about to happen was inevitable and beyond his control. Zen considered that in all likelihood only the bearers of death sentences would have such glances. Suddenly tenure did not seem so important.

His mind wandered. Maybe, he thought, they'd found Nitu and she was ..., but the thought was never finished. The spittle man turned and without even blinking smashed a fist into Zen's face. There was a moment of stunned shock, and then almost an eternity later the sensation of warmth running down his face. A further moment creaked by before the taste of blood registered and then swiftly forgotten as the pain kicked in. From then on it happened much more quickly. The blow and the pain coincided. No shock, no delay, the pain caught up with reality. From idle thoughts to stupid questions there was suddenly just a fist slamming into him, a head being thrown back and pain that momentarily blocked out the light. Still, though, he told them nothing. He couldn't tell them anything useful because he didn't know anything, but that wasn't the reason he didn't speak, he stayed silent because his mind had pulled away.

What was left of his conscious awareness did nothing but count numbers in a kind of catatonic rhythm beyond his control. Slam, pain, blood, count – he got to 1,000 before they paused, but only for a moment. They'd thought hitting him in the face would shock him, instil fear of being permanently disfigured, that the blood would terrify him, the counting told them otherwise, and the distant look in his eyes confirmed that he was stronger than they had guessed. Too late they turned their attention to his body, and there too they failed. After an hour the torture stopped. When Zen realised they were no longer striking him, he experienced some regret; he had been hoping to get to 4,000.

'He's one of them who can take it.' Spittle man said, turning to the older man.

The older man shook his head as if disapproving.

'He can't hear.' Spittle man said.

'He can.' Came the reply. 'Leave him until tomorrow.'

Without another word and barely a sound they left him. The door clanged shut behind him and all Zen could think was that he hadn't got to 4,000 and he didn't know how long it was until tomorrow.

Ω

Nitu's eyes fluttered open. They were uncomprehending, at least at first. Chepi held Nitu's hand against her face and at first touch their eyes met. Nitu's consciousness flickered to life and her eyes focused.

'What did you do to me? Some kind of drug?' This last was mumbled to herself. She still wasn't sure what she'd seen, if it was real or just some twist of perception, something Chepi had done.

'Welcome back.'

She closed her eyes again and let some semblance of control wash over her. Seconds flitted by and then she opened them again and looked around. The trees were the same as before. The bright green ferns danced with the same threatening pulse. She struggled to settle herself. 'Is …?'

'I have to show you something.'

Chepi stood and slowly pulled Nitu to her feet. She moved carefully and with patience, ignoring Nitu's furtive glances around her and the endless repetitive questions about what she had done. Instead of answering, Chepi smiled reassurances as they edged back in the direction they had walked, which to Nitu was seemingly only a few minutes before.

'What are these weird plants?' Nitu asked, her voice wavering.

'Healer vine.'

'Would they heal me?' She queried, her voice distant and uncertain.

'It would take too long.' Chepi linked arms and eased her along more quickly.

'Am I really ill then?' There was resignation in her voice.

'No, you're not ill it's just that they don't know you.

'Oh.' The answer made no sense but she was too distracted to care.

They walked on and Nitu did not recognise any of the ground they covered until they approached the entrance to the stone circle.

'I know this. It's ... but it can't ...'

Chepi's hand pressed lightly on Nitu's back and eased her forwards into the gap. Her curiosity for a moment overriding everything else, Nitu obliged and stepped through into the clearing. Whatever she had been expecting or disbelieving vanished in an instant. Arrayed before her in the clearing she knew so well was a thriving community bustling with life.

At first she could make no sense of the transition from what she'd expected to see. The open meadow sprinkled with unknown trees intermixed with familiar oaks and arbutus had lost its silence to the busy movement of people and the imposing presence of tall, stilted wooden buildings of strange and myriad shapes. Her eyes focused on the scene but her mind remained several seconds behind, and then she saw more clearly, these weren't people at all, at least not in the normal sense.

'What is this?'

'LIIyanhiviian.'

The whispered sound resonated within her mind as though it was as familiar as her own breath, but the word itself word made no sense, had no meaning, no reference point. Only the fact that the place had a name that Chepi knew gave reassurance. She gazed around without replying, taking in the strange, earthy golden people around her. They looked like elves, she thought, tall ones, elegant and almost too perfect to look at for too long. 'Is this dangerous, us being here?'

'No.'

A simple answer and then silence again. Despite everything that was happening Chepi's manner began to exasperate her. 'No, is that all?'

Chepi wore an expression that was unfathomable. 'They won't harm you. They're not taking any notice of us.'

'What is this place?' She asked again.

'I told you, LIIyanhiviian.'

Nitu stared at her. 'I know I'm dreaming.' She tried to sound confident.

'They have to ask you three questions, I can't tell you more until that has been done'

This was an archaeologist's dream, Nitu thought, to see exactly how the original builders had used a site. She wondered again if it was all some kind of weird prank. She was about to say so when she remembered the Sphere. In a world where that was possible she had reconsider everything. 'Is it real?'

'Yes, but that's all I can say until ...'

'The questions.'

'Yes, the questions.'

Chepi took her hand again and led her to the farthest most building set beneath the arched end of the long corridor of stones that bisected the stone circle. As they passed the inhabitants they looked curiously at her, but made no attempt to approach them.

'Where are the men?'

'No questions.'

'But ...'

Chepi guided her through the door of the building and led her up a twisting wooden stairway that spiralled around a large circular entrance hall. Every surface of the hall and stairway was covered with abstract carvings comprising vivid shapes and complex abstract symbols. She looked closely at them to see if they were the same as those they'd been studying on the stone pillars, but Chepi pulled her firmly on every time she paused. Bewildered by everything that was happening and still certain she wasn't merely dreaming or hallucinating, Nitu quietly followed.

After ascending for several minutes they crossed a horizontal walkway and began to ascend again on a spiral staircase winding the opposite way to the one they had used when first entering the building. She noticed Chepi begin to trail her hand over the carvings and whisper softly to herself. The whispers echoed off the walls but the words were unintelligible.

'What are you saying?' Nitu asked. Chepi squeezed her hand but didn't reply. And then, without warning, the light dimmed and darkness engulfed them. Nitu felt herself falling. She might have tried to scream but if she did it was lost instantly to unconsciousness and went unheard.

Ω

'Why don't you save your friend?'

Nitu's eyes blinked open. In front of her was the most perfectly formed face she had ever seen, and resting on her with quiet warmth were the most dazzling, piercing hazel eyes she believed could possibly exist. The voice came from the face in front of her and repeated the question. It spoke in English but the accent was light, musical and hesitant as though the sounds it made were unfamiliar and unsuited to those it would usually make.

'What friend?'

The eyes blinked.

'What friend?' She asked again.

'She doesn't know.' Chepi's voice drifted into focus from behind her. The sparkling eyes flicked in her direction and then returned to hold Nitu's attention. They lay easily and dizzyingly on her. The stranger spoke again. 'There are three questions.'

Nitu stirred impatiently and opened her mouth to begin reciting a list of questions far longer than three, but a finger pressed lightly against her lips. 'Only these questions.' Nitu hesitated but the resolve in the eyes was irresistible. She nodded.

'What purpose brought you into the world?' The finger moved. The eyes waited.

There were no parameters; Nitu didn't know where to begin. Did it mean her purpose in life, or here in the village or whatever it was, or the purpose of human beings in general? She felt irritated. Surely, she thought, growing increasingly edgy by the second, if you had only three questions they should be at least a little more focused. The question could mean anything. She decided to go with what she knew best. She was an academic and the first refuge for the academic was always some kind of generalisation, the more obscure the better, it left room to manoeuvre. 'To procreate.' She answered.

The eyes gave nothing away.

'What is your meaning?'

Nitu couldn't decide whether they were playing a verbal version of poker, chess or enjoying an alien's version of a first year philosophy tutorial. This time she said the first thing that came to mind 'The realisation of conscious awareness.'

The eyes blinked. The movement took Nitu by surprise. It became another thing to worry about; was the blink a gesture of astonishment or approval? Nitu couldn't help wondering once again if all this was an illusion, or some practical joke or governmental black ops to find out what she knew. Or in fact the dream she really suspected had come about because of something Chepi had done. Another thought came to mind, and she almost panicked. Maybe, she thought, I'm experiencing some kind of psychotic break. Saving her from further self-torment, the strange being asked the next question.

'What is your goal?'

Oh, is that all. She almost giggled. Nothing too hard then, just sum up the whole point of human existence by answering three short and somewhat ridiculous questions. She wanted a pun, a joke or a clever satirical comment to break the spell of whatever trap or trick, real or imagined it was that she had somehow stumbled into.

Try as she could nothing came to mind that would release her from the steady, insistent gaze. For the second time she grasped the first idea that came to her. 'Humans, we're toolmakers. We manufacturer, carve, paint, build, we create.'

The eyes shifted. There was no mistaking their disappointment. She searched desperately for another answer. The eyes moved infinitesimally away from her. She felt an awesome, inexplicable sense of loss. 'To create and preserve.' She added hastily.

Ω

The face in front of Zen was perfectly malformed. The gloved hand holding his throat and the clenched fist about to strike the side of his head for a time beyond counting was far from slender. He braced himself and the blow came fast and dark through the limits of consciousness and razed to nothing every thought except the number 3999. His unconsciousness smiled as the next blow came and the 4000th second of torture ticked off in his mind. He held that small triumph like a tiny, long awaited first child, and then all light faded and he slumped into peaceful oblivion.

'They'll kill him.' The aide said to the PM.

'So what.' Came the reply. 'It's all in the national interest.'

'With respect PM, his death serves no one.'

'Yes it bloody does. Can't let him go, he'll talk to every bloody news rat he can find and gibber endlessly like the frakking coward he his.'

He didn't look like a coward to the aide. His bravery almost made him want to cry. It was as magnificent as it was pointless. There were no comrades of war to save, no vital installation to stall over until something had been done to save it, there was nothing to hide; Macleod knew nothing, that fact was obvious to everyone, even the PM, he, though, had stopped caring about information several minutes early. He had found another kind of power, something his unconscious had always whispered to him but he'd never dared answer, but now he could. The reality of raw physical power gave him pleasure beyond anything he could have imagined. He buzzed with desire, felt boundless bliss, he could hardly believe how good it felt to be able to crush someone so remorselessly in the flesh, for real. Not just in a meeting, not psychologically like he had Marcoin, but in every broken bone drop of bright red blood. It excited him beyond anything he'd felt before.

The aide could see all of that and more in the PM's eyes. Politics had become hell in a way he should have foreseen, he had known they were all insane for a long time, but he had thought society could and would restrain them, and now he knew better. Seeing this, he knew he had to save Macleod, it would be a small thing compared to all the rest that had unfolded insanely around them, but it would be something.

'There are no news rats PM, you've blanketed everything, arrested everyone possible.'

'Then what about later?' The PM sounded as though he was talking to himself. His heritage was everything, he wanted to be remembered as the first and last of the great Canadian PM's. Set the bar so high no one would ever be able to follow.

The aide lied, and for the first time he understood how lies could be used for good instead of solely for self-interest. 'History tends to overlook small indiscretions in the face of greatness PM.'

'Bollocks.'

'It's true, look at Churchill's record as a military leader, and his earlier violent part against the UK trades unions. That all got forgotten after WW2.'

'Makes no difference, easier to kill the lying bastard.'

'And lose the chance to show compassion? Wouldn't it be better to have the record show that you interceded and saved him from certain death? That amidst all this chaos you still looked out for the little man and only did what you had to do for the sake of Canada?'

'The world.'

'Yes, PM.'

The words found their target. The PM saw a chance too good to waste; strong but compassionate, the warrior poet coming to the aide of all. 'Good point; I was thinking the same thing. A leader has to, there's no one else is there? It's hard up here.'

'Yes, PM.'

He wanted to see more, see how far it could go, how close to death they could take Macleod, how much pain he would be able to bear. He looked at the aide and the others standing behind him and guessed that it was now too late, if he pushed it even a little more they would think him a pervert. 'Let him go.'

The aide withheld a deep sigh of relief.

'I don't want him kept around here, shift him back to the Yukon and keep him there. He doesn't come back until I say so.' A saliva filled grin mirrored the grim arousal still reflected in his eyes.

'I'll get onto it PM.' The aide replied. He pulled down the blinds to hide the interrogation room from the PM's mad gaze of excitement. He didn't ask, he just did it, and then, as though it was nothing unusual he held the door open and the PM reluctantly made his way out.

Ω

Nitu open her eyes just as an eagle glided over her. Fearful of what new twist of reality might lie just outside her vision she watched it without turning for as long as she could. Finally it was gone, leaving only a blue sky and feint moon to hold her interest, crowd out the other darker thoughts slowly creeping back to steal her attention. She could sense Chepi standing near her and gave way to the inevitable.

'What the frakking hell was that all about?' She hesitated. 'Was any of it real?'

Chepi's mind ran through several meanings of the word real, but none of them came even close to describing what had happened. She tried the truth instead, which she reasoned Nitu was probably due and would definitely appreciate. 'It had a certain kind of probability.' She couldn't have been more wrong about their impact.

Surprised irritation spilled from Nitu like water bursting through a dam. 'Doesn't everything. I meant, was I there?'

Chepi was baffled, of course she was there, she'd thought Nitu had meant something else, something profound about time and history. She felt a pang of disappointment, this avatar wasn't anything like she'd supposed. ''There' as in the bodily sense you mean?'

'What other kind of 'there' is there?'

Chepi could think of several thousand, but Nitu continued before she had chance to say so.

'Yes 'there', with them, together, real, concrete, touching seeing things that actually exist, not things in my mind, hallucinations, illusions, visions or any of that mad, drug-induced stuff.'

'In that case, taking it that broadly, then I suppose you were.'

'You frakking suppose! What the shit is that suppose to mean?' She kneeled up and glared at Chepi. 'Was I or wasn't I?'

Chepi fidgeted and for the first time for weeks she wished the Sphere hadn't insisted on staying. It was all turning out to be more trouble than it was worth, and they hadn't even got that male Zen back yet. 'What kind of physically being there would please you?'

Nitu's eyes glinted with evil light. 'The kind that really happened.'

Chepi sighed with relief. 'Oh, okay, then sure, you were there. It was all real.' She smiled, the relief on her face immediate and unmistakeable. 'So that's that, let's go.'

In response Nitu squealed in bewildered rage. It was an almost not human sound that definitely got Chepi's attention back. 'What's wrong?' She asked innocently.

It was the innocent tone that almost spilled Nitu into violence, but caution hovered around her where Chepi was concerned. Whatever else was being held from her, she'd reasoned already that it was more than clear that Chepi wasn't normal, and not being normal in this case probably meant being very dangerous.

'What's wrong! Don't patronise me, that's what's wrong.' Nitu shouted. 'I know it's drugs, it's got to be, hasn't it, but frak knows why. Except that maybe you've got some weird kind of complex and like playing some kind of petty goddess from some cheap-rate science fiction television show.'

That offended her, so Chepi tried to jump in quickly, but Nitu was having none of it. 'No, shut up for one moment, it was drugs, just admit it.'

'But I ...' Chepi began

'Shut up Chepi.' She took a deep breath. 'Did it actually happen? No, that's impossible, so?'

By this point Chepi had grasped the point with which Nitu was having difficulty. It was quite elementary; she was having difficulty thinking about her physical body actually being in another kind of physical place, i.e. that it wasn't just her mind, which for Nitu obviously meant that it wasn't really happening. Clearly, the problem was with Nitu not having the faintest idea of what her mind really was. Sadly, Chepi could see that there wasn't time to explain, so decided that she had no option but to lie. 'You were physically there Nitu, I promise.'

111

Nitu's hands unclenched slightly as she battled successfully for self-control. 'Okay, that's more like it. No drugs, nothing like that?'

'No, I promise.'

'Okay.' She stood and stepped close to Chepi. 'Then where the frak was I and how did I get there?'

Chepi felt like crying, and then an obvious, completely safe and totally irresistible lie came to mind. 'The Sphere took us there.'

'WHAT? How the frakking hell could you get an alien Sphere to do anything?' She almost screamed. 'You must think I'm really, really stupid.'

To Chepi this seemed an even stranger and more intractable view of things than before. 'It brought me here.' She offered weakly.

Really?' It was becoming obvious to Nitu that Chepi was weirder than she'd imagined. She decided to try to be kind. 'Tell me, what kind of explanation is that?'

'The truth.'

'Okay.' Nitu said calmly. 'So the Sphere took me to another planet, or back in time. Now, I have problems with the ideas tied up with that explanation, but one thing at a time. So tell me first, why would it do that?'

'I don't know. It won't tell me.'

'So, you're actually some kind of alien abductee?'

'No. We travel a lot, it's just that it won't explain why I'm here.'

Nitu's face screwed itself into a nightmare of anger, and then as she hovered on the verge of uncontrollable rage some of the tension inexplicably eased itself away. She frowned, and tentatively asked; 'You mean it's sentient?'

Chepi let go a sigh of relief. 'Of course.'

Patiently Nitu weighed her words carefully. 'So, where do I start … you're telling me that you do what the Sphere says?'

It was Chepi's turn to frown. 'We share, but it often thinks it knows best, like now.'

'Like now, you mean us going to see those other people?'

'No, well yes.' She hesitated; Nitu had almost caught her out. 'No, that was my idea, partly anyway. Me being here, though, that was the Sphere's.'

'You mean it brought you here against your will?' She coaxed gently.

'Yes, no, well maybe. That's not clear yet.'

The charade grew tiring. 'What are you talking about?'

Chepi shrugged. 'I'm just answering your questions.'

Nitu smiled. 'Then just tell me why we're here and what the frak you are trying to do with my head?'

Chepi hesitated, she didn't like to admit that she didn't completely know what any of it was about, but, then again, she could see that admitting that got her out of a lot of questions. 'To be honest?'

'If that's possible.'

She was about to say that the comment was offensive, but under the circumstances she could see that some would think it fair. 'I don't know. The Sphere won't tell me. It says it's up to me to find out.'

'You're kidding, right?'

'No, the LIIyviian say it's probably something to do with trees, but, well that's all I know.' She also wanted to add that the second important thing was that Nitu was an avatar, and that maybe she needed to know that, but thought better timing was in order.

By this time Nitu was almost convinced that she was indeed dealing with some kind of gifted simpleton. 'Trees? Isn't that a bit vague.'

'Exactly, but you try telling the Sphere that.'

Nitu gave her a strange look. 'You're a bit childish aren't you. You're not going to last five minutes around here.'

'I know, that's why I need your help.'

'Is that why ...' She was going to say 'you drugged me' but falsely encouraged by her tone, Chepi jumped in enthusiastically.

'First of all we've got to rescue Zen.'

'Rescue Zen? What the frak d'you mean by that?'

'They didn't understand.'

'What? Who didn't understand what?' She took a deep breath. 'Look Chepi you and I have been together since we left the camp. There's no way you could know anything about what Zen's been doing, and nothing's going to have happened, okay?'

'He's very sick.'

'Zen?'

'No, the Canadian PM.'

Nitu crossed her arms. Despite the headache that was creeping across her temples the whole thing was beginning to have its amusing side, in an unreal kind of way. 'The Prime Minister is psychotic? They're all psychotic, that's why they go into politics.'

'Your leaders, all of them?'

'They're not mine.'

It was Chepi's turn to be baffled. 'You're Canadian, aren't you?'

'Yes but ...'

'I thought being Canadian was important. Anyway, psychosis, that's interesting, I hadn't considered mental illness.' She paused as though she'd just remembered something. 'But to be honest I thought you'd want to rescue Zen first.'

Nitu eyed her distrustfully. 'So what's happened to him exactly?'

Before Chepi had chance to answer, the mist that had been hovering around them some tens of yards distant cleared, revealing an army camp where, from Nitu's perspective, only minutes ago their camp had been. Nitu instinctively ducked down. 'Frak, where the hell did they come from?'

'They can't see us.' Chepi offered helpfully.

'Great, but how on Earth did they build that so quickly?'

Chepi looked at her sadly. 'It's been a few days. You still don't believe me do you?'

'You drugged me for days?'

'No, I told you.'

'Tell me again.' The look she threw in Chepi's direction was unmistakeable. 'I'm not playing games. There's an army camp out there and that's even slightly more weird than the stuff you've been waffling on about.'

Chepi looked miserable. 'I don't know what to say.'

Nitu closed her eyes for a long drawn out minute. 'Just for the sake of argument let's pretend you are somehow linked to the Sphere. So, how did it take us there?'

'Where?'

Nitu didn't answer. She looked unmovable.

Chepi had hoped that the confusion Nitu should have felt as a result of the trip would have meant she could save explanations until later, but it was clear that nothing else was going to happen until Nitu heard something she could accept. 'It was your mind really.' Chepi started to say.

So, Nitu thought, she had been drugged. She strained against rising irritation and managed to stifle the accusations striving to be unleashed.

'It's hard to know where to begin.' Chepi continued, seemingly oblivious to the effect she was having. 'Okay, seeing how you're listening.' She glanced quickly to check but couldn't really tell. 'So, you understand quantum non-locality?'

Nitu stared at her for a long time. 'Look, why don't you tell me what you think you know about Zen.'

Ω

The British Prime Minister and Chinese and US Presidents sat alone in a secure room on a remote Hawaiian island. The British Prime Minister, Grey, had his hand on the knee of the Chinese Prime Minister. He knew that it was an acceptable practice in Chinese culture and showed affection. Although it wasn't his own personal favourite way of relating to foreign heads of state, it did make him feel tolerant, knowledgeable in a worldly sense, and not a little superior, just as his aide had promised. Unfortunately he also felt rather effeminate.

The American President, Bettermann, thought the gesture daring and sophisticated, typically European in a way that all North Americans envied but would never dare copy. He knew such behaviour was acceptable to the Chinese, he'd been briefed on that, but he knew that it would be the end of him forever in the eyes of the American public if he did anything other than engage in firm, masculine handshakes and the occasional slap on the back. He regretted that he allowed 19th century conservatism to hold back his ability to network effectively on the global stage, and also to miss out on something that despite being a family man, looked like fun.

The Chinese Prime Minister, Han, knew that putting a hand on another adult man's knee in the UK was usually associated with homosexual behaviour, and although he quite liked the British Prime Minister he didn't want the further complication it could bring to an already over-stretched personal life.

Thus each in some way found themselves outside their normal comfort zone for no other reasons but pretention and a need to please the minority of the public who actually cared enough to notice they even existed on a personal level. This was the setting from which decisions about Canada were to be made, where the ultimate fate not only of their former ally but the rest of the world would be decided, a setting where impressions weighed more than analysis and balanced decision-making. There was technology and profit to be had, of that they had no doubt, and in the finest traditions of international relations, nothing could be allowed to stand in their way.

The Secretary General of the United Nations chaired the meeting. This was good cover for the G3, as it gave some semblance of international cooperation while at the same time keeping control well and truly where they wanted it. France and Germany might have had something to say about the arrangement if they'd known, but the US and the UK had been waging war together around the world for longer than either of the current leaders could remember. Germany and France had never wanted to play and therefore usually found themselves on the opposing side. Thus London and Washington believed that if it came down to the dirty choices instinct and previous practice told them would be necessary, neither could be trusted.

London was good at duplicity, it always had been, and it knew how to toe the US line as well. Especially after the famous labour government of the late 20th and early 21st century, when the then Prime Minister effectively annexed UK foreign policy to US whims and idiosyncrasies. Despite the fact that no one could understand what the UK had got out of the arrangement, it had remained that way ever since. Some had likened it to a child become now an adult taking care of the aged, senile parent, but others saw it more as elder abuse.

The Secretary General gazed as discretely as he could at the UK PM's hand on the Chinese leaders knee. He winced at the grotesque scene, hurt at the rejection of only a few days ago when he'd tried to take the PM's hand during an official photograph. At the time he'd put it down as cultural difference, but now he could see it was more than that. He'd needed the gesture for the audience back home, where handholding showed respect and familiarity, even fondness of a kind, but the chance of possibly a lifetime was gone, and yet there he was metaphorically fondling the knee of the Chinese. He felt a kind of sadness at the rejection that his sane, conscious mind refused wisely to investigate. He coughed to clear his throat and rubbed his eyes as though in tiredness and brought the meeting to order.

'Gentlemen.' He said authoritatively. 'We all know why we are here, to find a way of bringing Canada back into the fold of international cooperation. This won't be easy, but if we strive for fairness and understanding, if we overlook their zealousness and, I'm sure, their unfortunate misreading of the international community's responses to and interest in the appearance of this strange and momentous golden Sphere then I'm sure we can reach an agreement that will benefit all and bring calmness to what is at present a troubled and dangerous mood.' In an earlier incarnation the Secretary General had been a minor religious leader, it was something he'd never been able to throw off, nor indeed did he want to as one of the first things he'd learned as a young, argumentative child was that pious statements always slowed down the enemy as it forced on them unexpected and massive changes in direction as they sought to circumnavigate the bear traps of moral judgement that were so easily being scattered in their way. It won many debates purely from the fatigue his opponents experienced in trying to tie him down while at the same time avoiding appearing callous, vicious, ungodly, or, worse of all for a politician in the west, uncaring. But these were hardened men in front of him, and more to the point, not but them was listening with an open mind.

'Bollocks.' Said Grey.

'Kill the bastards.' Said Bettermann.

Han merely smiled and moved his knee, causing Grey's hand to slip down onto his chair. Grey pretended not to notice. He sat as still as he could for three or four long seconds, giving the impression that his left side had suddenly been paralysed by a stroke. Eventually the morbid attention of the others made him shift position, frown deeply as though he'd been in deep thought and then uttered the words the US had longed to hear ever since they'd told him what to say. 'We should go in and find out what the hell is going on.'

'Well said Peter.' Bettermann said.

Han smiled. 'Maybe we should consider this further. Wait for things to unfold. There is no hurry surely? The Canadians cannot act alone. Even if, as we fear, there are technologies involved that we all wish to possess, they will have to bring them to us. They cannot live alone.'

Bettermann almost panicked. What the hell did they mean by wait, he wondered fretfully. It bothered the US more than any other country that Chinese civilisation spanned several thousands of years. It made them paranoid. They knew they'd never last that long. For the Chinese waiting could mean hundreds of years if they thought it necessary he, though, had an election next year.

'I'm not sure waiting's an option Mr Han, or can I call you Zi? We're all friends here.' Han smiled. 'Okay, Mr Han, in the west we can't wait as long as the great Chinese people, we don't have your ...' He stumbled, but luckily Grey had been listening.

'Your resources Mr Han.' Grey finished.

'Yes, your resources; you see, the UK and I are one and the same on this.'

'But you have the resources to declare war on your friends?' Han said in an irritatingly neutral tone.

That was one thing the US hated about dealing with foreigners, it was never possible to tell if they were being naïve, devious or too clever by half. Bettermann blustered. 'Only as a last resort; no one wants an expensive war, but if the stock markets go down any more than they have been doing anyway, there won't be anything left to finance it.'

The idiocy of this remark struck the Secretary General particularly hard. 'So, are you proposing to destroy a huge part of the west so you can save it?' He asked.

Bettermann didn't hesitate. 'Yes, dammed right, better to go down fighting than give up.'

'But you have nothing to justify that, surely? So far as we know there isn't anything to have as of yet, so surely there is nothing to give up, to miss out on?'

'That's it exactly.' Bettermann squealed with false compassion and a complete misunderstanding of what had been said. 'We have nothing and the American people won't stand for that, whatever the costs.'

Han smiled. 'We should wait.'

Bettermann went to reply but Grey interceded. 'That's

difficult under our system Mr Han, but your views are key here, so, well, how long d'you think we should wait?'

'Yes, exactly.' Bettermann added, still not listening. 'Wait for what?'

Han's face grew serious. 'We cannot know. All we can say is that when a way opens we must be prepared. Peace is a snow flake blowing in the wind.'

The Secretary General nodded sagely, the UK PM did likewise, Bettermann went slightly red in the face for reasons that would never be known and Han smiled.

They all fidgeted for several minutes until Bettermann could take it no longer. 'Well, I don't know about you guys but I can't wait, Congress can't wait and by sure as hell the American people can't wait.' He lapsed into silence again without the slightest indication that he thought any further explanation was necessary.

'I don't know Bob.' Said Grey. 'Maybe Mr Han has a point. War's expensive, look what happened with Iraq, and then again with North Korea and Iran. I know there were personal reasons for all that and we went out purely to help everyone, but it cost us dearly. Once most of the public got off their backsides for once and voted, many careers were finished for good.'

'Fair point John, and there were a lot of lives lost.' Bettermann agreed.

'Yes, and that too.'

A longer silence followed. At last the General Secretary decided to intercede. 'Maybe you'd like to consider sanctions gentleman?'

They all stared at him. 'Need the trees Michael.' Said Bettermann. 'Lots of holiday homes going up once again in Arizona. Good for the economy.'

'And oil.' Said Grey. 'We're at £12 a gallon now, God knows what'll happen if the Canadians turn the taps off.'

Mr Han nodded wisely. 'We would help our friends. You only have to ask.'

The quick glances that flew between Grey and Bettermann were heavily tinged with pure fear. Being shut out of Canada was one thing but becoming dependent on China for sustainable energy was the nightmare from hell. 'Thanks.' Bettermann said.

'Then what do you propose?' The Secretary General asked.

Grey stared vacantly at nothing in particular. It was a kind of glazed absence that took the place of deep reflection. Of course he thought it made him look wise, but no one he wasn't sleeping with believed that for a moment. 'We'll have to threaten them.' He said at last.

'Good thinking John.' Bettermann beamed with relief.

'With what.' Asked Han.

'The 7th fleet, what else.'

'We'll help where we can.' Offered Grey magnanimously.

'We'd appreciate that John.' He looked meaningfully at Han, who merely smiled.

'Then it's decided. We'll blockade, say, Vancouver Island until that idiot they've got in power comes to his senses.' Full of confidence now he could take action instead of sitting around wasting time in pointless debate Bettermann got up and made to leave.

The Secretary General quickly interceded again. 'And, I know this is a difficult matter, but what exactly is the legal basis of this Mr President?'

Bettermann looked at him as though he'd gone mad. 'Homeland security, what else.'

The Secretary General wasn't quite satisfied. 'Can I just ...' But he was talking to himself. Bettermann and Grey had left, and to make matters worse as the door closed he saw them holding hands. He turned to the Chinese leader. 'Can't you do anything? The Security Council will never go along with this.'

Han smiled. 'We'll wait and see. Canada will need friends soon and the Chinese people are never in a hurry.' Then he left too.

The Secretary General sat down alone in the now empty room. A brief smile flitted across his face. This was a great opportunity. He knew that if he played his cards just right there could be a great role for him in the turbulence ahead. For the first time in several years he was glad to have become Secretary General, instead of a mere President of Morodelta. He could become famous, great even, perhaps a legend in the annals of diplomacy. He took out his cell phone and called Canada.

Ω

The blockade of Vancouver Island started almost immediately. US ships from throughout the Pacific region swept into the Juan De Fuca straight and brought to a halt all ship movements along the west coast of Canada. Freighters bound for the Island and mainland Vancouver were stopped, bordered and expelled from Canadian water. At least, that is, during the first few days, after which complaints from irate US citizens in Washington State that their brand new, shiny recreational motor cruisers and miscellaneous imports from China had not arrived brought on a rapid rethink.

The residents of Vancouver Island, arguably the area most to be affected by the US invasion, acted as though the blockade never happened. They did not seem to care. None of them bought large, foreign motor cruisers, preferring instead to drive around the windless Gulf Islands in sailing vessels with huge bowsprits built by obscure boatyards no one had seen or heard of for more years than anyone could remember. So far as general imports were concerned, Vancouver Island was far from being a consumer heaven and pot of gold for importers. The Island was instead a vast, disorganised cottage industry operating on the pre-internet marketing strategy of word of mouth. Impossible for visitors and the newly arrived, who could never find anything, it was a haven for small traders happy with the way things had been for the last 100 years, the homeless, who were tolerated better than anywhere else in the world, artist and writers who could never afford to buy anything anyway, and endless numbers of marijuana growers sprinkled around the endless small islands and uninhabited forests. It was, in general, a pre-industrial haven waiting for its moment to shine, which, as luck would have it, was exactly its fate.

Ω

Of course Ottawa did not care in the least what was happening in the distant, wayward, alternative world of British Columbia. Long being enraged at the glib, self-satisfied claim of being the most beautiful place on Earth and for being called 'British' Columbia instead of Canadian Columbia, for all the PM cared they could go and annex themselves to Alaska or the so-called Cascadian States, which in his view was something they should have done years ago, ridding the rest of Canada of the hippies, homeless, retirees, writers and dope growers who would then become a US problem.

World opinion, though, was another matter. In general the global view was split neatly into two opposing camps. One followed the Chinese view that despite the fact that Canada had reneged on all previous agreements to share technological advances, what was needed was a calm, conciliatory approach. Their detractors held the view that such a stance was either weak appeasement or fawning sycophancy. They believed only a firm hand would prevail, even if that meant the unavoidable, minor loss of lives. By which they meant other peoples lives, especially Canadian ones. In response, the moderate camp branded the USA, UK and their various acolytes as being nothing more than post-colonial imperialists, which, having being true for a long time, hardly raised an eyebrow anywhere.

Ω

'What are they doing?' Chepi asked.

'Going to war.' The Sphere answered.

'I know, I mean what the frak are they doing?'

'Rushing headlong into destruction in case they miss out on something.'

'Better to die than go without?'

'No one ever expects to die.' The Sphere replied.

'No one expected the Spanish Inquisition.' I read that somewhere.

'Cliché, but true.'

'Surely they know we'd never give them anything. They are way too primitive'

'No, not really, I don't think they grasp that concept. Everything is about trade to them.'

'Not to me.'

'But ...'

Chepi changed the subject. She was worried, and this was a new experience, one she wanted to explore to the full. 'What's happening to Nitu?'

'I thought you didn't care?'

'I'm worried about her.' The words sounded nice, made her feel significant in some way, as though she had a mission that, for once, actually meant something to her rather than the Sphere.'

'They've imprisoned her.'

'Frak. That really annoys me. She's mine so they've no right ...'

'Since when?'

'Since I decided it.'

'She thinks you're a lunatic.'

'It was just a misunderstanding.'

The Sphere didn't agree, but decided to stay silent.

'Can I rescue her?' Chepi asked, somewhat impulsively.

'What actually, or in principle?'

'Both.'

'You could destroy the whole planet if you wanted to.'

Chepi glared impatiently. 'Now why would I want to do that?'

'Just saying.'

'Well don't, try instead to answer the frakking question.'

'You swear too much since you got here.'

There was no reply.

'Rescuing her would cause a disturbance.' It added

'In the same way as appearing over that Vancouver place, or do you have something else in mind?'

'But I didn't do anything did I? We just ...'

'Pushed them onto the brink of something weird.'

'I wanted to give you something to work with.'

Chepi sighed. 'That makes no sense, but never mind. Can I rescue her or not?'

'Aren't you ignoring the fact that she thinks you're ...'

'A lunatic, I know, you said that already. Even if she really does think that, I still can't leave her down there in desperate peril.'

'Why not.'

Chepi bit her lip. 'I don't know.'

'You didn't rescue Zen?'

She pulled a face. 'That was her job, before she frakked off like that.'

'And who's fault was that?'

'Illiaeth wanted to see her.'

'So you say, but even so, you didn't handle it very well.'

'It's not my fault, you brought me here, and then Illiaeth got involved. How am I supposed to know how to deal with primitive aliens?'

'You could at least have moved more slowly, perhaps?'

Chepi was tired of having to justify herself. 'How long are you going to keep me here?'

'Until you sort out the mess you've created.' It lied.

'So I can rescue her?'

'There's no need.'

'Why, what have you done?'

There was no reply. Chepi sensed the Sphere retreat. 'And what about the frakking trees?' She mumbled to herself.

Ω

Nitu and Zen were sitting in the kind of wide, empty, starkly polished, echoing room that only the military can conjure into being. They huddled over large black mugs of coffee while tendrils of steam wetted their faces. The only place to sit was a hollow sounding plastic table and chairs placed purposely in the middle of the room for reasons they chose not to explore. Two unmoving guards stood at a distance to each side of them watching their every move. It was a cold place that offered no refuge for either their minds or bodies. This was how it was meant to be, their discomfort was the army's way of weakening them, bringing them to submission, or increasing their vulnerability. There was no rationale to this, no goal had been set, no outcome anticipated. It was simply what armies do when leadership is missing, when no one at any level really knows what they are doing; institutionalised cruelty filling the vacuum.

'Look at you.' Nitu reached out a hand but didn't dare touch the swollen mess that was Zen's face. Instead she let it drop onto his hand.

'Looks worse than it is.' He squeezed his eyes shut and sipped the coffee against the pain. It was harder one handed, arms tied for too long take time to find their way back to a world where things like lifting a cup come naturally once more. He wanted his two hands, and he wanted hers as well. It was soft, like it cared and it didn't even matter that much that it was hers, anyone's would have done.

'They tortured you?' She wondered if the question sounded cruel, or disbelieving. But she didn't know how else to start a conversation about horror

'Don't know if it was torture. What counts as that? Is there a grading system, start with shouting, then beating, then, what, cut pieces off, stick electric cables on you? How about rape?' He paused for a moment. 'I read once that someone in some army in a war against the Arabs used to push whole people into a ship's boiler so he could watch their heads explode. I think Lawrence of Arabia wrote about it.' He hesitated. 'But I'm not sure, maybe I just dreamt it. My God I hope so.'

His attention drifted and he looked away. Nitu was about to speak, say anything to kill the silence, but he turned back unexpectedly with sudden urgency, as though he'd just returned from somewhere long distant and had a vital message to deliver. 'Does it start with the first blow, or the anguish of the first threats? If it does, if it's that, then do we torture our children? Is that what we do? I want to know because if so I don't want to live. I don't want to be here any longer.' His eyes flashed and then settled uneasily into some kind of deep resolve. 'I don't want to disrespect those who've suffered more than me. That wouldn't be right.'

Nitu remembered something she'd once read and never before understood. 'We carry what we can.'

He surprised her. She'd expected to have to explain, use it to draw him out, but he got it straightaway. Is that what happens, she wondered, when you've been that far, far enough not to count and to know that, to see a complete absence of humanity in the eyes bearing down on you?

'If we don't die we're still here.' He said.

'Yes, I hope so.' The words escaped like the air rushing from a burst balloon.

'There's a kind of freedom too you know.' He almost smiled.

She squeezed his hand in gladness, in premature relief, but then saw it fail to reach his eyes. 'What d'you mean?' But she knew.

'They can only kill me. They know that now. That's all they have.'

She could see that something unnameable you expect everyone to have had gone. She felt it keenly, this thing not there. No cold hand of loss, but a vacuum. Once he was there, in their camp, whole, and next there was this … absence. 'I'll help.' She felt stupid.

'That's always been true.' She added hastily. 'They can only kill you. That's all they've ever had, we just didn't think about it; think that it meant us too.' She moved around the table and held him. She felt the tears come, first only hers and then his. Thousands of years of tears swept upwards and caught Chepi totally unawares.

Ω

'Frak, I'm crying!' She rubbed her eyes and stared disbelievingly at the wet palms dripping with her own tears. 'How the frak does this happen?' And then pain followed, tearing at her heart with remorselessness persistence. She could only whimper, coil herself tightly into a ball and feel the horror of a death she'd never have.

'Wake up little girl.' The Sphere whispered to itself.

Ω

The war with the Sphere lasted 45 seconds. Chepi swept across the 7th fleet and laid it to waste in 5 seconds of total confusion; at least for them, for Chepi things seemed all too clear. After the US fleet was gone she tore across the sky and destroyed everything military she could see. This included the Chinese fleet and every weapon anywhere that her sensors could detect. Globally, this left barely anything larger than a rifle. It was total, irresistible and awesome to behold. This is how it was from her standpoint.

Ω

'Okay, this should be child's play.'

'What are you thinking of doing?' The Sphere asked nervously.

'Going for a spin.'

'Maybe that's not a good idea, shouldn't you rest first? .'

'Get me one of those things. You know, the ones that will scare the frak out of them.'

'There'll be no going back.'

'There never was. You never meant there to be.'

'If you take a life ...' It was the only real concern the Sphere ever had. Life was everything, but so was this place it'd brought her to, so now it had to let her decide.

Chepi stopped and stared. 'There won't be any killing, what kind of person do you take me for?'

The Sphere didn't answer, it wanted to hear what came next.

'I'm going to disempower them. It's one of their words. I think their leaders hate that more than anything else.'

'More than death?'

'That's not relevant; they leave the dying to others.'

'So they're in for a surprise then, eventually.'

'Hardly, they'll be gone won't they; nothing is going to come after for them. No afterlife or reincarnation for a brain stem out of control.' Chepi answered.

'And then?'

'What?'

'After you've disempowered them.'

'I'll work it out.'

'Oh.' It had hoped for more.

'Got that thing ready?'

'Yes.'

'Okay, back soon.'

Ω

Chepi slipped down into the underside of the Sphere. What she'd asked for stood waiting and she wasn't displeased. It resonated with an awesome lack of symmetry, every angle superbly lacked purpose or fit. It jutted and curved to some pattern well beyond anything a rationale mind could handle. She felt her head throb just looking at it resting indecently against the golden deck. The contrast was almost too much to handle; the grotesque black pool of disjointed obscenity set against the persuasive, breath-taking equilibrium of the Sphere defied nature herself. It was an abomination even before it began to shimmer, lose focus and dance chaotically in front of her to some mad, micro rhythm spawned in hell itself. Her head whirled and she almost vomited.

'Frak, that's disgusting.'

She closed her eyes and edged slowly towards the monstrosity. The first touch made her retch again. It felt like cold pigs brains infested with psychotic cockroaches. As no human would ever get to touch it, this was a completely pointless embellishment. One obviously added just to annoy her.

'This is serious. Make it ...'

The surface shifted to a smooth, sensual texture.

'Thanks.'

The new ship left the Sphere at a speed beyond the reach of the human imagination. She paused for a single moment for effect and then screamed away.

Stopping briefly to pose was something she did seven more times, one for each continent, but mostly it banked and twisted in turns, climbs and dives beyond the laws of physics. It was fast, very destructive and, for Chepi, over far too quickly. She destroyed a great deal of stuff and was still back in the Sphere before the first members of the US navy were even remotely close to being pulled out of the Strait of Georgia by the bemused and polite Vancouver Islanders.

$$\Omega$$

For humans there was a very different timescale. Simply, it lasted far too long. For some it would prove to be a lifetime. It gave the expression 'living a whole life in a moment' a whole new meaning. One glimpse and a nervous breakdown from overwork seemed like a holiday in the mountains or some Tuscan farmhouse replete with the finest wines and cheeses. Minds crumbled and resolve disappeared in wave upon wave of self-pity. This was psychological warfare taken to a level way beyond the minds of even the hopelessly insane. Not even in the darkest bowels of democracy had anyone ever imagined the awesome potential for destruction contained within asymmetrical chaotic geometry.

Ω

For her friends on the ground things at first moved more slowly. It was several minutes before Nitu and Zen realised that the sound of crying wasn't theirs alone. Nitu was the first to move.

'What's that wailing?' She looked around and saw with surprise that the guards had left without her noticing.

'Sounds like its coming from outside, but don't get involved.'

The plea came too late, Nitu had already moved towards the now unguarded door. 'I'll be careful, she called back.'

He let her go. Leaving the security of the chair wasn't something he was ready to contemplate.

'I'll just take a look.' She said. He smiled. Nitu pushed open the door and peaked out.

The sight was a shock; the camp was deserted, or at least deep into the process of being deserted. All she could see were the backs of rapidly retreating figures, some running, others staggering and a few crawling away. Some glanced up at the Sphere, but most appeared to be fixated on the ground in front of them. Their heads were bent abnormally low as though they were carrying some enormous, invisible weight. If that was strange, there was something else even more distracting than a cowed retreat by an army clearly having lost control of its senses; the trouble was she couldn't quite put her finger on what it was.

'There's something really weird going on out here.' She called back to Zen.

He didn't react, for him weird was now normal. He shrugged silently, and instinctively gave thanks that whatever had taken place, it had nothing to do with him.

For the first time since they'd been put together, Nitu ignored him, she realised what it was that had been niggling her, all the trucks and buses had gone. There'd been dozens of them, mostly to be used to move people to some refugee camp they had been setting up, she'd been told, in some obvious but obscure lie.

'Unbelievable, all the trucks have gone. I didn't hear anything, did you?' Zen smiled but didn't reply. 'That's why they're walking I guess? I'm going to take a closer look.' She turned back to the outside and found yet another shock in wait.

'Frakking hell! What are you doing here?'

Chepi smiled.

Nitu called back to Zen. 'It's that frakking lunatic again.'

'I came to get you.' Chepi answered sweetly.

'Look, I know you're an idiot, some kind of simpleton who thinks she's an alien, but well, to put it simply, frak off.' She slammed the door and went back to her seat at the table. 'Can you believe her? She's stalking me now. Me! And right in the middle of army camp. What a freak.'

'I kind of liked her.' Zen offered.

Nitu gave him a withering glance. 'So they didn't cut off your doo daa then?' A feminist smile of condemnation almost made it out into the world, but, luckily, reality kicked back in just in time. 'Oh shit, shit, did I really just say that?' She slumped back in self-disgust. 'See what I mean, she's only been back for a minute and already she's frakking with my head,'

'They kicked it around a bit, but it's still there.' Zen said. 'Can't feel it but I've seen it.' He added, with seeming indifference.

'Frak.'

'They said no permanent damage.'

Nitu stood and began to pace up and down.

In truth they had never hit him in the genitals, he just wanted her to shut up.

'D'you think she might really be from the Sphere?'

Zen closed his eyes and didn't answer.

'Maybe she could be an alien. That would be weird wouldn't it, her being an alien?'

'Weird or insane?' He asked.

'Maybe that's what it would seem like if you met an alien and didn't know that they were.'

'Why would an alien come and see you? Of all the people in the world, why you?'

'And you.' She added.

Zen wanted to stop talking. It was too hard, and anyway he didn't see that it mattered. He was too tired, too reduced, too weak, too spent. He wanted to sleep and forget. This wasn't helping. 'She didn't take me off to meet strange people in a wooden village that somehow miraculously appeared out of nowhere.'

'Exactly.' She said triumphantly. 'How likely is that? She drugged me, like I said.'

'Why?'

'Probably a pervert.'

He shook his head sadly. 'And only a few days ago you were happy Miss Enlightenment.'

Nitu threw him an uncomprehending glance. 'Being stalked and drugged is different.'

'Well, for one, I hope she is an alien. Maybe she can do something.'

'Something about what?' He didn't answer. 'They've gone, the army, anyway. I guess that means we're free. We can just leave if we want.'

'That's not what I meant.' But she didn't hear. He hadn't intended that she would.

Ω

Chepi wandered across a great expanse of desert. It was a wild place, empty and dry like cracked, aged skin. Only small yellow shrubs long dried by the boiling heat that clung mercilessly to everything managed to break through the relentless red dust and clay that stretched in broken lines into the far distance where the sky invisibly met the ground. This was a harsh realm. The sun baked her relentlessly in its searing passage through the day, and then left her to freeze in the blackness of night.

If she had chosen to enter this place it might have been easier, but it had been far from her idea. The Sphere had said she needed time to think. She'd suggested something she'd found on Earth and now yearned for all too often, a long, deep bubble bath and a cold glass of cider; quiet music and candles. The Sphere said she was getting too girly and sent her to the desert. It had a point, when it'd asked what she was going to do after she'd destroyed virtually all the Earth's military capability she'd changed the subject. It'd wanted more, she gave it nothing. It was then it decided a sabbatical was a good idea. 'Sabbatical? It's not even Sunday.' She'd mumbled. And then it grew very hot.

Ω

The aftermath of Chepi's somewhat overdrawn rescue plan was unique in the history of dramatic interludes in human progress. There was no panic, no demonstrations, revolutions, implosions, military coups, religious fervour, heavy drinking, suicide, brawling or crying. People everywhere just stopped and waited. The world rapidly filled with silent tears and faces turned towards the sky. The despairing waves began in Seattle and spread out across the whole globe, with the exception, that is, of Canada, where national pride over the origin of the diabolical manifestation sustained everyone. A surge in nationwide confidence saw Canadians begin to imagine having true world influence. All, that is, except the military, which, like armed forces everywhere, seemed to shrink within itself and begin to fade from sight. Their tanks were gone, so too their fast shiny jets and sleek stylish warships. Their missiles had vanished and their manhood lay in tatters. Only Vancouver Islanders and their neighbours on the Gulf Islands remained totally unchanged, they just dismissed the whole thing as being a particularly effective piece of performance art. They carried their coffee to work in big, insulated mugs as usual, and patted themselves on the back once again for being smart enough to either have been born on one of the Islands or had the sense to move there. The refrain 'Nice show last night, eh?' could be heard far and wide. Their love of life was impregnable. They knew with unshakeable certainty that in the most beautiful place on Earth nothing really very bad could possibly happen.

For the Government of Canada all was very different. For them the castration of the military caused major problems. After all, what is a democracy without its armed forces.

'What d'you mean the Army's frakking lost it?' The PM asked, his hands shaking so hard his coffee spilled.

'Lost it. None of them have turned up.' The aide explained.

'Not turned up? What the bollocks does that mean?'

'Stayed at home playing golf perhaps. I don't know. There're a few Generals we can talk to but they're not much help.'

The PM paused and then eyed the aide with evil relief. There was someone he could blame. It wasn't down to him after all. 'Sack the buggers, get rid of them and find me people who can frakking well do the job.'

The aide fidgeted. 'I'm afraid we can't do that PM.'

The PM did a double take. No one had ever said no before, not even his mother.

'We can't sack Generals.' The aide continued. 'They're a military appointment.'

The PM frowned cautiously. Until he knew exactly whose fault it was that they couldn't be sacked, he knew instinctively to move carefully. It wouldn't do to find out later that it had been him.

'It's traditional. We let the military run themselves. We just appoint the very top people, tell them where to go and they do the rest.'

The PM's face radiated pure amazement. 'And that works? Letting the buggers do what they want?'

'Not what they want, so much as how they do what we want them to do.'

'And what's the bloody difference?'

The aide had to think quickly. 'Well, no one in the military even half way in their right mind wanted to go into Afghanistan, but we got them there. And same with the Brits and Yanks with Iraq.'

This sounded like tricky ground to the PM. He hadn't thought about it before but this kind of news could make it look dangerously like they didn't really know what they were doing. 'Well then, as long as they get done what's expected, what the country expects of them we'll let it pass for now.'

'Except that now it doesn't work that way any longer, PM.' The aide reminded him. 'And, to be frank, most of the country is in exactly the same mind as the military.'

The PM once again didn't know what the aide was talking about. It confused him when what he said wasn't instantly turned into some form of reality; when it didn't somehow materialise as a memo, a plan, some action, a cunning strategy, a news item or, best of all, some shiny new building or road laid out on land he personally had sold or lent or leased or made available in some way. This last made him feel like a true builder, a provider, and a man folding back the wilderness to create jobs and comfort for everyone. The fact that it usually made him very rich and bought him friends and influence everywhere was only natural.

He could sense that life might be changing. The rebellion by the army unsettled him. They were his, like his gang at school had been. The kids he'd supplied with endless cookies so they'd do his bidding. With them and his mother's endless baking he'd once ruled the whole playground and made it safest place in Ontario for him and his best friend. To his way of thinking it was the same now, but bigger and even better. Singled-handed he was making Canada the most secure and an advance nation on Earth. Him and the Sphere bound together to make real ...

'PM?' The aide tugged his arm. 'Sir?'

The PM's eyes slowly shifted into focus. 'What?' He bellowed.

'What should we do? About the paralysis?'

A glug of coffee bought him the brief few seconds he needed to think of a way to change the subject. 'What news do we have on the globe thing?' He asked as smoothly as possible.

He hoped the question would make it seem he had some kind of strategy in mind. The aide, of course, knew exactly what was he was trying to do but had no intention of playing along. Since the torture of Macleod he grasped every chance for payback that came his way, no matter how small. 'Seems also to be paralysed.' He answered unhelpfully.

The PM heard the 'also' and silently cursed. The next trick came to hand without pause, he grasped for humour, the politicians inevitable weak joke, pun or aside. As they all knew from birth, absurdity can win many a battle and defeat even the brightest minds. 'Well, it beats me, I'm not a bloody doctor.' He guffawed and would have ruffled the aide's hair if he hadn't since boarding school been clinically repelled at even the thought of touching another man.

'No sir.' And then he waited. No politician he'd ever known could stand silence.

'Well?' The PM roared.

'What would you like me to do sir?' Feigning acquiescence was always the perfect aggressive defence.

Thwarted, the PM had had enough of being pleasant. 'Get together with that bugger Marcoin and give me three sensible proposals in half an hour.' He stressed the 'sensible' so hard a small droplet of spittle hit the aide in the eye. The aide knew that the PM had seen it happen, he saw the pleasure dance across his eyes. For an instant they were both transfixed by this tiny dance of power and subjugation, and then the PM screwed his saliva filled mouth into a scowl and stalked off.

The PM thought he had won another trivial victory, but the aide had the last word. 'Marcoin is paralysed as well PM. In fact he's dead, isn't he.

These parting words caught the PM mid-step. They worked their brief magic and the PM's scowl shrank into his mottled face and vanished. Marcoin was dead; there wouldn't be any proposals on his desk in 30 minutes or any other time. He felt strangely naked and alone. His face greyed and he pushed on against the wind to find the sanctuary of the desk. Perhaps, he wordlessly hoped, just maybe there'd be some refuge, or, even better, some hint at what it was that had so dramatically, but obscurely, become paralysed.

$$\Omega$$

Chepi hated the desert, well, at least for the first few days. The 96 hours following her dramatic experiment with chaotic geometry were as difficult for her as they were taxing for the rest of the world's sentient life forms. The cetaceans were as phlegmatic as usual about terrestrial affairs, but even they were slightly agitated about the immeasurable, trans-physic shock waves that bounded and rebounded around the globe. Chepi, though, was as unaware of this as she was of anything else not confronting her directly. Coping with the sweltering, barren wasteland was as much as she could manage. Monotony and going without weren't things she'd ever been too well equipped to deal with.

It was when she was certain that the lack of something new to look at would surely kill her, that her perception of her surroundings began subtly to shift. At first it was no more than a gentle realisation that the desert wasn't as empty as she had imagined. Then slowly she began to see small plants of unknown types sprinkled in the previously empty sand, and spy rocks covered with patterns and colours that were almost too small to see with the naked eye. She paused to look at them and found herself transfixed by their variety and complexity. The early pauses became longer periods of careful scrutiny and then finally she sat for a whole day in a single spot while she absorbed the richness of the almost invisible life around her.

In reality what Chepi had found was an abundance of strange

and beautiful algae and mosses. It was a defining moment in her life, and one that won her over completely to acceptance of the infinitesimal difference that lay between life on a small scale and the greater visions and apparitions she'd previously thought so central to everything her life had been about. Galaxies colliding began to look remarkably similar to those startling greens and astounding reds formed from the tiny lives clambering towards each other over the reddish-brown, arid dust and boulders. In a moment of profound gestalt she knew without need for reflection what fractal meant. The endless perfection of infinitely repeating patterns of being pushed into her life with such irresistible power that in an instant it rewired the very architecture of her mind.

'Wow.' She said.

Gobsmacked beyond limit she sat in silent wonder for hours. Her presence was so inwardly silent that tiny animals came out of hiding and busily peopled the greying light of the day with a world of colour and textures. She saw them touch and feel their ways around their small universe of shades and affects. She felt the abstract calculations of her mind come alive with the movement of a million souls at her feet. And even she began to imagine the possibility that something profound was about to happen.

Her night passed in the company of moths, bats and owls, wolves, coyotes and a hundred other species, and when the sun came up the desert was filled with cacti arrayed with more colours than she could count. She undressed and rolled in the dust until she was as red as the ground. She brushed the earth with one hand; a long, slow sensual touch meant to help her remember, then she began to walk. Soon the walk progressed to a jog, and then the jog to a run. And then she ran as hard as was possible towards the horizon as tears ran across her cheeks and formed streams of orange mud down her face. She laughed until it hurt and she couldn't laugh any more. Then she smiled, and all the time she never stopped running.

Ω

Zen eventually left the army camp. He'd waited until boredom drove him from the scene of his terrible loss. Torture had taken away his sense of inviolability. Sustained abuse did that to the untrained, at least most of them, and Zen was like most others. That surprised him, he'd thought he was different, being an academic somehow above the material concerns of the ordinary, but life had held that surprise in store too. The body, he had to concede, always has the last say.

Nitu walked unhappily along by the side of him, struggling to show the sympathy she knew he deserved. Of course being an avatar made it hard for her to sense in any empathic way what he was going through, and not to be able to share his endlessly dismal observations made her surprisingly miserable. That she didn't know she was an avatar made it naturally even worse. She became convinced that she must by nature be hopelessly pathologically callous. This depressed her even more than Zen.

'Cheer up.'

Zen scowled. 'What is this place anyway? Why the hell did we have to come here? It's just bloody rocks and shit.'

This was the fiftieth time he'd said something similar. 'It's a wilderness.' She answered again.

'I know. You keep saying.'

'It's still true.'

Unexpectedly, Zen stopped. This was new and it momentarily encouraged hope. Nitu paused after a few steps and looked back at him. She had to wait several minutes before he spoke.

'I need to be alone.' He said at last.

She felt both relieved and hurt. 'Why?'

'I need to think.'

'But ...'

'I can't stand ... I keep thinking about you thinking about me. I don't like being judged and having to think about that. I've got to get focused. I need to be alone.'

Nitu tried to guess what he really meant, but failed. It never occurred to her that he meant exactly what he was saying. 'It's only a few more hours to the plane.'

Zen looked at the Sphere hanging just above the horizon. It'd appeared suddenly in this new place as they'd been walking. They guessed it was now over the stones. 'Five hours, maybe.' He said.

'You can decide when we get there.'

'I don't want to go back. I need time.'

'You can't survive here on your own.'

Even though he would never have known it, this was exactly

what he needed to hear. It was a challenge, something to focus on and overcome. 'You'll be surprised.'

But the land scared him, as it would anyone not used to real darkness and all its shifting sounds and darting secrets, she knew that and knew that he did too. 'But if you ...' She didn't finish. 'You want the food?'

'You'll need it.' He said instinctively.

'It's only five hours, you said so yourself.'

'It might not be there. You might be stranded.'

She smiled. It was meant as a gentle reminder of how long the Yukon had been a part of her.

'Not likely is it?' He smiled back.

'No, and anyway I wouldn't bet too much against that weirdo showing up again at any moment.'

'You shouldn't be too hard on her. Maybe she sees you as a big sister.'

'And the drugs?'

'Who knows; why not ask her?'

'She irritates me.'

'She didn't when we were working together.'

'No, that's true.'

'At least there's one thing you have in common.'

'What?'

'You shrug just like her.'

'Bollocks.'

'You do. It's a bit uncanny really.'

'If you say so.' She looked instinctively towards the Sphere. 'You sure you don't want the food?'

He couldn't be bothered arguing any more. 'Sure, okay.'

Three minutes later she walked off on her own towards the Sphere. She didn't look back but that didn't stop her feet dragging morosely at the thought of leaving him.

Zen had never been alone in a wilderness before. His dad had taken him fishing, and they'd had fun on the occasional camping trip, but all that had been when he was very young. He'd never understood why, but as he'd got older his father lost interest, not in fishing and camping, but in him, Zen. It was as if the reality of a child with a personality of its own was somehow too much, that the idea of a son had been an attraction that in the actual world didn't fit with the kind of person his father was or later became. Whatever his father's dreams had been, in the end a child called Zen was simply a child, a small person who got cold and tired and didn't really understand everything his father had wanted to teach him.

And then his dad left.

Zen read everything, especially books about travel if they had some kind of adventure in them. And then he progressed to anthropology and the environment. Until he was about 14 he would cry when they chopped trees down. Not so anyone could see, but privately at night, as silently as he could. If he had stayed his dad would have been proud of him.

As Nitu disappeared from view Zen strained to recall all of this, tried to remember the things his dad had said and the things he'd written in the half finished rambling, chaotic dairies and notes he'd left behind. These were Zen's greatest treasure from his childhood, still stored carefully in places of honour on his bookshelves at the University. They contained everything anyone needed to know to survive anywhere wild, places without people and modern conveniences.

There being no purpose in lingering he tentatively placed one foot forwards and left the trial for the unbeaten ground leading off in every other direction. He was surprised at the joy he felt at the muffled crunch of untamed dry earth and gravel under his shoe. The next step took away nothing he had gained. The steps came quickly and he was taken back to dry riverbeds and hidden pools of trout. His memory spooled a million images, sounds and tastes as the rolled vowels of his father's voice warmed him with recollections too bright and fast to slow him with sentimentality. He existed again back then, and found it once more in this newly found place of strangeness. His pace picked up and never slackened as he wheeled away to the West and left any chance of a certain reunion with Nitu far behind.

Ω

Still naked and dust covered Chepi stood staring out of the Sphere at the once more empty site of the stone circle.

'There's a lot of stuff going on out there.'

The Sphere wasn't sure what she meant.

'I said there's a lot of stuff going on out there.' She repeated impatiently.

'What kind of stuff?'

'Oceans of it.'

'What type of oceans?'

'The kind you could get lost in.'

'A normal ocean then?'

Chepi hesitated. 'Yes, maybe ... I don't know. What does that mean exactly?'

'What does what mean?' The Sphere asked.

'It being a normal ocean.'

'I was just humouring you.'

'Oh.'

'Where's Nitu?'

Chepi grimaced. 'Sulking.'

'I see, so it didn't really work out between you two.'

'I told you, she thinks I'm a moron.'

'No wonder, if she saw you like that.'

'No, don't you listen, before this. She thinks the LlIIyvian are just a figment of my imagination, that I drugged her.'

'Have you any idea at all what you're doing?'

'No, not really.'

The Sphere sighed. 'Okay, but when in doubt you should always act as comes naturally.'

Chepi scoffed. 'I did that before and you sent me on that bloody sabbatical.'

'I thought that being on your own you might learn something.'

'Thanks, I did.'

'Like what?'

'I told you, there's a lot of stuff going on out there.'

'And that's it?'

Chepi shrugged. 'It's a start.'

Ω

The PM spent the two days following Chepi's somewhat major digression from her usual indifference locked alone in his private office. There were many knocks on his door as the aide and various Ministers came and went but he ignored them all. His desk was tidy and his mind empty and that was the way he felt most comfortable. Literally, there was nothing on Earth he'd let in to spoil those endless quiet moments of inactivity and self-indulgence. He had unexpectedly found that solitude suited him. There was no need to perform, to listen, to convince, to argue, threaten, bribe, cajole, defeat, humiliate, bargain with, compromise, back down or retreat from. He'd found bliss. His room was neat and ordered and every thought he had passed uncontested and pure, liberated from the oppression of having to compromise to get by. He felt transcendent and in a moment of pure vision he decided that only through exercising complete autonomous control could he become the leader he knew he really was. He saw in an inspired vision that leadership without distraction was what Canada needed, and through luck it had in him the very person necessary to deliver that for them. There would be no side tracking, no concessions; single-handed he would unfold the world's greatest democracy. He had discovered the worst thing possible for a politician; he had found his big idea.

He called the generals to him, and added as a precaution the heads of Canada's various security services. They met behind doors closed so firmly that even the tea and biscuits tray wasn't allowed in. His aide was barred and federal and provincial Ministers were banned from even entering the building.

Some time later it would be recalled that twenty generals and departmental chiefs had entered the PM's office but 27 hours later only twelve left. The remaining eight had been huddled away after dark a few days later and were never heard of again. At the time no one in Canada or the rest of the world noticed.

What did hold everyone's attention at the time were the vast convoys of armed civilian trucks of all shapes and sizes that were seen leaving every town and city in Canada. Rumours soon spread that they were heading for a newly planned resettlement camp in the Yukon. Quite why one was needed wasn't at that time clear to anyone.

In fact, the PM's plan initially wasn't as sordid as it later became. Given his obvious limitations and staggering lack of insight he genuinely believed his plans to build a city close to Nitu's archaeological site and the Sphere was in the interests of Canadians everywhere. His master scheme was to create a wholly new township in the vicinity of the stone circle, to found a community entirely directed towards understanding the Sphere. He believed it would show commitment to understanding its purpose and an unchallengeable recognition that if the Sphere thought an ancient relic in the Yukon was worth its attention then so did the Canadian people.

Conversely, others argued that there was no evidence at all that the Sphere had any interest in the site or Canadians, and that its presence was likely to be directed at something else entirely, matters completely beyond their understanding. The PM dismissed those notions as being nothing more than idle speculation by people with too much time on their hands and too great a belief in their own imagination.

So, a small camp was built that was initially populated only by ardent believers in the mystical power of the Sphere. These were members of the myriads of quasi-religious groups who had travelled in thousands to Vancouver, and had left as quickly once the Sphere had vanished. These people weren't in the least interested in building, learning or developing anything even remotely in line with what the PM had naively hoped for. At first they industriously collected wood, cardboard boxes and anything metal they could scrounge from the military and built a vast variety of bivouacs and shelters. This pleased the PM no end and he would fly over the newly growing city, as he called it, at least twice a day to acclaim to anyone who would fly with him what a great and successful start was being made. Alas such progress, if it could be called that at all, petered out after the first few weeks and the vision began to flounder Instead of an emerging city, the project became instead a mere twilight spread of endless camp fires and folk music; tin whistles, fiddles, banjos and tambourines filling the air with laments for a life that had never existed. This wasn't at all what the PM wanted, and it wasn't long before his patience ran out.

'Kill the buggers.'

There was laughter, but it didn't last. When the silence grew too much someone braver than the rest ventured a response.

'I don't think we can do that sir.' It was General Smith, an aging veteran of many conflicts and a person who hated politicians as much as he hated war. He'd only joined the PM in the hope he could limit the inevitable damage.

'Why the frakking hell not?' The PM was almost speechless. 'You're the bloody army aren't you? Get the hell out there and do as you're frakking told.'

Another thing Smith disliked was swearing and bullying. 'It would be illegal. Even wars have rules of engagement. We have to follow the Geneva Convention. You cannot go out and start killing people willy-nilly'

His comments created a pause in proceedings lasting long minutes. Later Smith would go over this moment in his mind time after time, trying to work out if there was anything he could have said or done that would have changed anything. But like all such attempts it solved nothing, in life there's one chance to play a hand and then the game moves on, and this was no exception.

'You can shoot looters can't you?' The PM asked. 'People damaging property, rioters, saboteurs and gangs of criminals sent by foreign powers to overthrow law and order?'

The silence deepened, everyone in the room guessed what was coming next, the PM's long hoped for dream of ultimate power. The time when a State detaches itself from the pubic and works only for continued existence at any cost. It was the last trick in the bag, one that could only be used once because no one had ever found out how to put the lid back on. It was the cat out of the bag, a jar of worms, a sneaking, backsliding grasp at a shadow in the dark, a glittering jewel of the unconscious id, a deception spun from vanity and woven into a conceit, a fraught lunge to clutch at one last chance. It was the one thing every politician hoped for but never mentioned even in their most drunken nights and secret trysts with the rich and powerful. It was their skeleton in the cupboard holding the hidden fruit of desire, the apple they wanted more than anything to sink their teeth into. It was the last vast test of their greatness; would they be strong enough to beat, mutilate and murder men, women and children in the name of progress? Were they strong enough to wield absolute power in the name of the people?

Smith stepped in quickly. 'Parliament would never endorse such action.'

The PM hated Smith but had thought he needed him. His Anglo-Saxon name and all the misremembered history it invoked was enough to rile him in even his calmest moods. This unreasoned animosity was the final link in the chain of insane moments that led in only a matter of days to the downfall of the West and everything it represented. The PMs face glistened like dead pigs flesh. 'Smith, you're bleeding well sacked.'

Smith laboured successfully to remain calm. 'I don't think you can do that.'

'Get that bastard out of here.'

The words hung in the air waiting to be consummated by the first most wretched among them. But they all knew it was a step to be taken cautiously. There were human rights issues to be considered, and also the possibility of failure and banishment from reasonable society. Even prison wasn't outside the boundary of potential outcomes. All these factors and more had to be laid side by side with the promises of triumph and personal glory. It was no easy calculation but in the end vanity was the final decider. Each of them aside from Smith knew how well they were suited to times such as these. How their judgement and balance would bring something great from the terrible mess they now saw unfolding with unblinking resolve and certainty. The fact that nothing had actually happened that wasn't a figment of the PM's imagination escaped their attention. The eyes of self-interest can see gold in the most improbable distance future. And so Smith was escorted away and, for his own good so as not to rile the PM any more, was placed under house arrest, which in reality meant imprisonment in a squalid hut on the distant outer fringe of the about to be newly refigured Sphere City.

Martial law was declared a few minutes after Smith was taken away. At least that's when the PM declared martial law; the actual announcement in law and deed took a little longer. First there was Parliament to deal with. They proved obstinate and so the judiciary was bullied, threatened and bribed to support the PM. After a few days of tireless self-promotion and intricate plots involving kidnapping and sabotage the legislation was passed and the PM assumed total control of the whole of Canada, with the sole exception of British Columbia. Through some extraordinary subterfuge the leaders of BC managed to concoct an exemption. Through clever appeals to mythical reports, pledges and agreements in principle they managed to stall the legal process for long enough for the PM to grant them what they'd always wanted, a free democratic state of Cascadia, the new constitution of which bore more resemblance to Garcia Marquez's 'One Hundred Years of Solitude' then it did to anything else seen before in the West. Indeed the international community began quickly to refer to the new BC as British Macondo.

Of course this suited the PM completely, not least because he knew he'd never again have to open a letter pleading for the survival of white bears or trees whose only virtue was their luck at having been able to survive for a thousand years.

In the rest of Canada no such problems of that type had ever arisen. With the exception of Prince Edward Island the rest of Canada had always been more interested in personal wealth and consumption than in political freedom and environmental security, especially Alberta, the province that excavated 95% of its land area to produce oil to sell to China at prices so heavily discounted it was once calculated that it would take the three hundred remaining residents of the Province several million years to pay off debts incurred importing water, food, clean air and everything else needed to sustain life. From this background it was easy for the PM to win over sufficient support purely through making vacuous promises of jobs for everyone and unlimited wealth. Although there were some dissenters, overwhelming this new era of strong leadership was welcomed with open arms.

Having dealt with the minor political, social and legal issues standing in his way, the PM then moved on to the proper construction of Sphere City. With the help of the army he relocated tens of thousands of builders, architects and labourers to the Yukon. To fill the latter category, former ministers and local leaders, lawyers and BC citizens caught behind the quickly erected borders of New Canada found themselves transported to a world of toil beyond their worst nightmares.

It was an unlikely task force, but even formerly sedentary people can produce miracles of construction if there are enough of them. And so after only a few weeks the outline of a town rather than the city he'd hoped for began to emerge. Even a rudimentary infrastructure began to spring up. With the Government coffers quickly emptying to pay the army and unlikely to refill again with the natural wealth of BC having been traded for a good night's sleep, there was nothing the PM could do but let free enterprise supply what the State couldn't.

The first thing to develop was a food supply. The hippies and new age mystics of the first attempt to build the city began to drift back slowly to the site from the waterless canyon of their exile. Quite by chance, they would always contend, they began to sell bean stew, falafel and tofu burgers at exorbitant prices. Where they got their supplies from was much talked about but never discovered. The truth, though, was simple, they merely linked food into the extensive cannabis network that had since the 1960s spread its way around the globe, mostly thanks to the baby boomers. Some of whom had eventually became millionaires, but enough turned out to be happy enough attempting to spread vegetarianism and soft drugs to a world of people generally fixated on meat and beer. Their subsequent followers actually saw the move to the Yukon as a vindication of this special way of life, and, mirroring the PM's loss of perspective, believed it would somehow show the Sphere their worth.

Next came an elementary health service, comprising mostly the spouses and partners of those abducted by the state. They arrived after difficult and harassed journeys across untracked land and unmade roads pursued and besieged by the constant aggression of the military, as they followed nothing more than a map of rumours and innuendo.

Eventually, and against all the odds, they found their loved ones and enjoyed some brief moments of relief and innocent happiness. However, as it always does, reality had other shocks in store for them. The poverty, injuries and mental disorders they encountered in the growing city had risen to such an astonishing level, that without hesitation they set up impromptu clinics and health centres. The hippy and junkie food traders responded to their selfless attempts by making available at exorbitant prices medical supplies such as bandages, sticking plaster and painkillers. Later they managed via contacts in Asia to bring in antibiotics of horrendously low quality, which they nevertheless claimed were priceless. Inevitably payment became a problem, and so in the name of a reborn age of free love they demanded sexual favours.

With illicit drug use and sex work becoming quickly prevalent the army had to step in. At first this was a good thing but eventually they too wanted their share, and so military run protection rings came into being. This was the final piece of the jigsaw of the PM's perfect city. It had all the elements of any other city, crime, unearned profit, abuse, corruption, self-sacrifice and exploitation. The only difference was that it came cheaply. This especially pleased the PM, who, from a hill top enclave several miles away, watched his triumph grow as he basked in the glory of having helped make this hive of humanity come alive. He gazed with endless patience as each day a new building grew from the previously abandoned landscape. And he almost giggled with pleasure to see all the bustling human activity in a once empty and meaningless place. At these precious moments of self-congratulation he looked across to the Sphere hanging as still as ever in the sky a few miles away and wondered when it would rain its pleasure down on him in reward for the magnificent monument he alone had had the vision to build.

Ω

Showered and dressed in a long silken, hooded gown that she thought resembled something likely to have been worn in Avalon but which in truth owed its heritage to ideas tens of thousands of years older, Chepi sat on a large rock watching Nitu, who was in turn studying intently the newly sprawled city. Chepi wanted more than anything to be able to approach her, but feared the response. As she'd explained carefully to the Sphere, a person could only be called an insane moron so many times before it started to hurt. But, still, she wanted to make amends and show Nitu all the things she needed to know to solve the problem the nature of which the Sphere still would not share. Being alien she didn't even know how to begin, so she stood up and began to walk away, probably, she thought, for the last time.

'I know you're there.'

Chepi tensed, ready for the insults and rejection that always seemed to go hand in hand. She'd puzzled over that, wondering why it wasn't either one or the other. Any one of them would have worked, got her to leave, so using both of them appeared to be a bit excessive. She shrugged and waited but Nitu didn't add anything.

'I'm going, so you don't have to shout at me or insult me.'

Nitu turned around. 'Nice frock.'

Chepi tensed. 'It's not a frock.'

'Looks like one.' Nitu turned away again.

'Are you insulting me again?'

'You look like a virgin.'

Chepi tensed a little more. 'I am a virgin.'

'That makes sense.'

But it didn't to Chepi, it had all the baffling irrelevance and impenetrable obscurity that almost everything she had listened to or overheard had since she'd arrived. Which, she'd learned from watching endless television shows, meant that it was either deeply profound but essentially culturally arcane and thus beyond her, or, on the other hand, some quiet hint about something important that had so far escaped her. 'I don't think a person's sexual status has anything to do with dress sense or intelligence, does it?'

'Not usually, but in your case ...'

Chepi took a step closer. 'What if I proved I didn't do anything to you?'

'And how would you do that?'

'If you come here I'll show you.'

Nitu swung her head around slowly and cautiously. 'If you try to do anything I'll brain you.'

'That's ridiculous, I'll have to do something to show you something.'

'I mean don't do anything to me unless I say you can.'

Of course that presented Chepi with a big problem, as what she had in mind was very much about doing something she knew Nitu would never agree to allow. 'How can I show you something really extraordinary if I have to ask your permission first? One word about what it is and you'll start freaking out at me again.'

'Frak, you are such a simpleton. Why does everything have to be so difficult with you? Just bring it and show me.'

'You're insulting me again.'

'Look, show me what you want to show me in the next two seconds or I'm out of here.'

'Can I take you somewhere to show you?'

'If that involves another drug-induced hallucination then no.'

'It doesn't.'

'How far.'

We'll be quick, I promise.'

Nitu looked over to the Sphere. 'Taking me there by any chance?'

'No.'

'Thought not. Where then, and where's the transport? I'm not walking miles.'

'Then you agree to come?'

'Yes, but I'm watching you carefully.' She looked back at the city, half hoping it had vanished, but it was still there straggling shabbily in every direction. She turned back to Chepi, but she'd disappeared. Nitu was not too concerned, the ground around them was steep, so she assumed Chepi had already moved off ahead and dropped out of sight. Nonchalantly she picked up her pack and walked over to where Chepi had been standing. She moved steadily across the rocky ground.

After she'd taken only a few steps the rocks began to give way and her feet sank softly into yielding soil. Plants began to grow and seemingly millions of flowers burst out into the sunlight. The brown land that spread around her sank beneath fields of colour. The valleys filled with water until she was surround by lakes of staggering size. Islands appeared and trees sprang up to provide cover from the rapidly heating sun. In moments the world changed, and it was as though she could see for a thousand miles in each direction, gaze at everything there was as though she was flying above it all.

Chepi reappeared

'Where are we?' She asked, not really caring what the answer was, surprising herself that she felt so calm, but concerned about drugs once again. Instead of arguing, she decided to watch and wait.

'Where we were but a long time before.'

Nitu tried to coax something out of her. 'This feels real. Not like last time.'

'This is nearer. We had to go a very long way last time.'

'How long?' Nitu asked.

'This time?'

'Yes.'

'Millions of years.'

'How many millions?' The time didn't really matter, except as an anchor of some sort on whatever game it was being played.

Chepi shrugged. 'Not sure.'

'Some things don't change then, you're still a bit of an idiot.'

'I like it here, that's all.'

'If you don't know then how on Earth could you bring us here?'

'I found it by accident. The Sphere sent me on a sabbatical and ...'

'A sabbatical!' Nitu stared at her for a long time before adding anything. 'You really are alien.'

'I told you.'

'Where did you take me last time?' But she made the mistake of looking away as she spoke. When there was no answer she looked back and once again Chepi had gone and then in the next instant she seamlessly found herself back in Vancouver, walking towards the Urban Pit as though nothing at all had happened. She stumbled and almost fell, but Zen reached down and grabbed her.

Bewildered, Nitu stared around her. 'Where the hell am I?' She looked at Zen. 'How the frak did you get here?'

'They've closed the borders.' Zen answered unhelpfully.

'What frakking borders?'

'The BC borders, we've been sealed off.'

Nitu's vacant eyes scanned the bustling street. 'How did I get here?'

'You look like you need a drink.'

A light somehow switched itself on in her head. 'I think she is the frakking alien.'

Zen shook his head painfully. 'You're getting too obsessed, and, anyway, there's more important stuff going on.'

'What day is it?'

'Tuesday.'

'Date?'

'21st.'

'Shit. How the frak did you get back from the Yukon?'

'Grabbed a lift. What else.'

'How long ago?'

'About two weeks, why, where've you been?'

She ignored the question and instead peered at him intently. He looked too relaxed. 'And the dreams?' She asked, referring to the nightmares he'd had every day she'd been with him at the camp.

He smiled sheepishly. 'Sorry about that, but I'm fine. I've moved on.'

'That was quick. Sorry, that's great.' She glanced behind furtively. 'Sorry, I've just had a weird experience.'

'How about that drink?'

'Yeah, why not.'

They made their way to the Urban Pit and sat down in the same seats they'd had before the Yukon trip. They shared the obvious comments about water under bridges, what doesn't kill you makes you stronger, and all the rest of the usual patter people share when they meet again changed and confused about what they've been through. Nitu couldn't believe how well Zen appeared to have been able to put the torture behind him. They didn't refer to it, but she couldn't help noticing that if anything he was even more relaxed than before they'd started the trip north.

To Zen, Nitu appeared on the contrary to be yet more changed than the last time he saw her, and this time she'd even added furtiveness. He asked if she'd got dragged back into involvement with the military, but she denied it with convincing vehemence. He then began to suspect she'd met up with Chepi again and that this time she had either seriously got into some kind of drug use or had privately discovered that there was, in fact, impossible as it might be to believe, more going on around Canada than anyone really suspected. But, whatever had happened she was different in a way he couldn't quite put his finger on.

Not that life was that straightforward for him either. He feared brain damage. He believed only that could explain the walk that lasted forever yet only took a few days. A few days during which he apparently walked from the stone circle in the Yukon to Vancouver. A journey where he saw no one until the last morning he woke, only two days ago, and found himself buried in the refuse pile behind the Pit. Other than choosing where to sleep on that last night he could remember every step of the way in the clearest, sharpest detail. For someone who had been terrified of being alone out there it had been a revelation. Each step moved him further into something he'd never guessed would happen. Every valley he passed into and all the wide plains he crossed slowly grew denser and more exotic until he was entwined in a myriad of difference he couldn't unravel. It was another world, a separate country. There was nothing he could name and a thousand things he wanted to collect and keep. At first he almost cried for a camera and then it ceased to matter. Hunger and thirst left him, and tiredness only came with sunset and the ice cold light of untold heavens of stars uncannily watching his every thought. In those moments even his name ceased to matter.

'Penny for them?' She asked.

'It's nothing. Just thinking about the journey back here.'

'Yeah, how did you manage that? Thought you'd get eaten by a bear or something.'

'Never saw any. Anyway, how about you? You weren't exactly yourself out there. Nor now, to be honest.'

She took a deep breath. 'This seems to be the place for big revelations, so ...'

He wasn't listening. 'I think since the Sphere arrived all rules are off. Anything goes around here these days.'

'Maybe there's more. After ...'

'More happening than the global military being castrated, the world economies collapsing, Canada under military rule and BC declaring independence, where the have you been exactly?'

She could only stare.

'It's true.' He reached over and grabbed a copy of the 'Times Collectivist'. She took it, the front headlines were couldn't be missed: 'BORDERS TO B.C. CLOSED INDEFINATELY'.

'Shit. Is this anything to do with that town they're building near the Sphere?'

'What town?'

'Never mind. When did this happen?'

'It's news Nitu! It's in the paper. It's just happened, yesterday, or last night. We got independence and now they've cut us off from the rest of Canada'

'Yeah, well, it's a Vancouver Island paper so it could've been last week. It's all the same to them.'

'Well, whatever.'

Their drinks were brought over and they both took refuge behind the bustle of sorting them out. Nitu drank quickly but Zen only played sullenly with his. Nitu began to think she was intruding, or maybe it was disapproval at something she'd done or not done.

'So what's happening, what are people doing?' She asked.

'Surprisingly little.'

'Unsurprisingly little you mean, if Victoria's still running things.'

'Didn't think you were anti-Island.'

'No, I'm not really. Great place for a holiday.'

'I thought you would know. That someone would have been in touch, updated you or something.' He said.

So that was it, the loss of interest. He'd been hoping she'd have some miracle answer or a way back to the top. 'Sorry.'

For reasons neither of them could understand even if they'd tried, the mood between them shifted. Instead of being a reunion full of stories and warmth it became a burden, a distraction from nestling in their own thoughts with the weird memories that still felt so physically real. They ordered more drinks and drank them in silence. Zen was the first to leave. She watched him go with relief, back in the city she didn't have to feel any responsibility for anything that happened to him. Not that he needed those feelings from her, she knew that, and yet it was inescapable that she'd got him into the Sphere problem, the Yukon and everything that had followed. She ordered a third beer and wondered why in the middle of probably the most exciting time in human history, with Spheres, aliens and ancient cultures multiplying all over the place she felt so miserable. With half the beer gone she realised that a depressant wasn't the best choice, so she left and headed back to her apartment for comfort food, chocolate and a good movie, surprised and pleased that despite everything these things would still exist.

With happy but inane thoughts to keep her company life suddenly looked brighter, and she turned the corner only a few doors away from her apartment full of thoughts of hot baths, warm beds, wine and endless feel good films to bury herself into. In was then, in the middle of her reverie she saw Chepi standing by the entrance. She surprised herself by having mixed feelings. There was, naturally, the irritation, resentment, exasperation and mild anger she'd got used to, but this time there was a smidgeon of curiosity and, though she'd never have admitted it, some tiny trickle of affection worming its way into her life.

She decided to wait and see what Chepi would say about

what had happened without any prompting. 'What do you want?'

The question was terse and unyielding, but not exactly cruel or malicious. Chepi took that to be a good sign. 'Thought I'd come and see you.'

'I was going to have a bath.'

'Mmm, okay.'

'I'm having a bath. It's not an invitation.'

'I'll wait.'

Nitu was about to say she could wait outside, and then realised how petty that would seem. 'D'you drink wine?'

Of course Chepi had never tasted wine in her life, but thought better of saying so in case she somehow alienated herself again. 'Sure.'

'Then pop down to the liquor store and get some. Buzz me when you get back.'

She almost panicked. 'Er, I can't do that.'

'I'm not giving you any money.'

'They'll, er, they'll think I'm too young.'

'And are you?'

'No.'

'Well show them your ID.'

Chepi sighed, tired of always being on the back foot. 'Don't you ever listen to anything I tell you? I'm not from here and I don't have a frakking ID.'

Unfazed, Nitu carried on unlocking the door. 'Well you're not getting any of mine.'

'Fine.' She made to follow. 'You can be really childish.'

'I don't give a frak. And when we get up there just keep quiet, don't say anything until I'm ready, and then we need a serious talk about the way you keep abducting me.' Nitu was pleased with how calm she'd managed to stay, she was sure that most people would have thrown a fit.

'But I have something to tell you. It can't wait.'

'It will have to; first it's a bath, some wine and then food. Can you cook?' The look on Chepi's face said everything she needed to know. 'Okay, but you don't get to eat either. After all that I'm going to watch a film. When all that's done, if I can be bothered, you can explain what the frak has been going on.'

'You're a really selfish cow, d'you know that?'

But Nitu had gone and let the door swing back at her. Chepi caught it just before it locked her out.

Ω

Nitu's apartment was strange. If she'd known, Chepi wouldn't have been in the least surprised that Nitu never had anyone to visit. Her social life was always played out in bars, restaurants, cinemas, libraries, beaches, mountains, friend's houses and apartments; literally anywhere but where she lived. If she had known this, Chepi would have understood why. Even being limited to knowledge she'd gained from television soap operas she could see that there was nothing ordinary about Nitu's domestic habits. The two bedroom, spacious apartment was filled with plants, miniature trees, shrubs, ordinary weeds and endless other types of unnameable plants, and even a small pool filled with a intangible mixture of aquatic flowers, algae, reeds and things Chepi couldn't even begin to guess at.

Left to herself by Nitu's vanishing act into the bathroom she wandered out onto the balcony and found gigantic night blooming plants and smelled strange scents given off by a seemingly endless variety of exotic creeping plants winding their way through, across and over everything before reaching upwards along an iron stairway that led to the roof. She clambered up and found something even more completely different and surprising than anything below. The chaos of the apartment itself had been left behind and what had been created on the roof was a garden of imposing simplicity and perfect form. It was similar to a Japanese garden but lighter, almost empty, and tightly geometrical. Chepi guessed at the inspiration behind it and marvelled at how it had been brought about. Lacking stone and scale Nitu had created a facsimile of the essence of the stone circle. Its alignment and spatial integrity were perfect. Chepi knew, firstly, it shouldn't have been possible, and, secondly, that Illiaeth would have to be told. What Nitu had done really meant something, but exactly what was beyond her.

She wandered back down and found Nitu waiting for her in what would have been a living room in anyone else's apartment. She was smiling, and Chepi took that to be encouraging, she'd never seen her smile before, at least not since they'd stopped working together at the site, and then they hadn't been directed at her, nor even Zen, but at the work, the finds and the things they'd talked about. This time though the smile was definitely focussed on her.

'What?'

'Don't you ever take that hood off?'

'It's a cowl.'

'I want to see your face. Properly.'

Chepi ignored her. The consequences of Nitu seeing her were more than she was willing to deal with. 'How did you do all this?' She asked, hoping to be able to change the subject.

'So you're going to carry on hiding? Okay, but I believe your story about coming from the Sphere.' She waited.

'Later perhaps, first I want to know all about this stuff. It's amazing but well, why? What does it mean?'

Nitu raised her eyebrows, it wasn't the response she had been expecting. 'Does it have to mean anything?'

'Where did the idea come from?' She walked over and sat down next to Nitu. There was something in her expression that said she wasn't going to be easily distracted. 'What were you trying to do?'

'Why all the interest?'

'Because it's so awesome to have a place like this.'

Nitu wanted to ask what she meant but she thought she probably knew, and had done so ever since Chepi had taken her to wherever it was she'd just been. 'It was dreams. They started when I found the stones and then they just kept on getting bigger. Always the same, dense forests and miraculous things growing in the strangest ways, and then the stones would always appear, so smooth and intricate, not like they look now, and not like in that vision of LIlyanhiviian, or whatever it was, you showed me. So I started trying to build a small garden like it, to capture it, on the balcony, and then it grew until it got like it is now.'

'D'you know what it means?'

'It doesn't mean anything, I just like it. Look at this.' She got up and pulled Chepi after her to show her a small corner of the pool. It was interlaced with more different kinds of plants than Chepi could easily count. It reminded her of the algae and insects she'd seen in the desert, so much brilliance dazzling such a small space.

'This shouldn't be possible, should it? Can people do this kind of thing here?' Chepi asked.

'In Canada?' She was surprised by the question. 'People can do anything they want, within reason, it's just that mostly they don't want to, or maybe they're happy imagining it instead in a game or on the television.'

'Do you know what's happening in the world?' Chepi asked unexpectedly.

'Sure, why?'

'Did you hear about the Sphere destroying all the military armaments?'

'Zen mentioned it, I think, and I saw something in the paper in the pub.'

'And that's not interesting?'

'I guessed it was something to do with you. Like I said, I'm beginning to believe what you say about being an alien'

'Just like that? And if it had been me, it wouldn't bother you?'

'I was kidding.' And then she paused. 'I don't know. You've just taken me a million or so years into the past for real or through some amazing illusion, so either you are drugging me, but I can't see how you'd be able to control it so well, or you are from the Sphere. If you are I guess you could anything. Well, not anything I suppose, but much more than I'd be able to work out. So, yeah, you could have done it, or have done something just as weird for reasons beyond me Anyway, taking all that together, I'm just trying not to think too hard about what you do because to be honest if I did it'd probably freak me out more than it did when you gave me that LIlyanhiviian trip, I think that's what you called it, that weird illusion; probably. Anyway, that's what I think.'

'You can talk a lot can't you, when you want to?'

'I'm nervous.'

Nervous? Why?'

'I've never shown anyone this before. It's kind of, like sort of showing everything about me, like you could read my mind by just looking at it.'

Chepi glanced around. 'You've got to be kidding. That would be way too dangerous if this is anything to go by.'

Nitu sat down and clasped her hands between her knees. 'Is it awful?'

'Wondrous comes to mind.'

'As in unbelievable, or amazing?'

'I think astonishing would fit.'

'Well that's something, being able to astonish an alien.'

'That's the easy bit; everything about his place astonishes me. Like, what's that new town for, the one the being built right out there in the Yukon? And it's so near to the stones. Now why would anyone want to do that?'

'Apparently it's that idiot PM. He thinks it'll impress the Sphere.'

'And why would he want to do that?'

'So it'll give him things.'

'A headache most likely, if you think I'm a freaky, you haven't any idea what a freak really is until you meet that thing. Did I tell you it sent me on a frakking sabbatical into the desert?'

Nitu stood and peered intently at Chepi, her face heavily drawn with serious intent. 'You could be anyone, I could have had illusions and you could have done something to me, so, truthfully, are you, you know, having problems? Look, I don't mind if you are, I kind of like you, but if you need help we need to get it for you quickly.'

'There is a Sphere up there you know. Everyone's seen it and it's done some pretty peculiar stuff.'

'I know, but mostly it just hangs there. I kind of think it's stuck, acting arbitrarily. Why anyway would it send a young girl like you down here to plague me?'

'I'm not plaguing you.'

'You are.'

'I don't think so.'

'Don't bicker.'

'Whatever.' Chepi fidgeted uncomfortably.

'What?' Nitu asked.

'Don't get annoyed again.'

'What are you going to do?'

'Nothing, honestly, unless you let me.'

'You said that last time.'

'I mean it, and I meant it then. So, can I show Illiaeth your garden?'

'Who's that?'

'She asked you the questions.'

'And even supposing she's real why would she want to come here?'

'No, sorry, she can't come here, we have to go to her.'

'And take the garden with us? Just like that.'

'If you say we can.'

Nitu shook her head in disbelief. 'Sure why not, I'll open another bottle of wine and watch you. There're some empty boxes in the kitchen.'

'Thanks, and remember you said I could.'

There was only the lightest trace of wind in the usually still apartment that gave any indication that Chepi had acted without hesitation. Nitu sensed the change, the aromas it carried reminded her of LIlyanhiviian. It was a subtle shift and a fine, restrained memory triggered itself as the scent of the stones were stirred in hidden parts of her mind. She walked out onto the balcony to see the city and try to guess which direction the wind was coming from, but below her was a forest of such complexity that her mind gasped as she caught her breath with astonishment at the impossible vision of woodlands that shouldn't exist except in the dreams she'd never mentioned even to Chepi. She cried the tears that Chepi had found in the desert as her mind mingled with the soil of countless imaginings brought to one infinite completion. It was a lunacy of attainment gathered in by intelligences too old to give simple reasons for their existence.

Nitu saw her apartment reorient itself until every nuance of what she'd created mapped itself to some semblance of what lay below. The building dissolved and quietly she fell forwards into the boundless colours reaching out to embrace her.

Ω

In the rest of the world things weren't going quite so well. With the total disappearance of hi-tech weapons of war the balance of power across the globe shifted beyond anyone's expectations. When the only weapons available were those that could be held and used by a single person then population size once again became the single most crucial factor in deciding national status. As always in the primate world, it's the individual with the biggest gang who'll win through, and human armies are no different.

Of course at first politicians everywhere in the West pretended that nothing had really changed, and that with some minor readjustment in production new super armoured tanks, fast jets and stealth ships that looked like nursery drawings would roll forth once more to stabilise the world. Unfortunately for them, their hopes were in vain. Not only was the developed world in shock at the loss of humanity's global masculinity, the actual extent of that shock was inversely proportional to the lost wealth and status of the population. The net effect was that the West suffered far more trauma than the rest of the world. Realising this early on, the leaders of most developing countries calculated that population difference would impart to them a considerable advantage in any conflict. And so it was that an invasion greater than any other in the history of the world began.

Millions upon millions of poorly armed troops and civilians looking to emigrate spilled over from Asia into Europe, and via Russia across the Bering Sea into Alaska. They had nothing but farm tools, rifles and pistols, but the vastness of the numbers involved made it unstoppable. The UK, the EU and the US snorted disapproval, claiming that there was no precedent for such outlandish belligerent migration. If words had mattered their views might have counted for something, as it was they had no impact and the world reeled under the sustained suddenness of this unprecedented mass movement of people.

Given the weight of numbers involved it should have been the case that the West fell quickly and easily, and that might have happened if it wasn't for an age old rule about not moving so many people around before supply lines are built up. The invasion had been spontaneous and no such preparations had taken place. All too soon people began to die of fear, arbitrary and pointless gunshot wounds and various types of stabbings and puncturings due to their lack of training, but most of all, however, they died of thirst and hunger. Initially it was only the already weak and sickly, but quickly the numbers grew until hundreds of thousands of bodies were strewn unattended across both North America and Europe.

Some historians might later say that most of the ordinary people who invaded couldn't be blamed for ignoring the usual logistics of waging war, and will claim that they were rudely misled by the cunning of countries that had a long history of tricking the poor. It will be said that most of these people abandoned their homelands with nothing; that they had left everything behind for the promise of food and housing for free amongst the most glittering places their imaginations could conjure. The origin of these rumours and murmurings will no doubt be attributed to the UK Prime Minister, who when told that several hundred thousand people had crossed the Bosporus on their way into Europe had replied flippantly, and with a love of his own voice that has rarely if ever been equalled throughout recorded history, that they were all welcome, as always, and that there would be free food and limitless housing for everyone who made it to London. He was being sarcastic, of course, in the way only Anglo-Saxon politicians can be, but that nuance of British culture was lost on the millions who heard the remark and quite fancied a change of diet and accommodation at Europe's expense.

Thus it came about that the greatest sacking of a continent since history began started through greed, vulgar opportunism, vanity, ignorance, a total misreading of the situation, and misinterpretation of the Runes, the I Ching, the Tarot and many other prophetic practices too difficult to spell, and it ended as it was bound to, the West collapsed under the weight of dead bodies greater in number than could be accommodated by anyone. Millions became homeless, rootless, feckless and, from a resource point of view, surplus to requirements.

It was then, when things were about to get totally out of hand, that nature finally took over and spread terrible diseases so quickly that there was barely time in the newly constructed, post-electronic age for a telegraph to be sent pleading for help before yet another small pocket of humanity gave up the struggle and began to wander aimlessly from one empty, denuded place to another. The whole of Europe became like a vast film set from the latest zombie movie. There were tears and regrets all round, especially from the various enclaves in the Caribbean, the South Seas and the Azores providing refuge for governments of the EU in exile, as these various collections of bankers, corporate CEO's and recently redundant politicians called themselves. It has been reliably reported that they were heartily sorry for everything that had happened.

Events in the US initially evolved more slowly. Although Alaska fell in days, it was quickly given back to its inhabitants, namely the First Nations, Inuit people and the strange droves of those of European descent who had actively decided to live in the far north rather than somewhere warm and colourful.

Handing it back was an easy decision for the invaders, most of whom by that stage had already experienced quite enough of beautiful but bleak sunsets, horizons that were far too distant for a sane mind to grasp, and endlessly unpredictable weather. So, without pausing they wended they ways south along the coast eating whatever scraps they could find in rock pools until they got to the British Columbian border, and there things got even more difficult.

The problem with BC was trees, that is, the impenetrable rainforests that spread without break from end to end across the width of the former Province. To the invaders, rather than being a playground full of breathtaking landscapes, the forests were instead a frightening place of rain, fog and storms of mythically proportion filled with deathly cold winds that howled and swirled with endless energy as they ricocheted off strange mountains covered in snow deep enough to swallow anything that had the temerity to enter its icy boundaries.

If that wasn't enough, in addition to the climatic problems, the forest was also deserted. With the fragmentation of Canada and the collapse of the West, BC could no longer sell its forests to the highest and most convenient bidder. Trade with the U.S. died almost instantly and the forests emptied as almost everyone drifted south to warmer climes and the endless hospitality of places like New Westminster and West Vancouver where the homeless and jobless had always been nurtured, if reluctantly, by the favoured middle-class. Thus, there was no food or shelter of any kind to be found anywhere. And so, in short, in the face of overwhelming difficulties, the invasion of North America began to founder quickly.

Not so though, the invasion of the south of BC by displaced loggers. Under the stylish and totally unexpected leadership of a young former academic, the newly founded state of BC launched a programme of public works that put the economic renaissance of inter-war Germany in the shade. Infrastructure upon infrastructure burst upwards, driven by the irresistible force of an endless labour supply and wages so low Charles Dickens would have had a field day, and the 'Ragged Trousered Philanthropists' would need to be written all over again.

Elsewhere in BC, life carried on as usual. Artisans hidden away in small unreachable communities carried on painting and carving both great works of art and utter dross, both of which would never be seen let alone purchased. Boaters continued to motor about from anchorage to anchorage to barbeque fish under the same sunset in places they already knew like the back of their hand. Motor cruisers raced each other in their manly, traditional fashion, swamping anyone too slow to get out of their way. Sailing vessels chugged more slowly as they basked in a sense of superiority only they understood while they waited patiently for just the tiniest bit of wind or the day they'd cross an ocean. The other inhabitants carried on as normal, living their strange polite lives working as slowly as possible to fill the gaps between walking, birding, surfing, kayaking or talking about doing one or the other while they smoked a joint or two.

BC was, then, becoming a paradise. Either people could work themselves to death for the common good under the new leadership in the metropolitan south, or they could hang out elsewhere dreaming and playing. It was perfect. Some commentators even said that in effect nothing at all had changed in BC. Alas for the forests, nothing could have been further from the truth. And this, of course, is where we left the invading army of the East.

The forest won an overwhelming victory in the first few weeks. The intruders never managed to force their way through to the south, and the few who tried were killed by rampaging animals as eagles took children and other small people, killer whales charged up beaches and devoured those too afraid to rest in the forest and wolves ganged together in packs larger than any written account had ever documented or native tale recorded. These packs, especially, spun eddies of destruction through the deepest, darkest woodland as they laid waste to tens of thousands of the intruders.

For a time the usual pyramid of predation with only a few big predators at the top become more like a square, with as many carnivores patrolling the landscape as there was human prey trying to escape north to the Bering Sea. Where they all came from was never discovered. It was as though nature had held them in storage somewhere, waiting for this very moment to eke out some small vengeance for all the ills waged against them since Europeans had arrived.

This time of carnage didn't last long. As with all cycles, no matter how short or unexpected, a balance was eventually struck. Within a month the survivors had managed to barricade themselves into animal-proof fortifications. They had great hopes of founding a new way of life, but of course it could only ever be a temporary solution. Being an invading army they were almost all male and below 35 years of age, which meant, although they didn't know it at the time, their so newly found way of life would quickly die out from numerous random and pointless acts of violence between themselves, vain attempts to leave the forest and find a woman, and, in time, jealous rages over ownership of the least masculine looking among them. They didn't survive long, the last invader died of a broken heart as he gnawed on the last human bone he could find.

So, for BC the invasion from the East was a non-event. Most never even noticed it, and the few who did wrote poems that were never read and then moved on. Ignored, it quickly faded completely from collective memory.

Ω

While all this was happening, or at least for the first few, early days, Zen was barbequing fish in the cockpit of a sailing vessel he'd commandeered in Victoria's Inner harbour. It had belonged to someone from Calgary, Alberta, but as they would never again be allowed into BC, Zen took pity on the boat and decided to keep it for himself. On this particular occasion he was smiling to himself with satisfaction. Only a few days before he'd managed to evade a horror that, had it come to pass, would have been a source of soulless despair for years to come. In the moments of backsliding cowardice familiar to all politicians faced with an unprecedented national disaster, the leaders of BC had looked for any means to escape from any suggestion of responsibility for anything and everything that was happening around them. As would be normal in such circumstances, they looked for someone to carry the can who was sufficiently knowledgeable to be credible to journalists and trouble makers trying to exercise their rights under a democracy to challenge everything that happened, and yet naïve enough to believe that any such unjustified, ludicrous approach was in fact the break they always knew would happen, rather than see it as it was, nothing more than a crude and base subterfuge. They didn't have to look far. Still driven by a senile love for Nitu that should rightly have been medicated, Tantoning put forward Zen's name, in the hope that this would lead to his rapid downfall and thus clear the way for a late blooming romance that would rewrite completely the world of cross-generational adventure.

Despite still not quite being the person he had been before the Sphere arrived, Zen nevertheless grew suspicious when he started receiving strange phone calls from desperate sounding middle-aged men close to tears in their urgency to establish whether or not he was the brilliant young man who had on behalf of Government of Canada so skilfully led the early research into the Sphere. Even though the callers' total misreading of his role and status in the work on the Sphere attracted his suspicion, especially as, so far as he knew, being a victim of state torture wasn't a success as such, it wasn't the specific query itself that attracted his suspicion so much as the ever present voice in the background whispering urgent pleas that he be asked the whereabouts of Nitu. He knew instinctively that even a fraught politician at the end of their tether wouldn't resort to ventriloquism to confuse a potential ally at the very moment they were needed the most. He thus smelled the sticky hand of Tantoning and acted as anyone in his situation would.

Prevarication came easily to Zen, he saw it as an academic virtue that had saved him from many a rash judgement and mistimed conclusion, and so he was able to stall, delay, fail to return promised phone calls, and plainly deny any suggestion that he had agreed anything, or in fact refused even to confirm for sure that any of the tens of dozens of approaches they had made had actually taken place with an ease that everyone who didn't know him found breathtaking. He was totally in his element, rebuffing, rejecting, refuting, contradicting and disagreeing with everything and anything that in anyway involved him making a judgement, suggestion, proposal, offer or idea. It was scholarship in the finest traditions of the West and these conversations were, he'd later concede, his finest rhetorical accomplishments.

Finally, tired of the growing repetitive nature of the exchanges, he let slip the idea that they might be mistaken, and that for reasons of national security he had only been a cover for the true leader of the Sphere project. In fact, as an aside, this term 'Leader' evolved so completely from this first misrepresentation that it subsequently gained such an implausible concreteness that the title 'Leader of the Sphere' soon supplanted 'Prime Minister' as the preferred title for the head of the BC government. Of course nothing about this ridiculous fiction was lost on Zen, and later he would use this incident as an example of the kind of magic realist thinking in politics and the media that had so held back the progress of wisdom in the 19th – 21st Centuries, but in the meantime he gave them what they really wanted, someone so lacking in personal ambition and social skills that they might be capable of assuming responsibility without turning every action into a personal chance to gain immortality.

So, after much scheming and delaying, he gave them Simon Reboaten, a final year doctorate student at a college in Port McNeil in the far north, whose research was so outlandish and peculiar that no one dared criticise it in case it was later found to be the work of a genius, but nor did they dare pass it either, fearing that someone might discover later that had all been a hoax, or as some suspected, nothing more than a barrel of bilge water. And so, faced with this dilemma, those whom decide these matters quietly eased him out of the University of British Columbia and sent him on extensive periods of fieldwork to the north. In time the fieldwork turned into a permanent post as a laboratory assistant, funded by some slight of hand accounting on the part of the photocopying room at Port McNeil and a mythical clerical assistant at UBC. After ten years everyone forgot about him. Reboaten, though, loved every minute of his exile, and saw it as overwhelming support of his attempt to produce the definitive theory of everything human.

Zen had read his work the summer before and was impressed

by its brevity (it was only 109 pages long) its scholarship (he had managed to cite some of the most obscure of the Greek philosophers) its gravitas (it had mathematical equations sprinkled liberally throughout) and its boldness in that it claimed to be the final, unarguable truth about everything anyone needed to know to be able to form the perfect civic society. He was just what they needed and Zen delivered him to them with such aplomb and conviction that academics everywhere rushed out in unbridled, qualified support, glad at last to off-load their guilty secret and pass him on to the political establishment as their one true saviour.

As Zen munched his fish and quaffed chilled white wine in the golden glow of another perfect day's end he remembered these things fondly. With the pension he wheedled out of them he'd never again have to mark an undergraduate essay, nor attend a meeting about timetables. He was free, and it was a guaranteed freedom too, because Simon had said so.

Ω

Nitu's garden opened a pathway into a world that had been closed to the Earth since Antarctica had frozen over and the LIIyviian had left everything to the care of humans. Illiaeth had sent them out into the world in a migration that would see them spread throughout what would later become the Pacific region, where they would one day build the fabled city of Atlantis.

Nitu passed along this ancient pathway she had unexpectedly reopened and fond herself in the magical forest she had seen from the balcony of her apartment.

As this happened Chepi flitted back to the Sphere where she received a less than respectful welcome.

'What have you done to her now?' It asked.

'Why should I have done anything?'

'Because I think there's a pattern developing. You go down there, wind her up and then coming running back here.'

'Things have moved on. Don't you watch anything that's happening any more?'

'Not really.'

Chepi wanted to ask it how it spent its time, but previous similar attempts had produce answers so time consuming that she'd never yet heard the end of one. 'Well, just in case you are interested, she created this quite small reproduction of the enchanted Western Forest. It fitted perfectly into the portal and now she's gone there.'

The Sphere hesitated. 'And whose stupid idea was that?'

'Nothing to do with me, she made it herself, though don't ask me how.'

'Maybe because she's my avatar?' The Sphere sounded concerned.

'I don't see how, you've made her independent. You said so.'

'Yes, but she still knows things.'

Chepi smelled a rat. 'What's that supposed to mean?'

The Sphere tried to backtrack. 'Nothing.'

'Stop just where you are. You've done something you shouldn't have, haven't you?'

'You have. She couldn't have done that without you.'

Chepi shrugged and grinned widely. 'Oh dear, now you're trying to blame me are you? Is the big bad Sphere worried mommy's going to get angry with it?'

'You've learned some pretty stupid expressions down there. You do know that don't you?'

'Don't change the subject.'

'Don't they find you a bit juvenile?'

Chepi leaned comfortably against the wall. 'What exactly has gone on here?'

'To be honest?'

'It's always best.'

The lights dimmed. Chepi thought that was a bit over dramatic, but decided not to say anything.

'Illiaeth isn't going to be happy that an avatar opened up the portal.' The Sphere said.

'Why?'

'Don't ask me. She just said that if it happened she wouldn't be happy.'

Chepi's face carried an indescribable expression. 'Is that it?'

'More or less.'

'And the more is?'

'What?'

'And what more?'

'It doesn't work like that. There isn't any 'more', it's just an expression.'

'Mmmm.'

'Mmmm, what?' The Sphere asked with concern.

'I think you're losing it.'

'What?'

'Never mind, let's go back to Vancouver. No, make it Victoria, it'll be nearer to Zen.'

'I'm watching this creepy town being built.'

'Never mind that. BC's where the action is. D'you know thousands of people are being eaten by bears, cougars and wolves all over BC? And no one knows where they came from.'

'Where specifically?' It asked, hoping it would be near enough to nip back and to without missing too much of the soap opera unfolding below it.

'All over the mainland bit.'

'But you want to go that island.'

'We can check it out on the way.'

'Do we have to?'

'Leave some monitor things here.'

'It's not the same.'

'Don't sulk.'

'Why don't you just go there yourself, you don't need me.'

'Presence is everything.'

'By which you mean mine?'

'Of course.'

'What have you got in mind?'

Chepi chuckled. 'I'll tell you later.'

'There's still Illiaeth.'

'Don't worry, I think she likes Nitu.'

'Can you really be all that sure?'

'Can you stop arguing and just go?'

If the Sphere had been in the least humanoid it might have argued further, as it was it followed the pattern of thousands of years of practice, sighed deeply for maximum effect, and did as she asked, it blinked out of the Yukon.

Ω

'You shouldn't be here.'

Illiaeth had met Nitu as she emerged from the portal. She was standing in a clearing surrounded by trees that were so large it frightened Nitu to look at them. Their massive, twisted, whirlpool trunks and branches gave them the appearance of giant vertical waves hanging motionless for an instant while they waited for something unknowable before crashing down and obliterating everything around them. They were an impossibility made real, and if they grew at the same rate as normal trees she knew they must be the greatest things that have ever lived.

'I didn't mean to.' She answered weakly.

'The trees won't hurt you. They used to grow on earth.' She added wistfully.

'I wish they still did.'

'Is that why you are here?'

'Maybe. I don't know. Chepi said you'd want to see the garden.'

'You can't stay here. You must bring him.'

'Who?'

'Your friend.'

'Which friend?'

'The dreamer.'

Nitu didn't want to guess incorrectly, in seemed too important. She'd learned from the three questions that mistakes weren't just passed over. 'They all dream, it's what men do.'

Illiaeth waited.

'D'you mean Zen?'

'He sometimes dreams his way back to us.'

And then the forest disappeared and her apartment was back as it had been before she began to build the garden. It seemed empty and lifeless, but at the same time she felt a sense of completion. She rolled her thick duvet around her and fell into a deep sleep.

Ω

The turtle crawled out of the mud fully formed and with a smile on its face that Nitu would recall for the rest of her life. The recollection had more to do with the fact that she was aware that it wasn't actually a real smile but an artefact of the way its mouth had formed to best scoop food from the bottom of the ocean. But the truth made no difference because whenever she recalled the image in the future it was always thought by others that it was the smile that had caught her attention and not the fact that a turtle had been born unusually out of the mud. She let their misinterpretations pass. She knew that human imagination could only cope with something it has already thought through and filled with misinformation, and, anyway, at that time no one was prepared to believe that everything already known about turtles had been wrong.

At the moment the turtle appeared Nitu knew nothing about what hermeneutical mischief would later play havoc with her vision, and so she acted purely with the curiosity of the innocent and reached out and held onto its quickly accelerating shell as it swam swiftly and deeply on its unknown path through the dark, warm water of her dream and left the mud of its birth far behind.

The turtle swam with astonishing swiftness and the power of its strokes almost washed her from its shell; but still, despite the speed, everything passed by them as though in slow motion and so she managed to glimpse the lives of the strange inhabitants of the coral worlds and lost cities of imagination from the moment they were born until they died in obscure old age. She revelled in the vivid tales and amorous adventures she witnessed as the denizens searched for meaning in lives that were so short yet so full of potential. She cried frequently when a soul able to fill the world with endless light and wisdom blinked out in the darkest wretched misery. She mourned these unguarded souls who once conjured hope but were abandoned to rotting flesh by eyes that couldn't see.

She met mermaids so beautiful she dared not look at them for more than a second in case she drowned in despair at the bottom of the endless depths that lurked beneath every unseen moment of trickery the human mind was capable of encoding.

Her voyage was peopled with great shining beasts whose heads were so far from their tails that she was never sure if it was a series of great monsters circling her or was instead the single mythical creature of legend whose length was so great that its body circled the Earth and would one day grow so long it would merge with itself into a single massive ring so large it would stop the ocean currents and squeeze life from even the deepest hidden cause of all the new days the sun had brought.

She saw that all life was short and precarious and even the most hidden secrets of the universe depended on a chance flicker in a lover's eye and the miraculous bringing into being of hope to dwell close by in opposition to the gigantic voids of nameless extinction that pressed in moment by moment to second guess the turtles passage and blind her to some passing life that should be recorded but never would.

Her journey was a song for others to hear and grant immortality to moments beyond them. She bore witness to events brought into the light by powers that drove her onwards as they turned and twisted with disregard for everything except the current that carried her and the purpose that had no aim other than to fulfil intentions lost even before time began.

She gathered tales that will ever be told except to the oldest mind in patterns too large to grasp as all that has been before lightens and time never ends.

Nitu saw all of this and understood what Illiaeth had never told her and never would. She embraced the truth as she twisted naked in the unknown seas of her imagination and grasped a reality that had never been revealed except in the quiet moments of the solitary death of all life as it dreams extinction along paths so hard to bear that until their moment of relief, when all knowledge is removed and they survive only in forgotten realms where a single day is beyond counting, a year but a pause for thought, and peace beyond its grasp.

In this singular dream-song the tide drove her from the beginning of time to the end of the LIIyviian in a place and set of circumstances that would make everything that had gone before emerge as nothing more than the turning of a page.

She awoke with a passion that would never be satisfied and which would therefore grant her an ageless hunger for everything that would ensure she would never die. The day brought no fear and the sun made her smile like a turtle, and as quickly as it had begun the dream was forgotten and she was left with nothing more than the image of the turtle's face emerging from the mud.

Ω

'I'm going to find Zen.'

'Dressed like that?'

'I like it.'

'But they'll get suspicious if you never wear anything but that cowl.'

They're suspicious already.'

'Well then?'

'But look at me. If they see what I am it'd cause a riot.'

'He's on a boat, no one else is near him.'

'Will that make a difference?'

'I expect so.'

And so it was that when Zen woke in the middle of the night and went to investigate the sound of someone climbing on the boat he saw what he could only have suspected if his life had up to that point had been very different. As it obviously hadn't been, the shock took several seconds to fully register. Faced with a mythical creature that no previous artistic interpretation he'd ever seen had got close to representing in any realistic way, Zen said the only thing that came to mind. 'Look, this really had better be some kind of very expensive fancy dress costume or I'm out of here.'

'It's me.'

He recognised the voice but his brain was simply unable to link the adolescent, eternally hooded Chepi hidden beneath impenetrable robes with the slender, almond eyed and Elvin eared apparition that stood in front of him. She was like some kind of computer generated teenage fantasy, but even more so. She looked impossible. 'Is this some kind of joke?' He looked around quickly. 'Some kind of projection or something?' And then something else equally absurd occurred to him. 'This isn't a film set is it, because if it is ...'

'No, it's me.' She leant forward and touched him.

He stepped back cautiously. 'Is it completely necessary for you to look like that? Not only does it seem a bit of a cliché, but, well, you could get into a lot of trouble, and it's hardly going to go unnoticed is it.'

'I came to see you, not go on a parade up and down the High Street.'

'To be honest, looking back, I kind of liked the cowl. It was less … distracting.'

'Well, this is what I'm like, so you'll have to put up with it. You frakking humans, there's no pleasing you.'

'So Tolkien was right, you do exist?'

'Who's he?'

'The one who made elves tall and beautiful and not small, childish and somewhat idiotic.'

'You can be so insulting.' She fidgeted self-consciously. 'Aren't you going to invite me down there?' She asked, pointing down into the boat.

'I guess.'

He led Chepi below and made coffee, which she refused, and then tea, which she'd only drink if it was green. That way forty minutes passed before he got to ask her what she was doing turning up in the middle of the night dressed as though she was about to pull off the biggest alien seduction since time began. Of course she had no idea what he was talking about, or at least pretended she didn't, but to make sure there were no further misunderstandings she explained carefully and in full detail exactly why it was she could never in ten million lifetimes find a human attractive. She explained every facet of her distaste at least twice, and gave even more emphasis to smell than was strictly necessary.

'Okay, I get it.' He said. 'You find us disgusting.'

'No, not really, I just don't want to get too close to you.'

'Fine, and so you're here because?'

Chepi hesitated because she didn't really know. She had been worried about him but that had slowly passed when she'd found out he was on the boat. She guessed that like most humans she'd watched, he'd be happy pottering about doing nothing but feeling proud of himself for having conducted his life in a way that enabled him to merely float around on water eating fish and drinking beer. With this thought, she'd almost left him to his bliss and would have done so if she hadn't been curious about what he'd make of her if she showed up as her true self. It'd been a test run to judge how humans would be if and when she'd worked out what she was supposed to be doing and started mixing with them on a more open basis. But from Zen's reaction that looked like a non-starter.

'I'm just too beautiful, aren't I?'

'Actually Chepi, you're a bit of a freak. You look like something out of a ridiculous storybook. You've got a great face, except your eyes maybe, they make you look a bit like a cat, but, anyway, to be honest I like women to be a bit more normal. I'm sure some people have thoughts about aliens, you know, thoughts like that, but not me. I wouldn't even be surprised if you had a tail under that frock. You are simply very, very strange.'

Chepi wound her tail in tightly against her. She felt like crying. She had been going to show him that next, she thought it really suited her. 'You're a pig, d'you know that? And it's not a frock it's a gown.'

Of course it wasn't true, what he'd said, her appearance was something beyond any dream, but being told he was disgusting to look at and smelled like bad breath from a camels arse he had no refuge but denial and counter attack.

'Whatever.' He said unhelpfully. 'But now we know we're not going to fall madly in love with each other can you tell me why you're here and why it's now that you've decided to come out of the closet and show that, without any doubt, you must something to do with that Sphere that, incidentally, seems to have no purpose in life except to hang around distracting people from getting on with their normal lives. And, in fact, in that sense, from what I know about you, you seem to have an awful lot in common.'

'We have a purpose.'

'And that is?'

'We have to wait for Nitu.'

Zen looked up in surprise. 'Nitu's coming? And she knows about this?'

'Yes and no; she's coming but she doesn't know I'm here. And when I say coming, I mean she's coming over to the Island. I don't think she knows you're here either.'

'So, basically this is all about, what, jumping out and shocking her again?'

'No, nothing like that.'

'Then what?'

'We'll have to wait and see. I'm not really sure' She added hesitantly.

Zen frowned. 'I don't understand, you've come to meet her when she gets here but you don't know why?'

'No, yes, well not exactly; not just that. I don't even know why I'm here on this planet, why the Sphere came here. It seems like I have to work it out myself.'

Zen sighed impatiently but decided that the ludicrousness of that statement was too much to deal with right then. 'And what's Nitu got to do with this? She's right you know, you have been kind of stalking her.'

'I know, but she was my link to here. The only person who might lead me to what I had to find.'

Given Nitu's interests that seemed reasonable. 'Because of the stones?'

'Yes, and the fact that she's not human either.'

Zen laughed. 'You can say that again.'

'No, really, the Sphere made her. She's an avatar.'

Zen stared long and hard. 'A robot?'

'Don't be ridiculous. She's a real living being just like you are, but not one born here, that's all.'

'And that's all?'

'Yes?'

'You don't understand us very well at all do you?'

'No.' She openly admitted.

'You don't even try.'

'I have no interest to be honest.'

'Except in Nitu.'

'And what it is I have to do here.'

Zen wasn't finished with the need for explanations. 'And me? I thought we were kind of becoming friends.'

'I think you're important, otherwise Nitu wouldn't have picked you.'

'Important?' He waited. 'I guess that will have to do.' Chepi didn't say anything. Zen changed the subject. 'So she knows she's an avatar? I only ask because knowing you I really think you probably haven't even told her'

'Well, no I haven't and she didn't. I mean she probably does by now.'

To Zen this type of situation was becoming all too familiar. 'You've done something, haven't you?'

'She did it, I just helped.'

'Care to tell me?'

'No.'

'Why? I thought I was important.'

Chepi didn't answer, she could tell that as usual with humans the discussion was going nowhere. Teetering on the verge of boredom and lacking any direction from either the Sphere or anything else, she decided to do something completely different. She stood and walked the length of the cabin, and began to touch everything strangely and with great care, as though everything on the boat had inexplicably become an important part of some unknown ritual. Bemused, Zen watched her without comment. For once he didn't want to interrupt. Whatever she said next he wanted it to come straight from her. He thought that maybe that way she'd say something meaningful for once.

When she did finally did communicate it wasn't with words but a slowly beginning transformation that gathered pace with every sweep of her hands across the unclean surfaces of the boat. Strange insects began to fill the cabin with flapping wings and chirps, and softer sounds that almost made music to the rhythm of the colours that dazzled every corner. Creatures he'd never seen before flashed into existence and began moving with purpose beyond instinct. They were creating something, he sensed that, but what it was lay a long way beyond him. He heard them whisper and saw Chepi respond, and as though following her instructions the lives she'd brought from wherever it was they belonged began to fade into the wood and cause deep etches to appear along its surface. He traced a finger along one of the patterns they left behind and he heard a silent voice talk to him in a language he couldn't understand. He looked up and saw Chepi watching him.

'What have you done?'

'Brought these old lives back to us.'

He heard the 'us' in what she said and it filled him with some strange kind of hope that somehow she'd decided there was a link, something to bind them to a common purpose, but the rest didn't sound right, the lives had gone, spent themselves into the dead body of the boat. 'And now they've gone again.' He said.

She frowned, and then realised his mistake. 'No, they've returned.'

'Were they supposed to tell me something?'

'We have to go.' She climbed back up to the deck. Zen followed.

The boat had been changed outside as well as in the interior. The etchings covered the deck and mast, and Zen guessed the hull was changed too.

'You chose really well.' She said.

He knew what she meant. 'I like wooden boats.'

'Can you make it go?'

'To where?'

'The shore, for now.'

Glad for the chance to regain some control, Zen lifted the anchor and using the slight breeze of the approaching dawn he let her sail slowly deeper into the bay until they were only feet from the rocks at the side. He dropped the anchor and made it fast and then looked back to Chepi. She didn't say anything, instead she turned away from him and let the gown fall, and he could see that she did, indeed, have a tail.

Now you're just showing off, he said to himself.

Her appearance switched in an instant as her skin rippled with changes of colour until it matched the forest behind. In much less than a second she blended perfectly into the landscape. So well that even on the boat he found it hard to make her out clearly. She smiled and her white teeth made a line in the dark camouflage of her face. 'Want to come?' She asked.

'Where?'

'To find Nitu.'

She held out her hand. He moved towards her and they linked hands. He was careful to maintain eye contact.

She squeezed his hand with unexpected strength. He tried not to flinch, but the pain distracted him. Beyond the discomfort, it transformed him in someway, he felt differently somehow. He unconsciously followed Chepi effortlessly onto the steep rocks of the shore. From the rocks they flowed silently into the forest and then flitted like shadows deep into the interior.

They travelled for an hour or more and then stopped. Chepi sat on a fallen tree and looked carefully around her.

'What is it?' He asked nervously. She looked concerned and that didn't seem to bode too well for where they were.

Chepi shrugged. 'I think I'm lost.'

If she had hit him with a dead rat he wouldn't have been any more surprised. He couldn't believe that was possible. 'You think you're lost? You're kidding, right?'

'No. I mean I don't think I know where we are.'

'Okay, let me get this right. You transform yourself into some kind of mythical creature, conjure up alien insects that bond themselves into the hull of my new boat, turn into a chameleon and all so you can get us lost in the middle of some forest? Nitu's right, you are an idiot.' He stood. "Okay, point me in the right direction, I'm off back to the boat.'

'It's not your boat.'

'What?'

'You said it's your boat but I know for a fact it's not.'

'Does that really matter?'

Chepi was about to reply but Zen's patience was waning. 'Just don't interrupt, okay?'

She kept silent.

'And anyway, it is now.' He watched her carefully for any sign of disagreement. He hated the thought of her spreading rumours about him being a thief. Knowing that any kind of disagreement would irritate him, she kept quiet.

Zen heard the silent peace offering and shifted back to complaining about her getting them lost. 'Fine. So, why d'you have to be naked, why camouflage yourself somehow, flick your tail, which does suit you by the way, and then drag us both off into the middle of nowhere?'

'Thanks, I thought you hadn't ...'

'Don't interrupt! Why drag us through the forest like meandering ghosts on speed when you can't even navigate properly! Have you ever considered sitting down and making a plan instead of running around all over the place at random?'

'Mother nature doesn't work like that.'

'No it doesn't does it. Instead of sending someone who could solve whatever it is you're supposed to be doing, it gave us you.'

'She never ploughs a straight furrow.'

'She? No, never mind, the last thing I need is a goddess story from you. The only thing that's relevant, if anything is, especially in a crisis like now, is that rather than getting to the point, the natural world, or whatever mystical beings you people claim magically run everything, tend to zigzag around for millennia trying to find something that works, all of which sounds more than a bit like you.' When he'd finished he was left with the sense that he was starting to drift off the point too. He blamed Chepi. 'Anyway, what's nature got to do with you?'

She shrugged again.

'That's a bad habit you've got.'

'What?'

'That shrug.'

'Don't be petty.'

'So, anyway, what's the explanation?'

'I didn't want it to know where we are.'

'It?'

She pointed upwards. 'The Sphere.'

'And having a sense of direction somehow gives you away does it?'

'It usually shows me where to go.'

'Well, you're a big girl now, maybe you should start working it out for yourself.'

'That's what it says.'

'God, you sound like my twelve year old niece. Just how old are you?'

'I'm very old, but not all that experienced in dealing with beings like you, or any other primate types. You think all this human stuff is natural, but it's not to me. All the weird things you do. I'd have to be insane to make any sense of it.'

'Like wearing clothes.'

'Yeah, if you like. What's the point of that?'

'Warmth.'

'Freakish taboos more like. You're a very strange bunch of people. I don't know why the Illivian bother with you.'

'The who?'

'Nitu's people.'

'I thought she was a robot.'

Chepi stared at him with the most inscrutable expression he'd ever seen. 'Don't be childish.'

'Whose being childish?'

'I don't believe it, you bicker like the frakking Sphere.'

Zen shook his head. 'If it has to look after you all the time, I'm not surprised.'

'I said don't be childish.'

He bit his lip and breathed deeply. 'Look, are you going to get us out of here? And while you're at it you could put some clothes on as well, if that's okay.'

'Do you really find me that disgusting to look at?'

'Chepi, just get us out of here.'

'Where d'you want to go?'

'Didn't you have somewhere in mind?' He asked sarcastically.

'Not really; to be honest I was just showing off.'

For the first time he felt his temper slip. 'And why the frak would you do that?'

'Research?'

This pressed a button that Zen had thought well hidden. He hated research; he saw it as the first and last refuge of the vain and over excitable. Although it'd been his career up until the Sphere arrived, mostly he'd only used it as a way of earning money, gaining prestige, and avoiding manual labour, especially anything outside, where it was invariably cold and wet. He researched in the warm and dry confines of the University while he focused on his personal development. In his heart Zen had always wanted to be a writer. Not an ordinary writer, he didn't care about money and film rights, but someone who could make a difference. That had been his dream, and it still was. He believed it was a way to do something extraordinary, whereas research he saw as mostly the poorly written ramblings of people with minds so disciplined to mediocrity that they would wouldn't recognise a new idea unless it popped up unexpectedly painted in the brightest crimson and wearing a funny hat.

Chepi saw his face distort with unknown emotions. 'I thought you liked research.'

'Not really.'

'You must be a good actor then.'

'You have to be.'

'I told you. You humans, you're weird.'

'Just don't do any more research, okay?'

'Then how can I found out what I'm supposed to be doing?'

'Believe me, if it's important it'll just come to you.'

'Just like that?'

'Yes. Or just make something up, that often works.'

She stood up. 'Maybe there's hope for you after all.'

The forest blinked out and Zen found himself sitting in the Urban Pit with a beer in his hand. He whirled around to find Chepi, and panicked momentarily. Luckily, though, she was dressed and back to her normal self, except for the woollen hat she had pulled down over her ears.

'Thank God for that.' And the he peered closely. 'Where's your tail?'

'Still here.'

'Must be uncomfortable.'

'Not really.'

He sipped his beer. 'So we weren't lost?'

'I talked to the Sphere.'

'Bet that pleased it.'

'Sure, it loves me.'

'Yes, I'll bet it does. But we're here now because?'

'Nitu's just about to come in. It should be fun.'

Zen looked at her closely. 'Fun? Why?'

There was no time to answer. The door behind them swung open and Zen could tell by the gasps around him that something else had been sent to spoil his barely begun retirement.

They both turned to face the door and were greeted by hundreds of multi-coloured humming birds streaming in behind Nitu. They filled the bar with dazzling wings beating a myriad of fast rhythms resonating into strange melodies that slowed hearts and plucked tears from happy faces as their numbers swelled until the whole room danced with light like a waterfall of rainbows crashing around them. People stood and clapped and others cried with laughter.

Nitu found their table and sat down. Before Zen could speak someone brought a carafe of something. It was carved strangely with patterns like cascading glaciers that matched exactly the three glasses that were so cold the frost collecting around them cracked and hissed like a tumbling icefall. Liquid was poured and a cold mist wafted up and chilled the air around them.

'Some entrance.' Zen observed, deadpan.

Nitu glance at him before sipping her drink. Chepi followed suit and then they exchanged words Zen couldn't understand. 'You should try it.' Nitu said to him.

He took a tentative taste, and then a longer swallow. As the icy tang slipped down easily and cooled his thoughts he was certain he could hear a message being beaten out by the hasty wings all around him. It was only a fleeting sensation, and one quickly overtaken by the shift in mood of the whole room as kaleidoscopically pattern bats followed the humming birds into the bar. They were quickly followed by a wind of leaves that filled the gaps between dazzle and songs already threaded into every tiny space. Soon the light from outside failed to find a way through and the bar became like a sea of colours and sound so tangible that people tried excitedly to hold it against them in happy, carefree embraces.

The light of rainbows grew so bright that the roof disappeared and the walls vanished. There was nothing left but light and shade, and eager faces waiting for the next turn of magic to daze them into beliefs they'd never known existed.

These moments began Nitu's transmogrification from avatar to Faun. Although later those in the bar would be able truthfully to claim they were there when the world shifted and a creature of long-lost legend reappeared, they would never be able to describe how beautiful it was, how stunning was the creature that came amongst them at that ordinary time on a wet Vancouver Monday morning. Zen could, he'd been watching closely and he kept his cool throughout. At the precise moment she switched and vanished, he turned to Chepi and asked her what exactly it was she thought she was doing.

'Don't ask me.'

'Where's she gone?'

'Don't know.'

'What did she say, when you spoke?'

'Not much, she just said 'watch this', and then you saw the rest.'

'Watch this?'

'Roughly, it's hard to translate.'

'So nothing crucial missing, perhaps?'

'The sense of it maybe, but nothing objective.'

'And the sense was?'

'Big.'

In exasperation Zen turned to drink the strange concoction Nitu had somehow ordered, but like her it too had gone. Working hard to avoid being irritated, he grabbed for the beer instead.

'She took it with her.' Chepi explained, stating the obvious.

'Kind of her.'

'You'd think so if you knew what it was.'

Zen froze. 'Like what exactly.'

'Hard to translate.'

'But I'd guess something disgusting?'

'No. But, well, with you humans who can tell.'

Zen was about to tell her when something else caught his attention.

With Nitu gone the enchantment she'd had woven with the birds and bats began to dissipate, and as the last few left, the roof reappeared. Even more miraculously, as though on queue everyone in the bar quietly moved back where they'd been before it had all begun. Some of the peculiar atmosphere nevertheless somehow remained, and in the newly hushed silence it was allowed to linger like a favourite taste as they quietly pondered the vision that already seem almost impossible. Finally, as the fading colours shifted back to the grey light of the city all trace of what had happened was lost to sight. It was a hint to leave, and almost as one everyone but Chepi and Zen obediently filed out of the bar in silence. Familiar music echoing from the walls that closed behind the last of the departing was all that was left.

'That was really strange.' Chepi volunteered.

'D'you really think so?

'Yeah, sure, they all just upped and left.'

Zen didn't bother to respond. He sipped his beer and tried to work out how he could get back to his boat without having to take Chepi with him.

Ω

The Canadian PM's hopes of building a spiritual city of the North, a Rome of the new age, came crashing down the moment the Sphere vanished from the Yukon and reappeared over Victoria. As luck would have it, or not in their case, that happened at the exact moment two of the Generals were explaining to him that with all the prostitution, drug dealing, fraud, smuggling, police brutality, false imprisonment, and illegal military activity taking place it might be a good idea to reconsider his plans and relocate back to Ottawa as soon as possible.

The PM took the timely disappearance to be a sign from the Sphere that the comments were not only unhelpful, after all driving everyone back to the East would be expensive and time consuming, but also probably blasphemous. He had them crucified, not literally of course, but in the sense of making sure it would impossible for them to work again, let alone hold a commission in Her Majesty's armed forces. Which actually they no longer held anyway, as the Queen had withdrawn her patronage from Canada and transferred it to British Columbia on the pretext that given that the old Canada had acted illegally the true Canada became de facto BC. Of course that wasn't really true, she just happened to like BC more, it reminded her of Scotland before her ancestors destroyed it with aggressive logging practices, the overstocking of red deer for hunting and through filling the place with sheep to make a quick profit. The Queen didn't like sheep, but she was a fan of irony.

Faced with his disastrous rejection by the Sphere, the PM launched his final great project. Bringing all his troops together in a last great assault against reality he marched his army from every corner of Canada and amassed them on the border of BC some two hundred miles north east of Vancouver on the Alberta border. It was to be a pincer movement that would have put the Romans to shame and the plan was so well drawn that even his few remaining Generals looked forward to a quick victory and a salmon supper on the deck of some commandeered yacht before the week's end.

It started well and the army made 40 miles through almost impenetrable forest during the first two days. Their progress at this time was unimpeded and, as any army would, they found this reassuring. Alas, though, their confidence was misplaced. They took their progress to mean that the BC army lacked the courage to face them, the truth however was very different, the fact was there was no

BC army. No one, not even Simon, had thought to create one. It was thought to be both a waste of resources and oppressive, and clearly the last thing that would gain favour in the land where whale worship came into being so fast that within days no one could remember a time when orcas hadn't been gods. British Columbians prayed to nature, they didn't go to war.

Which as luck would have it was exactly the right thing to do. Nature heard and in terms of warfare that meant the same creatures responsible for destroying the army from the east. They drifted in one night with the casualness of supreme confidence and didn't leave until there was nothing left to consume. Even the PM comfortably at home in Ottawa didn't escape, nor did his family, nor anyone he cared about. The newspapers reported his death as the strange incident of the domestic cat gone mad, but those who knew better knew differently, and no one else believed it either. This started the long road away from nature on the part of new Canadians. Even pets became taboo. The fear of domestic pets began a long chain of influences that slowly spread across the globe as people everywhere but in BC closed themselves off from the natural world, and in pursuit of the illusion of safety devoted their time to watching television and tweeting about how safe they felt since they'd stopped going outside.

Ω

In BC, and especially on Vancouver Island, things couldn't have been more different. Ever since the Monday Bugle carried photographs of a beautiful, naked, alien looking young woman running through the forests surrounding Victoria, the capital city, a sudden renaissance of naked tree worship emerged. Deep down inside human beings had never really been happy about being clothed, chaste and far too disciplined. All they had been waiting for was a sign from the heavens, the afterworld, their ancestors or some random prophet with the answer to everything at their fingertips and they were ready to shift back to the old ways in a jiffy. So when surprisingly and against all the odds there appeared suddenly a naked doe-eyed alien with a neat body running around forests in broad daylight without being metaphorically flogged in public by a repressed religious group, or beaten by political police protecting the corporate social order, they joined her as fast as they could. Public nudity and blatant tree-worship, both great threats to democracy, were literally out in the open.

'I see they've published that photograph of Nitu running about starkers in Sooke again.' Zen casually commented.

Chepi flipped her tail but otherwise didn't answer.

'How long did you say you were staying?' Zen asked.

'I told you, as soon as I've worked out what Nitu's up to.'

'Tree worship isn't it, to add to the whale thing?'

But Chepi wasn't listening. 'I told you, as soon as I know what she's playing at.'

Truth be told, Zen was no more interested than she was. 'It used to be as soon as you'd worked out why you're here.'

'I think they're connected.'

'Why the Sphere doesn't just tell you is beyond me.'

'Me too.'

Zen put the newspaper down. 'You don't seem to care very much.'

Chepi gave him an odd, worried look. 'We're not married you know.'

A trace of horror at the thought of being married to someone out of a storybook flickered across his face. 'God forbid.'

Chepi smiled. 'Orca forbid, you mean.'

'New age hippies.'

'They've always been like that, you just never noticed.'

'Vancouver was saner.'

'I like it here.'

'Make the most of it, it won't last. The animals won't protect us forever and when the rest of the world gets its weapons of mass destruction back online we'll be in for it. There are too many mines and trees here for us to be left in peace forever.'

'I'll zap them again.'

'For how long, a thousand years, two thousand?'

Chepi sat up. 'You're right, all this very nice but it doesn't actually change the problem does it.'

'And the problem is?'

'People.'

'Why?'

Chepi was about to answer but stopped. 'Mmm, good point. Why not just leave you to get on with it.'

'And?'

But she'd vanished.

Ω

Illiaeth was waiting for Chepi to uncoil herself from sleep. The Sphere had warned her that it might be a long time but she waited patiently, silently watching until her first stirrings sent ripples through the stillness. Chepi stretched and yawned and flicked her tail at the sun as though in protest at the world pressing itself back into her consciousness.

It had been a month since she'd been pulled away from Zen, and during that time she'd travelled like no other member of her species ever had before. It'd been a gift from the Sphere and from Illiaeth. She travelled to an ice filled world peopled by fur-clothed races of tall, lithe movement and charmed songs who lived in a place where the night and days fell equally and trees grew to heights that stretched above the towering cliffs cutting through their lands and made it a labyrinth of hidden vales and lakeland plains. She danced through the night with a black skinned race of giants dwelling on a parched land of heat and beauty as they welcomed the dawn on a special day when their seven suns rose together to bring the dawn. The web-handed races of the blue world of endless seas made her a princess and so she lived with them for a thousand years before their passage to the stars left her to chose between a life as a spirit or a return to her journey through worlds of the seven Peoples. She returned and drifted through space and time with the massive beings dwelling in the centre of the most magnificent blue bright stars the universe had willed into being. Their wisdom wrapped itself around her in a trillion tales of understanding as they filled her mind with the last secrets of their ancient kind. Leaving them she travelled alone on a colossal sailing vessel that could navigate the stars as well as the oceans of the greatest planets that had ever formed. And on the most azure of them all she came across the fishers of truth who blessed each day and every life they shared with prayers and blessings so profound she cried each day at the fortune that had brought them into being and made them whole. They sent her on her way with the skills of the ocean navigator and the good sense of people who had lived long enough to know a life of value is found at its nexus. They pointed her towards a world of mountains and cool air as clear and intoxicating as the purest mountain stream that tumbled down its endless waterfalls. And in the mountains she found her own kind guarding the ways of the magical West as they created the heavens in tales told by ancient pillars of stone carved with the lives of souls dancing in bright colours on wings as fine as the breath of life itself. They held her tightly to them and wrapped her in tales that finally stirred the sense of purpose buried deeply inside her that had been left there quietly resting while she found her way in the worlds in innocent pleasure. She was the child of them all brought into being to bring a new mind to grasp the wonder of the creations and tilt the balance of life in favour of a small light that grew unsteadily in the distant realms. Her life was to learn, else its nature blink out and be lost forever. She curled around them and embraced a million caresses before she left and found her way back so the old lives could be retold and correct the strange path that no life had expected would ever come to pass.

She came back to a Sphere that none before her had ever known and warmed to the life brought to her by the seven worlds through the dreams of Illiaeth and the friendship of LIlyanhiviian itself, this village of life nestled at the very beginning of time. Glad that the seconds of her absence were over the Sphere touched her with light floating like cosmic dust around her until she slept, only to awaken as meaning and propose were finally resolved.

'Frak, what was that all about?' She asked dreamily.

No one answered. She shrugged and curled her tail briefly around Illiaeth before leaving to talk to the trees.

Ω

Zen waited a few days before deciding that Chepi wasn't going to return. Eventually bored with waiting he lifted anchor and set sail first for Cortez Island and then on to the more distant lands beyond. He made good time and two days later he dropped anchor in a remote, unnamed bay. He sat idly for an hour or two basking in the pleasure of a passage well made before the growing sound of movement on the bank behind him broke through the scattered daydreams of a tired mind. Turning he had expected to find a few bears foraging along the shore, as they always had been in the stories his father told him. Instead the beach was lined with more grizzlies than anyone could easily count, and more wolves than you could shake a stick at mingled in amongst them like infantry between the heavy armour of an invading force.

He shifted nervously, ready to haul the anchor if any showed the least sign of entering the water. But none of them moved, they just stood silently watching, hardly stirring as some unknown purpose bound them to the land. He stood and shouted and waved his arms hoping to trigger some reaction, but there was none. Unnerved he was preparing to leave when the largest cougar he'd ever seen made its way through their ranks to stand at the very edge of the water, and following behind came Nitu, or at least what Nitu had become.

'You're either very brave or very stupid.' She called over.

'Listen who's talking.' She looked different. 'And what's that you're wearing?'

'Nothing, it's me.'

'So she got to you after all.'

'Who?'

'Chepi, who else.'

'Not seen her.'

'Are you coming over, or have we got to shout like this all day?' He asked.

'I'll come over.'

He hesitated. 'You're not dangerous are you?'

'Not to you.'

'Hang on though, what exactly are you now? The last time I saw you, you were running around naked.'

'I didn't see you.' She said, surprised.

'Not actually saw you, I mean in the newspapers.'

'Oh, that, that was months ago. Took me a bit of time to get the hang of this.'

He still wasn't certain she was safe to be with, or wouldn't bring one of her pets with her, but he couldn't see any other way of finding out what she was doing. 'Okay, come over. D'you need me to get the tender?'

'No.' She dived into the water and seconds later came up

alongside the boat. 'Pull me up.'

Once she was on deck Zen found it hard to work out what he was really looking at. 'Is that really you, or is it body paint?'

'It's me.'

'You kind of look like Chepi.'

'I don't think so. She's not really female anyhow, well, at least not in the human sense.' And then she looked at him intently. 'Hang on, how would you know?'

'How do I know? Because, you both seem set on turning this place into some kind of nudist colony for the deranged.'

She couldn't hide her surprise. 'You mean she looks like this now?'

Zen grimaced at the memory of their strange flight through the forest. 'For a while, I've no idea why. She got us lost in a forest trying to hide from the Sphere, or so she said, and then the next thing we were in the Urban Pit waiting for you.'

She laughed quietly to herself. 'Yeah, sorry about that, but it was awesome, don't you think?'

He wasn't listening, instead was trying to peer behind her.

'What the frak are you doing?'

'You got a tail?'

'No, why?'

'She had.'

'She's different.'

'I know. That much would be obvious to anyone.'

'No, I mean really different.'

'And you're normal I suppose?' He paused. 'Look, I know you were never really one of us.'

'Not one of whom?'

'Chepi told me you're a robot.'

'I think she probably said avatar. And, yes, I know, but now I'm something different.'

'What?'

'I'm Faun.'

'D'you know how stupid that sounds?'

She sat down and stretched her legs across the cockpit. Zen tried successfully not to look too closely beneath the patterns, which somehow gave the safe illusion that he wasn't actually having a conversation with a completely naked version of the woman he'd fallen in love with the moment he first saw her.

'Life's full of surprises.' She said.

He decided he could play games too. 'What I mean is, if you were a Faun you'd have a tail and the legs of a deer.'

'Don't believe everything you read.'

'So, anyway, just out of interest, what exactly is the difference between a Faun and a naked woman wearing body paint?'

Nitu held up a finger and a flower sprouted from its tip. It opened slowly into a bright bloom of vivid reds and pale green.

Zen feigned indifference. 'Could be a trick. But, have to admit, your eyes are different, they make you look a bit like Bambi.'

'Whatever.' She shifted position self-consciously. 'But it's not 'a' Faun, it's just 'Faun'.'

'As in a kind of collective sense?'

'Bit more in the sense of there being only one.'

Zen wondered momentarily if this new bit of information was worth thinking about. He was growing tired of all the relentless weirdness. 'Look, is there a point to all this or are you and Chepi simply misguided freaks of nature?'

She jumped up suddenly, as though she'd remembered something important. 'I'd love to explain, but right now I've got to go and address the United Nations.'

'Dressed like that?' Not the most useful thing he could have said, but under the circumstances it was all that came to mind.

'No, most of them are probably perverts, I'll put a frock on.'

'Maybe a gown would go better. Fit the occasion.'

'Don't fuss. You sound like my mom.' And with that she dived back into the water and disappeared.

It took Zen a few hours and a handful of cold beers to take the edge off his frustration. All he'd wanted to do was enjoy his amazingly early retirement, not get dragged into the mad lives of mythical beings. Worst of all, he knew events were far from over. As he stared into the dozens of eyes of the still unmoving bears and wolves watching him with an intent he didn't exactly relish, he could sense, as anyone in those circumstances would, that none of what was happening was taking place purely by chance.

Ω

Although at this time the United Nations was no more relevant or influential than it had ever been, it was nevertheless the only organisation that could in any way even pretend to represent humanity, hence the hurriedly convened meeting. Thus in many ways what was happening was what had always happened, with the exception that this time the pointlessness of the exercise was more apparent.

Although no one would own up to it, being addressed by an alien entity was in many ways no different from being summonsed and dictated to by the US, the permanent members of the Security Counsel or some deranged leader of a country hounded into submission by gun toting children and psychotic adults. Except, that is, on this occasion the power involved was bit more impressive and certainly more inscrutable than even the murkiest gathering of power mongers or commodity company Chief Executives and their militarily intelligence lackeys. This was the real thing, and for the former powerful it was a bit like the transition from the playground of the infant school to the concrete acres of the big school down the road. From being at the top of the heap, in control and able to steal anyone's candy they were now metaphorically huddled behind the unwashed masses waiting for some slim chance to join the next gang, no matter what the admission fee might be. Except for those who had already done so, in situations like these they'd sell their own mothers and feed their children to anything hungry enough to want them to get a head start on the next big thing. As politicians and business leaders always did, they knew that the next major opening was always the last major opening, and that this time, rebuilding from the chaos of destruction that now surrounded them was a once in a million life times opportunity not to be missed at any cost. They even had a strong sense of purpose to motivate them further. People had been killed to get them to the meeting, and that wasn't something to be squandered easily. After all, like anyone else, they did have a conscience.

The Sphere's message to meet came as the biggest shock in politics since the birth of the last major prophet. No one had expected it and therefore no one was in a position to make the first move. The Permanent Members were, of course, not on speaking terms. Even considering long-standing mutual agreements over the exploitation of the world's resources, the invasion from the East had tended to unbalance everyone. This meant that even a quick phone call to manipulate a cast iron veto for no other reason than naked self-interest wasn't possible. And so, when Nitu arrived to address the General Assembly she didn't face a cynical fait accompli, as was the norm, but instead a frightened bunch of people who felt abandoned to their own resources. It was a terrifying time for them, and they all, in the greatest show of hidden agreement in human history, pledged in secret to themselves that they wouldn't say a word until they found out just how they could wring something out of the event, no matter how small and personal.

So it was a hushed, divided and totally self-absorbed audience that greeted the first non-human to address the best of humankind. Or rather the lamentable best the world's democracies could cobble together to provide a mockery of representation. The shallowness of the gathering wasn't lost on Nitu, one look and she wished they'd acted a thousand years earlier and been been able to address the Althing in Iceland instead. She almost turned to go, but they'd caught a glimpse of her and gasps of shock resounded around the assembly room. After that, she couldn't resist walking out to show them what they had missed out on by choosing technology over the ancient forests. A few different decisions down the line and they could have had someone exactly like her leading them instead of semi-illiterate financiers and lawyers from the back end of beyond whose only value was as a reminder that left unshepherded, most human beings were basically despicable.

Whatever they had been expecting, her appearance staggered them. She was Faun, there was no doubting that, even though none of them had the slightest idea what it meant. When out of courtesy the Sphere had told them what she was, hurried research had led them to expect a half human half antelope hybrid of possibly disquieting appearance. Some said it was Pan arriving from hell to punish them, and yet others, the majority, with no official briefing to help them, had no view whatsoever. So her entrance came as a surprise to all. Tall, slender and strangely beautiful in an unmistakeable, unknowable way, her appearance bewitched them. She calmed the timid, cautioned the brave and put the fear of God into those of strange tastes who had secretly thought that for the good of mankind they would seduce her at the earliest opportunity. Faced with the reality of perfect humanoid potential, they had to conclude that power was not, after all, the greatest aphrodisiac.

She sensed all of this in the briefest of moments and acted to warn them that all was not as they would wish. In an instant she changed. Her aura no longer gave encouragement, her eyes touched no one with fondness or welcome, her movements scared them and brought to mind dark places from the wilderness of their biggest fears.

She reached the podium and stood silently for several minutes. Scholars would later argue vehemently through the deepest hours of the night about what the gesture had meant, but in truth it was merely a whim. Having once almost been human, she understood how unexpected silence could torment those with too much to say. Which so far as she could recall, meant almost all of them.

When the silence ended words of condemnation were spoken, their sound chiming like the song of a mermaid.

'There has been a mistake.' She said.

Above them a three dimensional Earth appeared. It was spinning slowly on its axis. Nitu pointed and the along the Pacific Northwest, all the Pacific Islands and the West coast of South America nearly all the lights of cities blinked out as the land turned green. This blanket then spread slowly across the globe until only the densest areas of human habitation were left untouched.

'Move your people before the forests consume them.' She suggested helpfully.

It wasn't what they'd expected. They'd thought she would have the wisdom of Solomon or Moses, and would enchant them with tales of the magnificence of humankind and amazing futures that lay ahead. They'd expected her to show them the way to profit, the stars and instant fame. Instead she sounded like a member of the Raincoast Protect League at some Stonehenge gathering of the International Tree Huggers Convention. It was a huge disappointment.

The Globe vanished and she left. Not grandly with a swirling exit of pomp and circumstance, she just left, One second there and the next gone.

The meeting sat silently and unmoving for endlessly long

minutes while they waited for something else to materialize, some sign to show itself that the meeting wasn't over, that the best was being kept for last; that she'd return and give them something for being such a good audience, a prize for not only being human but for being especially good at it.

They waited, but nothing more happened, and so eventually they began to leave. Cautiously, quietly, only timidly making eye contact with the person nearest to them they filed out in sombre mood. It was only outside in the blaze of television cameras from all over the world that they regained their composure and began glibly to lie about everything that had taken place. And when that solemn duty had been fulfilled they smoothly made their various ways to their country estates or elegant town houses, packed everything of value, their great works of art borrowed from somewhere or another and never returned, first edition books collected on behalf of the People and kept in their care for the good of everyone including posterity itself, fine wines to covet and to bribe, and lastly their partners and children.

The essentials of life taken care of, they quickly removed themselves from any source of danger and headed for the safety of the biggest city outside the Green Zone, as it became to be known. It was only when all this was done, had been coordinated across continents through silent complicity with a degree of perfection that would have staggered the best Roman Centurion or beach master at the Normandy landings, it was only then that they made the news public.

$$\Omega$$

Reluctantly, Nitu travelled to the Sphere to talk to Chepi. Since her transformation she had become obsessed with forests, trees and wild life, especially the dangerous kind, which she now saw as the ultimate source for good in the world. Given that gnarled oaks and scruffy, large mammals were now her thing, she found the perfect symmetry of the Sphere somewhat offensive, and that alone was enough to start her complaining endlessly about the injustice of everything she no longer valued.

'Stop moaning.' Chepi urged. 'You were the same when you thought you were human, always going on about something or other.'

'You've got room to talk.'

Chepi looked affronted. 'I've never complained about anything, except the way I'm treated by you and this thing.'

'Well, anyway, what d'you want?'

'I just wondered how you were going to get everyone moved from your Green Zone into the cities, and then keep them there?'

'Why is that my problem? They've screwed up and now they'll have to accept the consequences.'

'Bit callous isn't it?' Chepi asked.

'And when have they shown any sympathy for my trees? So many of those ancient, precious souls lost, all the animals displaced and left with nowhere to go, or murdered for fun.'

'Your trees and animals?'

'According to this obscenely shiny thing we're in, I'm the custodian now. Don't tell me it didn't tell you?'

'No, it didn't.' She wasn't too pleased at the news. 'So what does that make me exactly?'

Nitu smiled as nicely as she could. 'You've done your bit. You made all this possible; brought me to Illiaeth and helped me become Faun.'

That was news to her; no one had yet told her that this newly emerged shambles was what she had been supposed to bring about. To her it'd all seemed like a big mistake, a chaotic mess bumbling its way through her life for no reason except to cause her unparalleled levels of inconvenience. Now it seemed that having thousands of people eaten by wild animals, disrupting all life on a planet, banishing a complete species of almost sentient beings to a life of poverty and squalor in tiny industrialised enclaves where natural resources will never again be available, had for some reason been her mission in life. Condemning them to die horribly and miserably, solely so Nitu could get a bigger garden and a wider variety of pets. 'You've become very self-obsessed you know.'

Nitu shrugged. 'I've always been self-obsessed. You made me think I was human don't forget, and what they call middle-class as well. No point in making a wheel and then complaining that it rolls downhill.'

'Maybe it's me, you know all the experience I've had travelling around the universe looking at stuff, but I don't really think my whole purpose here was to enable you to run around naked befriending dangerous animals.'

'Then why is all this happening?'

'Because you're self-obsessed, I just said so. And for some reason the Sphere's going along with it.'

Nitu crossed her legs and leant back against the wall. To Chepi she looked annoyingly comfortable. 'It's what Faun does.' Nitu explained unhelpfully.

'And please stop referring to yourself in the third person. It sounds pretentious.'

Nitu raised her eyebrows. 'Can a mythical being be pretentious?'

'It would seem so.' Chepi replied snootily.

Nitu fidgeted, clearly bored and ready to leave. 'Can I go now? The wolves need feeding.'

'That's disgusting.'

'So you expected them all to die peacefully did you? Either that or you thought I'd role over and let those humans assassinate anything that could run around, and burn everything else that couldn't so they can sit in their cars and planes and get fatter and fatter filling their photo albums with pictures of some great wilderness or other that they were so lucky to see before it got chopped down to make teak decks for some pornographer's super yacht? There are no half measures with these people. They have insatiable appetites and an unswerving ability to trick themselves into believing they are somehow the chosen species.'

Chepi wanted to cry with frustration at the impossibility of being able to play fair, save the world, if it was what they wanted, and not hurt anyone. 'I don't know do I? I don't see the point of human beings anyway.'

'Well then?' Nitu got up. Chepi could see that she was eager for action.

'No, wait, we can't just kill them all.'

'Why not?'

'It's immoral.' Chepi said unconvincingly. Even to herself she sounded hesitant. She'd never had to think about ethics before, prior to arriving on Earth everything had worked so well. Things just happened and the universe unfolded as it was supposed to. Humans, though, they had to be different.

'You're right, I suppose, they do tend to think about themselves far too much.' She admitted reluctantly.

'They have a philosopher called Kant who would argue that it's okay to kill all of them.' Nitu offered

To Chepi that seemed possible but highly unlikely. Although throughout human history there had always been people willing to commit genocide over some idea or another, she knew there were also worthwhile people down there and she thought they deserved a chance. There were people with very little, going to work at ridiculously early times for long hours so they could feed their children and send them to college, and others with virtually nothing spending their days helping those with even less. Their were groups of activists devoted to protecting the environment Nitu cared so much about, or doing what they could to ensure that democracy remained more than an experiment, an abandoned dream. She was sure that some of these were worth saving.

'Nothing you've said is wrong, but it's not the whole picture.' She said, hoping that Nitu would pause and reconsider.

Nitu struggled to remember someone she knew who was worth rescuing. It was hard, her mind was no longer human and the concepts she needed were difficult to bring back. 'Zen, maybe.' She said at last, unsure but ready to concede.

'Yeah, maybe.' And some people seem to have taken your lead and started hugging trees with a vengeance.' She added. 'They seem unworldly enough to make a good life for themselves in the forest.'

'Maybe, BC's a cool place.' Nitu grudgingly admitted.

'And what about Polynesian people, don't they deserve a second chance? They were having a great time before the Europeans arrived.'

Nitu nodded. 'And the first nations people, they always showed respect.'

'Yes, them too. When you think about it, it's the industrialised nations who were the problem, and among them, the one's with the most money' Chepi urged.

'I guess so. Some people in cities haven't even seen a cow, so what do they really know?'

Chepi didn't know what that meant, but thought better of admitting so. 'Really? Wow.'

Nitu eyed her suspiciously. 'You do know what a cow is, right?'

'Sure. An animal.'

'Why on Earth did they pick you?' Nitu asked no one in particular. 'Never mind, don't answer that.'

'So, you can't go and kill them all, it wouldn't be fair. We could save everyone in BC, the Polynesians, first nations people, and all those poor people in, say, London. We could even give them a cow each, if that'd make them happy.'

'Give them a cow each?'

The idea of giving gifts really interested Chepi. She'd never had the chance before. 'Yes, I'll do it if you like. You'd probably freak them out.'

Nitu shook her head. 'You are an idiot. You do know that don't you.'

'I just don't want to kill millions of other beings unnecessarily.'

'Billions, and if we don't they'll kill themselves anyway.'

'Billions?' Chepi asked.

'Yes.'

"How did that happen?'

'At the expense of everyone else, they made themselves way too confortable.'

'Even to Chepi, that appeared to be excessively self-indulgent. She had a moment of self-doubt. 'Maybe we should just let them wallow in their own lack of foresight?'

'And allow them to kill everything else as well? This is the whole point of what I've been saying. You can't trust them.'

'Maybe we could just unmake them?'

'What? Can we do that?'

'Yes, of course.'

'Unmake them?'

Chepi looked at her distrustfully. Clearly Nitu found this possible new form of destruction as potentially interesting as the more brutal kind. 'I don't mean literally. I mean we could go back a bit and make sure the Europeans don't get here.'

Nitu stared in amazement. 'Just like that?'

'Well, we'd have to check with the Sphere, and maybe even Illiaeth, but, yeah, sure, we could do that.'

'And that's not like killing anyone?'

'No, they'd never have been alive.'

Nitu began to think that maybe Chepi wasn't taking the issue too seriously after all. 'But they are alive now, right?'

'Yes. Why?'

'And if we go back and unmake them they won't be here when time goes forwards?'

'No, they won't be here. I thought that's what you wanted.'

'So you'd stop them from existing?'

'Yes.'

'And that's different from killing them, how?'

Chepi laughed, but a little uncertainly. 'Because they will never have existed.'

Nitu shook her head. 'That can't be right because they do exist now.'

'I know, but in the other universe they won't exist.'

Nitu definitely did not like the sound of that, it was this universe she was interested in, not some other place Chepi would pull from her sleeve in a cosmic conjuring trick. 'What other universe?

'The one we'll make.'

'The one we'll make?'

'Yes, what else.' Chepi couldn't see what the fuss was all about. It seemed like the perfect solution.

Nitu wasn't convinced. 'I'm not interested in what happens in another universe. This one, the one that exists now, it'll still exist won't it? Because if it does then ... '

'No, well yes, but only theoretically.'

'Only theoretically?'

'As a possibility.'

'A possibility?'

'A possibility declined.' Chepi explained. 'When the times comes.'

'A possibility declined when the time comes?'

Chepi glanced at her doubtfully. 'Are you getting this, or d'you just like repeating everything I say?'

Nitu ignored her. 'But we haven't declined the possibility, it's here with us now.'

'Only because we're observing it. That bit is obvious, surely?'

'And what happens to something when we decline it?'

Chepi could tell that she was getting angry. 'The quantum wave front collapses.'

'Don't start that quantum stuff again. The truth is they die, don't they.'

'No, definitely not.'

'Idiot.'

'Look, I don't get this, you wanted to slaughter all of them a few minutes ago, and now you're fussing over a collapsing quantum event.'

Nitu shifted uncomfortably. 'I just can't stand euphemisms.'

Chepi watched her warily. 'Death yes, that's okay to you, mass slaughter, no problem, but a play on words, no, not for you at any cost. You're the idiot.'

'If we're going to kill them let's be honest about it, and have good moral reasons for doing so.'

'Well, I prefer the 'not existing' scenario, but if you're set on murdering them all I'm leaving.'

'Leaving where?'

'This planet, where else.'

'And leave me to do the dirty work.'

'Your Faun, it's your job.'

'We need an emissary.' Nitu said suddenly.

'A what?'

'One of them to decide whether we should collapse their wave front or kill them all.'

Chepi wasn't sure. 'Isn't that a bit devious?'

'Sure, but who better than one of them.'

'Okay, but how do we get one?' Chepi asked.

'We could advertise.'

'Take too long. Think about all those résumés we'd have to go through. You were human, can't you think …?'

'ZEN!' They both said simultaneously.

'He'd hate it.' Chepi said.

'Maybe, but since they tortured him he's been carrying

around a bit of a grudge. It could make him more a bit more objective.'

Chepi shook her head. 'You wouldn't think so if you'd listened in on the phone calls he got when they wanted him to be PM of BC.'

'What phone calls? No, never mind. So we get Zen to do it?'

'Sounds good to me.' Chepi agreed.

They sat smiling to themselves for a couple of minutes and then Nitu zapped back to Vancouver Island to talk to Zen.

Ω

'About time.' The Sphere said.

'Are they always like that.' Illiaeth asked.

'I don't listen most of the time.'

Ω

After several nights Zen was getting used to the constant company of wolves. The bears had eventually left, but the wolves appeared to either have more patience or got hungry less often. Their persistence eventually carried an unexpected treat; it led them into his dreams. At first it was no more than a newborn's whimper, a new life beginning as a crack of light opening into a new world.

From small beginnings he soon wanted more, and in his eagerness he wrenched back the layers of foreign senses that seeped in whispers into the night like some opening to another world. They heard him and eased him from this world into theirs, and he ran with the pack in a world of a million smells that held him in a tangled rapture of unnamed textures. He was seduced by their easy gait as they looped along through forests and stealthily zigzagged meadows for tens of miles in gliding trails and soundless conversations. He joined the hunt and became one of those perfect bodies locked in a million year dance to the death as his jaws closed and opened the promise that he almost didn't dare taste. As the blood flowed he turned his mind away and jumped awake, as startled and unsure as all the times before.

Each time he awoke he climbed up onto the deck to see if the wolves were still there, and as though they knew his thoughts they always jumped up and watched him eagerly. He would sit down and wait. It was a dangerous time. He knew he was still held by the dream and had to fight the desire to swim ashore and be with them. He ached to go, but a lifetime of civilisation held him back.

'They'll kill you if you go.'

He didn't need to look round. 'Nitu, how nice, you're back.'

She ignored the sarcasm. 'Yes.'

'Wearing anything?'

'No.'

'Still Faun?'

'Yes.'

'What a waste.'

She didn't respond, at least not directly. 'What's it like to be a wolf?'

He answered without thinking. 'Easy.'

'Life is easy.'

'Not for people.'

She felt lucky. 'That's what I've come here to talk to you about.'

'Let me guess, doomed humanity? I thought you'd got all that worked out.'

'Maybe not.'

'Power's not everything then?'

'No.'

He turned around and looked at her. 'The faun thing suits you. Now I've got used to it.'

She ignored him. 'What's the best thing to do?'

He turned away. 'Frankly I don't care.'

'It's your future too. Don't you want to get married and have beautiful little children.'

'Not sure what little Faunettes would look like.'

She stiffened.

'Just kidding. Then again, look at you, how could anyone …?' But he didn't finish.

'No need to be so suggestive.'

'Sorry, it's easy to forget.'

'Back to the point, what should we do about them? There isn't much time'

'I know, I've seen the news on the internet. Thousands dead already.'

'What's best for them?' She insisted.

He felt like saying they should be left alone, but he knew it wouldn't help. 'How much of this d'you want to keep?' He waved his hand vaguely at the surrounding rainforest.

'All of it.'

'And just as it is, or d'you want it bigger.'

'It should be everywhere.'

He shrugged. 'Then kill them all and get it over with.'

'We thought maybe we could keep some indigenous, non-industrial people?'

'Just them?'

'And a few others. Those who deserve a second chance.'

'Why bother?'

'Chepi thinks genocide is a serious matter.'

He laughed. More lightly than he would have expected. 'Good for her.'

'The thing is, if we let all of them survive they'll start destroying everything again.'

He turned back to her. 'Look, why does any of this matter?'

'I'm Herne, so that makes me a sort of goddess for humans; well some of them anyway. So I guess that means I should think a bit more broadly.'

'I thought you said you were Faun.'

'I have other names.'

He shook his head. 'I'm not sure I understand, but to be honest I don't really care? Anyway, I thought 'it' was male, some kind of hunter with the head of a stag and body of a human?'

'Only animals have sex.'

He hoped not, but kept that to himself. 'Really, then what's all that stuff about the universe being half male and half female?'

'It's not true.'

'Oh.'

'Human's are, so your world is, but it's a kind of quirky thing Illiaeth thought up.'

'Promise me something?'

'Sure.'

'Please don't ever explain that to me.'

'Why?'

'Just don't.'

'Okay.'

He smiled. 'D'you know, you sound more like Chepi every time I see you.'

'I came here for your help, not to be insulted.'

'Okay, but tell me one thing. You're this mythical forest being and probably immortal and infinitely powerful, so why don't you sound a bit more intelligent than you do?'

'It's a language thing.'

'Excuse me?'

'Tell me about your dream.'

The way she asked brought the images back. He wanted to be back there right that instant. Running with the pack as they mingled in each other's lives and smells and hopes and hardships, unspoken and inseparable. 'It's too hard.'

'Like this, deciding about them?'

'Like this, talking about it.' He corrected.

It was then she glimpsed what had to be done. He was changing somehow, and that it could be what they had been looking for all along. She spoke to Chepi quietly so he couldn't hear. 'I have to go.' She said after a few moments of what he mistakenly and sadly saw as the beginning of an awkward silence.

'Sorry I couldn't help.' He said forlornly.

'Maybe we need to teach you another dialect.' And then she vanished.

He stared at the empty space. 'Brilliant.'

Ω

'Do what?'

'Give them what they need, a deity to watch over them.'

'But that's what you're supposed to be.'

'No, that was never the plan. Ask the Sphere. I'm here to clean up the mess.'

'But they already have their Gods.'

'Sure, but they're not much help are they.'

'But do they really need another one?'

'I don't mean another half-cocked idea of one, or a wild belief in something obscure and unreachable, I mean a real one.'

'Okay, fine.' Chepi said, growing a little exasperated. 'We'll ask someone if there's a spare, unemployed human-oriented deity hanging around anywhere.'

'Not human.'

'Then what? If we don't really know what we're doing how can we pick a goddess for them?'

Nitu went to answer, but whatever it was she thought she was going to say, the words never got passed her subconscious. 'I don't really know. Thought you might have an idea.'

Chepi buried her head in her hands. 'This is so embarrassing. You know they're listening to everything we say.'

'Well that's not my fault, if we could meld or something maybe we'd do a little better?'

'I know, but they're afraid of the consequences.'

'What consequences?'

Chepi shrugged. 'I don't know, they just said that and then wouldn't explain any further.'

'Typical.'

Chepi went and sat down next to her. 'Look, there's something missing, like a reason for all this, why are we bothering?'

'Because you don't want to slaughter everyone.'

'No, I mean why are we here. It's just a tiny planet in the middle of nowhere. Who cares what happens to it? Out there.' And she pointed upwards as though that helped. 'There are GALAXIES actually COLLIDING into each other. And who's doing anything about that? Not the Sphere, it takes me to watch it all unfold in brutal detail as though it's some kind of educational outing. TRILLIONS of things die when that kind of thing gets out of control, but does anyone care? No, not even the smallest fig. On the other hand, this crummy little planet overrun by semi-intelligent apes gets everyone's attention. So, you have to ask don't you, why is that exactly?'

'Okay, calm down, it's not my fault.'

'Sorry, but don't you think it's likely that somewhere along the road we've missed the obvious?'

'And that would be?'

Chepi could feel her frustration rising. 'I don't know, I just told you that.'

And in a moment the Sphere would later claim was pure serendipity, Nitu walked over to a console and put some music on.

'What the frak is that?'

'Music. It helps me think.'

'Only you could find the sound of animals copulating tuneful.'

'It's not that, it's a tree growing.'

Chepi sighed wearily. 'I thought they were the strong silent types.'

'They're everything.' She said absentmindedly.

Chepi stared at her in surprise. 'Frak they are!'

Nitu couldn't be bothered arguing about it. 'I'm the spirit of the forest, remember, not the animals. It's just that they're a bit more active, physically. Being with trees can get a bit wearing at times'

'No, I mean 'Frak, they ARE.' They are everything.'

Nitu's mood picked up a bit. 'So we can kill all the apes after all?'

Chepi ignored her. 'That's why they made you a Faun.'

'Faun.' Nitu corrected.

Chepi blinked several times. 'I … never mind. They made you Faun.' She looked over to check. There didn't seem to be any disagreement. 'Called Herne.' She checked again. 'Who's a forest spirit.'

'A wraith.' Nitu corrected.

Chepi looked surprised. 'A ghost?'

'Get to the point please.'

'Why a forest wraith?'

'To look after the forests.'

'Yes, because the trees are key to everything!' Chepi added

'D'you know, Chepi, that's hardly new. We have been talking about saving the trees for a while now. Try to stay focused.'

Chepi grinned as though she'd just won something. 'We've been talking about the environment, your bears and all that animal stuff, we've not been talking about the trees per se. Which is crazy because Illiaeth said it was all about them when I took you to see her. I thought at the time that it was a euphemism, but maybe it wasn't.'

Nitu shrugged. 'Easy mistake, but to get to the point, what the frak are you talking about?'

'Yew trees in England are up to 3,000 years old, and Bristlecone Pines in the alpine deserts of the USA about 5,000 years old.'

I know, and Sequoias can be over 3,000 years old. We know that, that's why we have to save them.'

Chepi looked like the cat that had got the cream. 'Can't you see what that means?'

She couldn't, but she pretended not to mind. It wasn't easy. 'No.'

'They must be the oldest living things in this universe.'

'How d'you work that out?'

'The speed of light of course.' She explained.

'The what?'

'Dark matter; the less of it there is now this universe is older and more complexly formed the faster light travels, and this planet happens to be in this most recent bit of the universe, so compared with almost everywhere else time here is relatively faster, or more compressed, contains more information. A few thousand years here are worth billions of years in the earlier parts. The oldest being here would be the oldest being anywhere in this part of the multiverse.'

Nitu was highly doubtful about such reckless speculation, but in case they got side-tracked again she stayed quiet.

'This is what we've been missing.' Chepi triumphantly announced

As her words echoed around inside the Sphere the light changed and they felt it depart, leaving them in a place that had no form or texture.

$$\Omega$$

Long moments of deep solitude followed the Sphere's departure before the dim shadows surrounding them shifted to the deep red of a perfect twilight. They found themselves on a sweeping desert of reds and gold flickering in the light of a 1,000 setting suns. They were standing next to a giant tree that looked more dead than alive. It's gnarled trunk looked lifeless, but despite its appearance they could feel it vibrate with a vitality its sparse foliage belied.

Chepi reached out and touched the oldest living being creation, the first soul in the infinite multiverse, and Nitu wrapped her arms around it in a tight embrace. The tree held her and she dissolved into it, vanishing completely. Chepi asked the tree why, and a branch fell in a silent crack of relief as the tree folded in on itself and melted away into the earth.

Chepi took the branch and for seven days fashioned a gigantic etched arrow and longbow from the gifted branch. When it was finished the bow was longer than she was tall and the arrow measured six feet from end to end. An eagle as light as the wind came and gave her four feathers to make the flight, and a snake gave her its skin to make the bowstring. And then she waited.

$$\Omega$$

Nitu carefully explained to Zen that the trees were the oldest living things in the universe. He argued, lining up his arguments one by one to prove that the earth was young and that there had to be planets out there in the void that were older by tens of millions of years, if not more. With great skill and even more patience she countered every play and towards the end of the discussion she explained what Chepi had told her about light, how it changed it's speed and the fact that light from the end of the universe was slower than the light here, meaning that the Earth was the first place to have life, and that the trees were the oldest things so far created in this part of reality. He countered by saying that trees were different, that trees a million years ago were not the same trees as now. She said they were the same. He refuted everything and said that it was known that the world was four and a half billion years old and life was only a few hundred million. Nitu said that on the timescale of the cosmos, of the stars at the beginning of the universe, the ones he thought so important, the Earth was only 5,000 years old. And then, finally, she explained that this was the exact moment when time began.

'Okay, I give up.' He said. 'Its crazy, but you believe it, so tell me, what difference does it make that you think that? Or even if it was true?'

'They know everything that ever happened in this place. That's obvious, isn't it?'

'And how would that be obvious?'

She took his hand. He almost flinched, but didn't. 'Everything that happens, happens everywhere.'

'And that's true because?'

'Chepi calls it quantum non-locality.'

'She would.'

'It's true.'

'I know.' He said. 'I did physics, but what could that possibly have to do with trees knowing everything?'

Nitu wanted to explain it all, but there wasn't time. She pulled him to his feet. Something he couldn't read flashed quickly across her insanely unreal but nevertheless irresistible eyes. 'Make love to me first and then I'll tell you everything.' She said.

That was the last thing he'd expected. He flushed with surprise and embarrassment. 'Wouldn't that be kind of perverted. You not being human anymore?'

She laughed. 'I promise I won't let you exploit me.'

'Yes, but ...'

'It's a yes or no kind of thing. If you make me try to persuade you, I think that with everything that's happened I'll probably just burst into tears.'

He turned away to stare at the wolves.

'Look at me.' She said.

He looked at her..

She saw what she needed to see. 'Not here.'

She took his hand again and in an instant they were stood on a remote hill with the ocean below and the horizon dancing with light and promise. It was golden in another dawn, and it made her wonder if the Sphere was watching and whether it approved.

'Let me undress you.' She asked.

'Pervert.'

They both laughed and Nitu cried a little.

She undressed him, said nice things about his body and then held him close.

Ω

Chepi waited until the sun was clear of the horizon and then she lifted the huge bow and fired the arrow high into the heavens. She watched it climb away out of sight into the morning sky and then she left the Earth.

Ω

Nitu took Zen's face in her hands. She held his eyes with hers and watched the flicker of surprise cross his face as the arrow buried itself into his brain and travelled through his spine to anchor itself into the rich ground beneath his feet. There would be only brief instant before searing, fleeting pain would find its way into his dying mind, so she reached into him and closed her hand over his senses. The pain was never felt, and the stygian cloak that fell only paused on its way somewhere else.

Nitu stood back and stroked the wolves that had followed her. Together they watched the second genesis of the Earth.

'You could have let me bonk him first.' Nitu complained.

'Sorry.'

'It was always going to be a long time after he went. It's not as though there are going to be many people to meet from now on.' She said dejectedly.

'You can bonk me if you want.' Chepi suggested.

Nitu glanced at her. 'I might need to think about that for a while, but thanks anyway.'

'You're welcome.'

'Faun and a …? What are you exactly? You've never said.'

'Illiaeth says I'm some kind of feminised representation of universal intent.'

Nitu shrugged. 'To be honest I'm not sure what that means.'

'Me neither.' Chepi said, hesitantly.

They walked on in an awkward silence for a while.

'Feminised representation? Really?'

'Apparently.'

They paused to gaze over the forest below.

The Sphere and Illiaeth have had a big falling out.' Chepi said.

'About us?'

'About me, the Sphere wants me back, but Illiaeth said no.'

'How do you feel?'

'I'd like to see what happens here. See how it turns out for Zen.'

'They call him the Yggdrasil.'

'That's nice.'

'He had a crush on me you know.'

'No, I tend not to notice things like that to be honest.'

'They worship him.' Nitu still felt some affection for him so it pleased her to see that the deity strategy had turned out okay for him.

'How long has it been for them?'

'In their time, about a thousand years.' Nitu said. 'They become more like the forest every year. The big change came when we managed to phase out opposable thumbs. They are less fixated on fiddling about with gadgets and have more time to develop their minds, and emotions. The next few thousand years could produce a big intellectual breakthrough for them.'

Chepi thought that was probably for the best. 'All's well that ends well I suppose.'

'I guess so. Pity about all the deaths we caused, but what did they expect?'

'They never expected anything.'

'Maybe that was the trouble all along, they never seemed to learn much from anything they did.'

They walked on quietly for a while. 'What should we do now?' Nitu asked.

'Be patient. Watch them carefully and hope that this time they meet their potential?'

'We've taken care of their obsession with tools, all we need now is to stop them getting into farming.'

'And keep the numbers of males in check.'

'Definitely; with social primates there always seems to be a fine balance between social and intellectual stagnation and the aggressive hierarchical accumulation of resources.'

'I know, it's a problem.' Chepi was happy to help, but she didn't want to spend too long on a wild goose chase. 'We'll give them ten thousand years and then see how far they've got?'

'Okay.'

She wanted a fall back position before she would commit fully. 'And if we don't see any progress?'

'I think we'd have to get rid of them one way or the other, and keep the Earth as a sentient, boreal library nexus for the transfer of ideas across time and space?'

'Okay.'

Their plans decided Nitu suddenly felt exhausted. 'I need a break. Fancy a holiday?'

'Perfect.'

ΩΩ

About the Author

Alan Dean is an independent fiction writer with a focus on magic realism, satire, fantasy and science fiction. Alan is also B.Sc. biologist and Ph.D. anthropologist with extensive experience of wilderness travel and working with people from a wide-range of backgrounds and cultures. He lives with his wife and daughter on Vancouver Island, British Columbia, Canada.

www.raincoastimages.ca/raincoastfiction

Other works:

Sangian: Returning

An urban fantasy and mystery involving an ancient sect finding its destiny in a 21st century world.www.raincoastimages.ca/raincoastfiction/sangian-urban-fantasy/

Magical Thinking

A collection of poems influenced by magic realism and surrealism. The content spans inner drives, war, terrorism, aging, and political and social commentary.
www.raincoastimages.ca/raincoastfiction/magical-thinking/